MW01487270

Cover Design: Jay Aheer
Editing done by Jenny Sims Editing4Indies
Proofing Julie Deaton by Deaton Author Services

Interior Design by CP Smith

To finding love and never letting it go, no matter how scary or how much it might hurt!

THIS IS LOVE

THE THIS IS SERIES

PROLOGUE

VIVIENNE

Ten Years Earlier . . .

"HAPPY BIRTHDAY," KARRIE says, holding up a glass of champagne with a smile. I raise my glass of champagne with my own megawatt smile and clink it against hers. "Twenty-one and legal." I nod and bring the glass to my lips. Karrie has been my best friend since I transferred to America from France when I was a senior in high school. We clicked as soon as I bumped into her on the first day.

"Merci." *Thank you*, I say in French. Even though I've been in New York for five years, I still slip into my mother tongue. I take a sip and then close my eyes as the sweet bubbly hits my tongue. "God, this is so much better when it's legal." I laugh.

"So, what are you doing tonight that you couldn't go out with me?" Karrie asks with a smirk as she takes her own sip.

I shrug my shoulders and try not to smile as though I'm hiding something. "Nothing."

"Nothing, my ass," Karrie says, putting down her glass and leaning over to me. "Is it your mystery guy?" she whispers.

"He's not a mystery guy," I say, taking another sip to hide my eyes.

"You have been with him for over two year, yet I have never met him," Karrie points out.

"He's busy with work," I tell her, swallowing down the champagne that a minute ago was sweet and is now a touch bitter and sour. "Besides, I need to make a dent in my American Express this month, and no one does it better than you."

"Changing the subject now, are we?" She smirks and then holds her hand up to get the bill. "I do need to get myself a graduation present," she says, pushing herself from the table to sign her name on the bill. "Let's go shopping."

We spend the next six hours doing all of Fifth Avenue, and when I kiss her goodbye, she gives me the biggest hug with promises to call her tomorrow. As I make my way back down to my apartment, I spot something out of the corner of my eye and turn, not sure if I actually saw it. But I did, and my heart sinks.

I stand here for a minute taking in the scene before turning and walking back to my apartment. The doorman, Harold, spots me and smiles. "Ms. Vivienne," he says, his eyes lighting up. "I heard happy birthday is in order. Or as the French say, Joyeux anniversaire."

I smile at him. "Merci or, as the English say it, thank you."

He grabs the bags in my hands. "I am expecting more," I tell him as he walks me inside the marble entrance toward the waiting elevator.

"I will have all these brought up with the rest," he tells me, and I nod at him, knowing he'll be up in about twenty minutes.

He pushes the button for the sixteenth floor, and I watch the numbers go up one by one. My head is going around and around with everything I just saw. When the elevator opens on my floor, I walk out into the hallway and come face-to-face with my red door. Once I get into the apart-ment, I walk down what I call the gallery hallway. It is why I bought this apartment; the way the molding was all down the wall reminded me of France. I pass the kitchen on my right and the hallway to the bedrooms on my left as I walk into the huge living and dining room with a wall of win-dows that faces Central Park. Bouquets of roses scattered throughout the room are all from the same person, except one from my grandmother in Paris and another from my parents.

The phone beeps in my pocket, and I reach in and grab it.

I'm running a bit behind, but I'll be there by seven.

I swallow, letting my purse fall to the floor beside me while I walk to one of the couches and sit down. I don't get up when I hear a knock on the door, knowing the doorman will leave the bags in the hallway. I stare ahead as the light in the room ever so slowly fades until the glow of the moon is all that remains. My eyes focus on the stars outside, look-ing at one that seems to be blinking. Or maybe it isn't, and it's just me.

I hear the key in the door and grab my phone to see the time is 9:35. I put the phone down and hear his steps coming down the gallery. He turns on the light and spots me sitting here. I look at him, this man who I love with everything I have and would do anything for. He's wearing the same suit I saw him wearing this afternoon except he doesn't have a tie on.

"Hey there," he says, smiling and coming over to me. "There she is, the birthday girl." He squats down in front of me and leans up to kiss my lips, and I let him. "Why are you sitting in the dark?"

I take in his brown eyes that look almost black, eyes I've stared into for over two years now. Eyes that promised me the world. "I was thinking," I say softly, and he grabs one of my hands and brings it to his mouth.

"I'm sorry I'm late," he says, and I take a mental picture of him, not that I need to. "Stuff came up."

"You mean your wife," I tell him, and it suddenly hits me. I mean, it hit me four months into the relationship when I found out he had a wife. But he promised me he was leaving her. She was his high school love, and it would take time, but he loved me. And only me. It. Was. All. A. Lie.

He continued to woo me with exotic vacations when he knew I was fed up, but I can't blame him. I have to take the blame myself.

"Mon amour." *My love.* He uses my nickname, and I shake my head. "You know I'm working on it."

"Really?" I ask him. "From the looks of it, she's about eight months pregnant, so you must really be working on

10

something," I tell him. The color drains from his face, and I laugh bitterly. "I mean, the writing was on the wall really."

"I can explain," he says. I push him away from me and stand. Going to the window, I look out, refusing to show him how much he just hurt me. I won't give him that. I blink it away and push it down, then turn to look at him. He stands there with his hands in his pockets, wearing his gold Rolex—a birthday present from me—on his wrist. I wonder how he explained that to her, or maybe he didn't have to.

"What can you explain?" I ask him but then just continue talking. "How, for the past eighteen months, you strung me along by saying you were leaving her?" My voice rises a bit. "How, for the past fucking eight months, she was pregnant with your child, and you didn't bother to mention it? Nothing!" I shout the last part. "I waited for you and believed you."

"I love you, Vivienne, with every—" He starts to talk, but I stop him.

"Would you just cut the bullshit?" I finally snap angrily. "For once, why don't you just admit it? Just admit I was your mistress."

"You know you're more than that," he says. "You have to know."

"I've been sitting here for the past four hours thinking about what excuse you must be giving her. Wondering if she suspects that you're a liar and a cheater, or are you just that good?" I put my hands up. "I mean, I believed you every single time you walked away saying it was almost over."

"She got pregnant by accident," he says, and I suddenly see how fucking stupid he sounds.

"By accident, you mean your dick fell into her vagina or

what …?" I shake my head.

"You know that isn't what I mean," he says. "I was going to leave her, you know that, and then she got pregnant, and I didn't know how to tell you."

"So you lied to protect me?" I rub my face. "Then how long would it be before you told me?"

"I was going to tell you."

I roll my eyes. "Oh, for sure. Happy Birthday and oh, by the way, I'm a father." I fold my arms over my chest. "Get out."

"You don't mean that," he says, trying to come to me, and I walk away from him to the other side of the room. "We can talk about this."

"The only thing I want you to tell me is where to send all your shit," I tell him. "Holy shit, we were partially living with each other. What could you have possibly told her that she believed?" He opens his mouth to answer. "You know what? I don't care. It isn't my problem anymore."

"Why don't we talk tomorrow?" he says. "I'll call you to-morrow." He turns to walk away.

"You can try, but you won't get through." He stops and then turns back to look at me. "After tonight, you will no longer be welcome here. You will never see me again, not even in passing."

"Baby," he says softly. "I'm sorry I didn't tell you. I need you."

"No," I say, shaking my head. "You need to go back to your wife and your child."

"But—"

"But nothing," I tell him. "Get out." I walk toward my bed-room, slamming the door behind me and locking it. I fall back onto the door and slowly slide down, listening to him walk to the front door. Only when the door closes and I count to one hundred do I allow the first tear to fall, but then it is like a dam opening and the sobs rip through me. I don't know how long I sit here, but my whole body feels like it got run over by a truck. The only thing I know is I will never, ever let myself fall in love again.

ONE

VIVIENNE

Present Day . . .

*W*ALKING INTO THE restaurant, I spot Karrie sitting in the corner with her head down as she types something on her phone. "Bonjour," I say, leaning over and kissing her cheeks when she looks up. Her hair's tied up in a ponytail, and she's wearing a white shirt with a black blazer. I look down at my sleeveless white silk button-down tucked into an olive-colored pleated long dress that falls to my mid-thigh. I accessorized with gold bracelets on my wrists, and my open-toe nude Louboutins match the camel Hermes purse I'm carrying.

Karrie is the closest person to me in the world, and I tell her everything. When we met in high school, we bonded over guys and trust funds, and from the first day, we were attached at the hip. Karrie's father owns the biggest communications company in the world along with a bunch of other things, including the hockey team New York Stingers.

"I just got here. The kids were all over the place," she says, mentioning her four children. After she graduated at the top of her class in public relations, her father hired her to be someone's chaperone. Well, little did she know he would turn out to be the love of her life. I mean, it was love at first sight for him, and he hasn't let her go, not even for a second. With just the way he looks at her, it's clear he loves her with everything he has. It's a look I have never been on the receiving end of, but I've made my peace with that.

"How are my favorite kids?" I ask her as I lay the white linen napkin across my lap. My family resides in Paris, and although I visit a couple of times a year, I consider America my home. It's where my life is, and it's where my home is now.

"They are fit to be tied." Karrie starts talking. "It's almost back to school, and I can't freaking wait." She stops talking when the waiter comes over and tells us the special. We nod at him, and he walks away. "The back-to-school shopping is done, courtesy of Auntie Zara's Closet." She mentions one of Matthew's younger twin sisters who is a professional shopper and now owns one of the most sought-after closets. If something is going on and you need a one-of-a-kind dress, she'll find it for you. "The only thing I have left to do is get them dressed and drive them to school."

"You really are the best mom ever," I say, grabbing the glass of water and taking a sip. "I honestly don't know how you do it."

"If you dated the same man for more than two dates, this

could be you," she tells me, smirking as I grimace.

"You aren't helping your case," I tell her. "When was the last time you slept for longer than four hours?" She doesn't say anything. "That, right there, is why. I sleep eight straight hours."

"I hate you," Karrie hisses. I laugh, and we talk about everything and nothing. We talk every single day, sometimes more than once, and we still find things to discuss.

"We are having a pool party at my house next weekend," Karrie says. "Matthew is throwing an end-of-summer, welcome-back-to-work barbecue," she says, and I sit up and wink at her.

"Does this mean fresh meat will be there?" I ask her, and she just shakes her head. "I'm single and ready to mingle."

"We know." She laughs, and for the first time in a long time, I think back to that fateful day I have locked away tight. The minute I close my eyes, I see it all over again, and just like that, I close the box back.

"Anyway, what do I have to work with?" I ask her, and she just shrugs.

"Regular people, I guess," she says, and I don't say anything. "Oh," she says between chews. "There is a new dad. Well, single dad."

"Abort mission," I say, pointing at her with my fork. "I am all about having sex with a daddy, but I am not going to be a stepmother."

She throws her head back and laughs. "Only you would think about having sex with the father before even asking why he's divorced."

"It's like you don't even know me." I roll my eyes, and she

17

laughs. "Anyway, is Zoe going?" I ask about Matthew's other twin sister. She's the last single one left of the girls. His other sister Allison eloped with his enemy, but now they are two peas in a pod.

"She is coming. I think she is going to come down on Saturday," Karrie says, and I take out my phone and text Zoe right away.

Me: *Me, You, Train, Wine.*

It doesn't take her long to reply.

Zoe: *Me, You, Car Service, Wine......*

I smile and answer her back.

Me: *So much better than train. It's a date.*

"Okay, I'm riding with Zoe," I tell her. "In other news, I really, really need to have sex."

She looks up at me. "Like now?"

I shake my head. "Not like now," I say and then look around, seeing no one who really piques my interest. "I mean soon. Like tonight or tomorrow."

"So, go out and get it," Karrie says, drinking a sip of water. "What is with you lately?"

I look at her and lean back in my chair. "I have no idea. I think it's the changing of the seasons. I spent the weekend in the Hamptons this year."

"You do that every year," she points out.

"I know, but this year, I didn't even suck one dick." I lift my hands. "Not one blow job. Not even a hand job." I shake my head. "Every year, you know I go there, and it's usually a buffet of men."

She closes her eyes and shakes her head. "Yes, I'm aware. Remember when you made a spin card game, and it

18

would tell you what color hair the guy you had to have sex with that night had?"

I smile, thinking back. "Those were some good times. Now all I do is sit on the couch and read."

"There is nothing wrong with relaxing," Karrie says.

"I complained my neighbors were loud." I lean in and hiss whisper, "Me."

"I mean, you are hitting close to thirty-two," Karrie says, and I glare.

"Yes, Dirty Thirty. I need to be dirty for my thirties," I tell her.

"That isn't how it goes," she counters, trying not to laugh.

"Why are we best friends again?" I ask her, and she throws her head back and laughs.

"The list is very short. I think number one is I named a kid after you," Karrie says, and I nod my head. All her kids are named after the most important people in their lives. Their first child is named Cooper Douglas after Matthew's stepfather and Karrie's father. The second child is names Frances after Karrie's mother who passed away, and then obviously, the perfect child is Vivienne. Although, truth be told, she really is the perfect one—great in school and never in trouble. It's like my namesake is dwindling. Chase is the last one and he has to be the cutest little thing ever.

"That could be it. I do love those kids," I tell her and grab my own glass of water to take a drink.

"I will remember that when they wake you up on Sunday," Karrie says. I dread the sound of feet when the girls run down the hall to wake me up. Cooper not so much anymore; he's too cool for that.

"Anyway, I have to get out of this funk," I tell her, and for the rest of the meal, we make plans for the weekend. When I hug her goodbye five hours later and start my walk back to my apartment, I do it slowly. New York is the perfect place to people watch.

When I finally get home and walk into the cool apartment, I slip off my heels and make my way to the kitchen. Grabbing a bottle of water from the fridge, I realize I don't have much in there besides fruit and a couple of prepared meals that I have ordered in.

When I enter my office, my feet sink in the plush white carpet I had put in the room. I turn on the lights just a touch and walk over to the white desk in the middle of the room. Putting down the water bottle next to the vase of pink roses, I turn on the computer. As I wait for the computer to boot up, I sit in the white plush chair and look out the window. The mirrored hutch catches the reflection of the sun, and I look at the picture frames that I placed on the top. Most of them include Karrie, and the picture of us from high school when both of us dressed up for an NSYNC concert is my most treasured one. The other frames are of me with the kids taken in the hospital as soon as they were born. The whole room is my private area, and no one really comes in here except the cleaning lady and Karrie. Grabbing my agenda, I look at my schedule and see that I have an article due for the magazine tomorrow and a blog post to do by next week.

What started off as a pastime has snowballed into my career. After the whole heartbreaking episode, I knew I was never going to fall in love again, so I became a serial dater. It was also at a time when blogging was just coming out into the world, so I started my very own little blog. Not thinking anything of it, I called it Life of a Serial Dater. At the beginning, I would just journal my dates, even if it included sex, and slowly but surely, my following built to over three million people. It was then that the magazine called me and asked if I would like to do a "Dear Serial Dater" article once a month. Readers would mail in their questions or opinions, and I would select a few to post and answer. I was shocked by how big it became, and now I also do an online part to the article every week.

No one besides Karrie knows what I do. They just think I'm living off my family's money, and I work for them by taking care of their websites. I open my emails and start getting my article ready.

How much sex is too much?

I read my first email.

My boyfriend and I started dating and have only been intimate twice in four months. I want to have sex more. Should I ask for it or just be happy with what I have?

Signed, Sexually Frustrated.

I shake my head. "You aren't the only one sexually frustrated, my sister," I say but then get into serial dater mode.

Dear Sexually Frustrated,

There is nothing wrong with asking for more sex. In fact, it's a healthy thing. I mean, would he rather you ask him for sex, or you go out and get it on the side? You have two choices here. One: ask him for more sex and hope that he agrees. Two: get really familiar with the closest sex shop as you will be visiting them for new toys every two to three months. In case you chose number two, here are my list of top vibrators that keep me company on a cold night …

I answer five more questions and then start my blog post while I'm on a roll. The sun has long set, so I turn on the salt lamp in the office for a soft glow. I also pick up my laptop and walk to the gray velvet chaise I have in the corner.

Another Summer Recap

It's time to pack up the sunscreen, put on the shutters, and drain the hot tub. Summer weekends in the Hamptons are almost over. I can't believe how the time has passed. It feels like just yesterday I was packing my bikini and a box of condoms. Although this summer has been tamer than the others, I'll still miss rushing out of town at just the right time to avoid the dreaded traffic. But all that traffic brought in all the man candy I could want, and did I ever sample.

Now it's time to cover up my naughty bits. Until next year, Hampton!

I attach pictures of the beach, one of my legs in the hot tub, and one of me by myself because I somehow became a hermit. I shut down the laptop and put it on the side table, then get up, stretching. "Fall, I am ready for you," I say to the universe, not knowing that I was, in fact, not even close to ready.

TWO

MARK

"*Y*OU HAVE TWO meetings this week." I put my cup of coffee down on my desk in my home office. My assistant, Tracy, sits in front of me with her planner open while she takes notes.

"What meetings?" I ask her, looking down at my own agenda. I am finally back in the city after spending the summer going around the US. From the minute the season was over, I had a detailed travel schedule. Every other week, I was in a different city visiting my businesses. As well as goalie for the New York Stingers, I am also a multimillionaire business owner, but no one really knows. There is a reason everyone calls me PM, Private Mark. Don't ask because I don't tell. I keep my stuff private and only give what I want to give them. The reporters know that if they ask me about anything but hockey, I have no time to talk to them.

"We have two more stores opening, one in Milwaukee

and one in New Orleans," she says, and I turn in my chair and look out the floor-to-ceiling window. It's a sunny day today, and the water looks almost blue. You would never know you're in New York.

"Did we confirm the leases for those two locations yet?" I ask her. Fifteen years ago when I first started out in the NHL and was drafted fifth overall for Nashville, I moved out there on my own. At only eighteen, I had my own little studio apartment, but I was lonely as fuck. My mother is Italian, and my father is Greek, so to say I have a big family is an understatement. It's also expected that they'd be in my business. No matter how many times I told my mother it was a secret, her sisters or her cousins always found out somehow. Now here I am all by myself. My family is in Canada, so I have myself an English Bulldog I call Brutus. Except I didn't think about what I would do with him when I was gone. I needed someone to come over and feed him and walk him. Getting someone was impossible at times, and more often than not, he ended up spending a week in a kennel.

It was while I was taking him to the vet for kennel cough that I came up with an idea to get a dog walker. I created an app with the help of my brother to connect people who could walk the dog with people who needed the service. So here I was, starting the Walk 'N' Licks Dog Walking App. It blew up right before my eyes, so then I opened my first doggy daycare in Nashville under the same name. The demand just kept coming in from all around the world, so now I've opened fifty locations all across Canada and the US. And as of two years ago, I even added a grooming service.

Getting up from my desk, I walk over to the window and

look out at the boats in the water. "So is that a yes?"

"What?" I turn and see Tracy sitting there, tapping her pen.

"You went off in your head again." She shakes her head and laughs. "The SPCA is throwing a huge event, and they would love the support of Walk 'N' Licks."

"Send me the email, and I'll look it over," I tell her. As she makes a note, my cell beeps in my pocket at the same time the phone rings.

"Hello, GM," I say, laughing. "To what do I owe the honors?"

"Very funny," Matthew says. "You still busting my balls over that title."

"I don't think it's busting balls if that's your title." I laugh.

"Yeah, yeah," he says, and I have to say he has his work locked down tight. Two years ago, he hung up his skates as the captain of the team and is now the GM for the team. He's making smart moves although his latest had me scratching my head. "I was wondering if you were back in town."

"Got in last night," I say. "Why?"

"I'm having a year-end party at my house for my kids and their friends, and I invited Viktor," he says.

"I have to check," I tell him, knowing I won't be going to that. Too many people with kids running around everywhere. I like kids; I mean, I like other people's kids when I don't have to talk to them or be next to them. Which is strange, considering my mother has eight siblings, and my grandmother has twenty grandchildren, including me, and twenty-seven great-grandchildren. Christmas is a madhouse. Now on my father's side, there are five of them and only nine grandchildren. The great-grandchildren numbers aren't as grand, since everyone is too busy with work. My brother and I are the only ones from both sides who don't have any kids. We are twelve months apart and mostly look like twins. He sits behind a desk all day making sure everything for my business runs smoothly, so he isn't as athletically built as I am. He also hates hockey and barely knows how to skate. Both of us have black hair so dark that it looks purple in the sun sometimes, and our eyes are dark green, but they look almost black at times. He doesn't have a beard whereas I'm too lazy to shave, and the ladies actually love it, so I keep it.

"Okay, I'll take that as a no." He laughs. "But I will see you tomorrow at the rink."

"Bright and early," I tell him. "Anything I should know?"

"Well, you haven't been cut, so no." He laughs, and I just shake my head when he disconnects.

"What else did you have planned?" Tracy says, and I look up at her. She is beautiful, and the perfect kind of girl I go for. The only problem is she works for me, and I'll never ever cross that line.

"Nothing. I have a workout in thirty minutes," I tell her, looking at the calendar on my phone. "I have Saturday afternoon free," I tell her. "Schedule the meetings for that day." She nods and gets up, grabbing her bag and putting her stuff in it.

"I'll be around if you need me," she says and smiles as she walks out of the room. I listen to her heels click on the floor as she walks down the marble hallway toward the door, then hear a soft click when she leaves. I make my way out of the office and grab my pre-workout shake prepared by my chef. All I have to do is put it in the blender. I walk past the library and dining room toward the kitchen at the end of the hall. Opening the fridge, I take out the shake and put it in the blender. Once it's finished, I turn around and walk out of the sliding door onto the terrace. I got this apartment five years ago when I got traded to New York. Besides the perfect location, the corner two-story penthouse has a wraparound terrace on both levels. I drink the shake while I look out at the calmness of the water. It's still warm for New York, but in just a couple of weeks, the leaves will be changing, and fall will be here. And with that, the hockey season begins.

I think to how it all started, how at ten I asked my father if I could play hockey instead of indoor soccer. His face was filled with surprise, and I expected him to say no because we really didn't sit down and watch hockey. We were more soccer people. World Cup fever would hit, and as much as my father had pride in his country of Greece, we all wore the Italian jersey with pride.

I didn't even know how to skate. I couldn't skate backward, and in order to stop, I usually just crashed into the boards. I shake my head, laughing at the memories of my first tryouts. I was so happy I didn't give a shit. My father bought all my equipment secondhand, but I got out there and played my heart out. When the goalie showed up for one game and then came down with the stomach flu while getting dressed, I was the one closest to his size, so they put me in his gear and put me in nets. I was made for it. When I turned sixteen, Tri-City Americans scouted me, and three years later, I was drafted. I played for Nashville for four years before finally being traded to New York, and I've been here ever since.

After finishing my shake, I get up and go back into the kitchen. Putting the cup in the dishwasher, I make my way upstairs to my bedroom. My phone rings, and I see it's my dad.

"Hey, Dad," I say to him with a smile.

"Markos." He uses my legal name, and I can hear the smile in his voice. "How are you, my son?" He has been in Canada almost all his life, but if you listen close enough, you can still hear the accent. Now my brother, Christos— he calls himself Chris—and I lived in Canada our whole life, and no matter how much Greek school we had growing up on Saturday mornings, we still cannot understand it.

"Good, Dad," I tell him, grabbing my workout shorts. "Just got home actually."

"Good. How was the drive?" he asks. I spent the last week with them at my summer house in Kelowna, British Columbia, and I stopped in Toronto and then decided to drive down to New York.

"Good. I got to zone out for a couple of hours, so it was peaceful," I tell him. Even when I was younger, I was always the quiet one, and then once I became a goalie, it just got even worse. I am always in my head, always quiet, and always assessing the situation. Before the games, I don't talk to anyone. Instead, I put on my music and get in the zone.

"Your mother already misses you," he says. "She wants to come down for the opening game."

"No problem. I'll get you tickets," I tell him. "I'm getting the official schedule this week, so I'll let you know the dates."

"That sounds good," my father says. "I just wanted to make sure you got home okay." I smile because even at thirty-two, almost thirty-three, he still wants me to call him as soon as I get home.

"I'm home," I tell him quietly. "I'm going to go work out now, so I'll call you sometime tomorrow or when I get the schedule."

"Sure thing, son," he says. "I love you," he says in Greek, and I say one of the few Greek words I know.

"Love you, too," I say and disconnect the phone, grabbing my stuff and heading down to the gym. Once I get on the treadmill, I put the Air Pods in my ears, and for the next two hours, I just run, trying to shut down my mind. But instead, I make mental notes and lists for later. When I walk back into the apartment, I grab a bottle of water and hydrate myself.

"It's going to be a good season," I say to the empty room. Little do I realize exactly how big this season will be.

THREE

VIVIENNE

"*D*O YOU KNOW you've carried me more than any other man before?" I say, giggling as Matthew tosses me over his shoulder like I'm a bag of potatoes. "I mean, I've had men carry me before, but I got the happy ending after they did."

"No happy ending here, Vivi," Matthew says, opening the back door to his truck and placing me in gently. We got to Long Island earlier in the day and started house hopping and finally ended up at Zara's where Matthew and Max swung over to pick us up.

"You have a good guy there, Karrie." I lean forward in my seat, my head spinning a little more than I'm used to. It all started out so well, and then the talk turned to love and sex. Since I am without both at the moment, I started to feel sorry for myself, and well, that doesn't end well. Ever. "He's the best guy there is."

Karrie nods her head with her eyes closed, and Matthew

gets into the truck and groans when he hears me talking. "Are you guys going to go home and have sex?"

Karrie peeks up now, sitting up. "Um, yeah, we are," she says and leans over and tries to whisper in his ear but because she's drunk, there is no whisper. "We are going to have hot, dirty sex."

"Oh, yeah, you are." I giggle in the back, clapping my hands together.

"I'm going to ride you like a bull in Spain," she says, and I have to roll my lips when Matthew groans even louder. "Like this," she says and pretends she's riding a bull in the front seat. But it looks like she's just thrashing all over the place.

"Isn't that sexy?" I say, and Matthew just shakes his head. He pulls up to the house and turns off the truck.

Looking over his shoulder at me, he asks, "Can you walk in or do you need to be carried?"

"Matthew, I never need to be carried," I say, grabbing the door handle. "I need to be pushed up against the wall and fucked seven ways to Monday."

"I don't think that is the saying," Karrie says, trying to open her door but failing. I get out of the truck at the same time Matthew gets around to Karrie's door. "Matthew, can you push me against the wall and fuck me seven ways to Monday?" She giggles when he doesn't answer. "Remember that time I didn't wear panties, and you did me against the truck?"

"Please stop talking," Matthew says, but she doesn't.

"Vivi, it was so good, the best. It's always the best with him."

"Good to know," I say, walking behind them while Karrie

tries to kiss his mouth and instead licks his face.

"Lick my tongue, Matthew," Karrie says to him. "Lick my tongue and then lick my—"

"Okay there," Matthew says loudly when we get into the house, and he walks up the winding stairs to their bedroom.

"See you all tomorrow," I say, going toward the stairs leading down to my guest room. I don't bother turning on the lights nor do I bother getting undressed before I pass out.

When I hear little footsteps the next morning, I open one eye right before they try to shake me. "Who sent you?" I grumble, and Vivi and Franny laugh.

"Daddy said the coffee is ready," Vivienne says, jumping up on the bed and getting under the covers with me. "Bonjour." *Good morning*, she whispers in French, and I grab her around her waist and bring her to my chest. "Aunt Vivi, your breath smells." I laugh and kiss her neck. Turning to get out of the bed, I spot Franny going through my makeup. "Don't mix the colors like you did the last time," I tell them and make my way to the bathroom. From the time they were little, they knew that whatever I had they could have, so they would always come and wake me up and then do their makeup. Matthew freaked the first couple of times, but now he just goes with it.

After washing my face and brushing my teeth, I make my way upstairs, and the sunlight hits me right away. "Why is it so sunny?" I ask. Walking into the kitchen, I see Matthew cooking and Karrie with her head down on the island, her hand on a coffee.

"There she is," Matthew says with a smile, and it is more

irritating that normal.

"Shut up, Matthew." Glaring over at him, I grab a cup and fill it up with coffee, drinking it black.

"What's up with her?" I motion with my chin.

"She hates me," Matthew says, and Karrie grumbles in agreement, but her head doesn't come up. "She is never drinking wine again." He then leans in. "And I broke her vagina."

With that, Karrie raises her head a bit. "That he did."

I throw my head back. "God, I'm thirsty."

"You're drinking coffee," Matthew says. "How can you be thirsty?"

"I just am. You can be drinking and still be thirsty," I tell him, walking over to the stool next to Karrie. "It's a girl thing."

"You are probably dehydrated," he says, turning to continue making pancakes.

"You have no idea," I say quietly and then take a sip of coffee. Matthew finishes breakfast while Karrie just tries to lift her head.

"Karrie," I tell her, and she looks over at me. "I've decided that if you die, I'm going to marry Matthew," I tell her, and she just looks at me, her eyebrows pushing together.

"Um, thanks, I guess," she says.

"You're welcome," I say to her. "Besides, you don't want him to get with someone who will actually love him, do you?"

"True …" she starts to say.

"Exactly. I'll marry him, and he'll never love me or have sex with me, so in the end, you'll be winning."

"What happens if I die?" Matthew says, and I look at him.

36

"Oh, she's going to find someone else, and she'll be fine," I say, and now Karrie smiles.

"Why do I get stuck with you, and she gets to date?" Matthew asks, putting the plate of bacon down in front of us.

"Matthew, I don't make the rules," I tell him. "It's just the way it's going to go."

"Great, so I get to marry you, and then she gets to marry some guy who is going to love her," Matthew says, glaring and folding his arms over his chest.

"That sounds about right."

"I'm going to haunt her from the grave," Matthew threatens.

I look at Karrie. "Don't worry about that. We are going to sage the house."

"I'm not having this discussion," Matthew says and calls the kids.

"There is no discussion really. You get me, and she gets, I don't know, Chris Hemsworth."

"He's married," Karrie says from beside me.

"Karrie," Matthew hisses out.

"What? You're dead. You don't want me to be alone for the rest of my life, do you?"

"Um, yeah, I see nothing wrong with that. Since you're leaving me with her." He points at me.

"Hey, I am good eye candy, but I'll also need like a hall pass to go and have sex with other people."

"If you are going to have sex with other people, then so will I," Matthew says, looking at me.

"Absolutely not. No husband of mine is going to have sex with another woman."

"Enough," Karrie says. "No one is dying." She gets up and walks over to Matthew, but she is walking funny.

"Did he get the wrong hole again?" I snicker into my cup when she turns to glare at me.

"I told her it was a bad idea, but she kept begging for it," Matthew says, his chest puffing out again. "The cry after? Not so good."

"You have to relax, Karrie, and just let it happen," I tell her, and somehow she tries to glare at me again but she's so out of it she closes her eyes.

"I'm hungry!" Cooper yells as he walks down the stairs, and then the girls come in, and I swear I did not know I owned that much blue eye shadow, but Vivienne is wearing a green and then a blue, and Franny has blue and pink.

"I'll get the face rags," Matthew says, kissing Karrie on the head. "You go eat."

We sit at the table with the kids to eat and then get excited when the guy with the blow-up castles arrives. The rest of the afternoon flies by, and the number of people arriving is just overwhelming, I don't remember half the names.

I do know that I am always with a mimosa in my hand, and when the car finally gets here to drive us home, I beg to sit in the back seat. I get in and lie down, my head still spinning or maybe it never stopped. Zoe gets in with Viktor following her, and I have to say if the guy was available, I would give him a ride. But one look and you know he's not even there.

I close my eyes, and before you know it, we are in front of my building. I hear Zoe call my name, and I get up, grabbing my bags with me. "It was lots of fun," I tell them, then look at Zoe. "Give me a call this week, and we'll grab lunch."

She nods at me and kisses my cheek, and I walk into the lobby, nodding at the security guy who is here on the weekends. He looks cute. Maybe I should … and I'm saved by the ding of the elevator.

The cool air hits me right away, and I bring the bags with me to my closet and dump them there. Then I walk to the bathroom and fill up the tub. All I need is a good soak and a full night's rest with a detox in the morning. I slip my bikini bottom off and then the top and see that I've gotten a little bit of a tan. My face is a little red, and when I slip into the bath, I lean back and just clear my head.

I stay in the tub until the hot water turns a lukewarm. Getting out, I then slip into bed naked only to wake the next day at noon. I sit on the couch while I go through my emails and then see that I can make the two o'clock Pilates class. I grab my white shorts and slip them on with a black bra and a leopard print silk button-down shirt that I leave open at the top and tuck in the front.

I grab my open-toe black heels and my Chanel purse and make my way to the studio. I do the class, and then afterward, I get one-on-one instruction from a trainer who helps work all my muscles. I end it with a sixty-minute yoga class.

When I walk out of the studio a few hours later, my body feels more relaxed than it has in a while. I look down at my phone and am not watching where I am going and walk smack into someone. When firm hands grab my waist and his smell hits me right away, I know it is a man. I even know what this man looks like. It isn't the first time I get his smell all over me.

"I'm so sorry." I look up into his dark green eyes that light up when they see it's me.

"Well, well, well." His voice comes out smooth. "Would you look at the luck I'm having," he says, his mouth widening to a full smile. I step out of his touch so I can think clearly.

"Look at you," I tell him, looking at him up and down. He's wearing navy blue shorts and a baby blue button-down linen shirt open at the collar showing his smooth, tanned neck. A white baseball cap on his head covers his thick black hair. "You are so tanned. Were you jet-setting around the world?"

"Oh, yeah," he says, putting his hands in his pockets and making his shirt pull across his chest. "I was down in Greece for a couple of weeks just enjoying the sun."

"Well, it definitely suits you," I say, looking down and thinking of ways to walk away from him.

"I was just going to get something to eat. Would you like to join me?" he says, and everything in my head tells me to run the other way. When I hesitate, he adds, "It's just dinner, Vivienne, nothing more."

"Ah," I say. "But what if I wanted the something more?" I walk closer to him. "What if all I wanted was dessert?" He shakes his head.

"It's all coming back now," he says, laughing. "Let's go get something to eat, and we can talk about the dessert."

I roll my eyes. "Fine. I have to eat anyway." He puts his hand on the lower part of my back, and I feel his heat through the silk shirt.

"This way," he says and walks me around the corner to a little restaurant. His hand remains on my back, and the only thing I can concentrate on is not tripping over my heels. My heart echoing in my ears blocks out whatever he is saying, and when I finally sit down, I say a little prayer for the strength not to give into him.

MARK

I SIT DOWN and look at her, and I have to stop myself from doing something stupid. The last thing I expected today was to run into her, but the minute I heard her voice, it was like electric currents went through me. I watch her as her eyes roam around the room taking in the decor, smiling at the waiter when he hands her the cardboard menu, I lean back in my chair. Looking around my favorite little Greek restaurant, I admire the pictures of Greece hanging on the walls, and it takes me back to the summers I used to spend there.

"This is a cute little place," Vivienne says, looking down at her menu.

"It's the best Greek food you will get in New York," I tell her, nodding at the waiter who comes back and fills our glasses with water. "I mean, besides my yaya," I say of my grandmother.

"Really? Now I'm excited. When we visited Santorini last summer, it was the best food I have ever eaten," she says, looking back down at menu. We listen to him talk about the special, but my eyes are on her as she takes it in and smiles.

"Start with some tzatziki, some tarmosalata, and melitzansalata," I tell the waiter who just nods his head. "Some white wine and a bottle of sparkling water please," I tell him, and he walks away. "So, tell me, Vivienne," I say. She mimics my pose, leaning back in her chair.

"What do you want to know, Mark?" Her face gives away nothing.

"Two years ago, you said you were going to call me," I say to her with a smirk. "I haven't changed my number."

"Two years ago, you told me to give you a call when I was ready," she says. Sitting back up now, she puts her elbows on the table and folds her hands together. "I was making you sweat it out." Her sly smile comes out.

I laugh now. "Is that so?" Leaning forward, I put my elbows on the table, too.

"What is the saying that Americans say …?" She stops talking when the waiter comes back and pours her a glass of white wine. After tasting it, she gives him a nod. "Good things come to those who wait."

I nod, grabbing the glass of water in front of me. "They also say you catch more flies with honey." I wink at her.

"The only thing I know about honey is that it takes at least three showers to wash it completely off." Now she winks at me. "But I do have one question."

"I'm an open book," I tell her, and she throws her head back and laughs as I take another sip of water. My throat

44

and mouth are becoming dry.

"You know they call you PM, right?" She tilts her head. "And I'm assuming it's not for private masturbation." The minute she says this, I choke on my water and feel the burn as it tries to come out of my nose. I cough as I try to get some air in and get the water down. "I didn't think so." She takes a sip of wine, not even noticing I'm about to die. "So why do they call you that?"

I drink another sip of water and am finally able to breathe. "They call me that because I'm private, so I don't give anyone anything. It's Private Mark." I shake my head. "I almost died."

She shrugs and rolls her eyes. "You were fine." She then stares right at me, and I'm mesmerized by her blue eyes. They are crystal blue today especially now that she's joking. "I mean, if that was just a way for me to give you mouth-to-mouth, it was a little dramatic."

"Trust me, if I wanted mouth-to-mouth, I would just take it," I say, and her eyes shift. If I wasn't looking at her, I would have missed it. The outside of her blue eyes turns just a touch darker, and she gets blue dots in the middle.

"Is that so?" she asks. I don't get a chance to answer before the waiter comes by and places our appetizers in the middle of the table.

"Are you ready to order?' he asks us, and Vivienne looks at me.

"I'll let you decide," she tells me, taking a piece of pita and dipping it in the tzatziki. When she moans, my cock gets rock hard in the blink of an eye. I order a bunch of stuff, and I am sure it's way too much food, but my brain wasn't getting the blood flow it needed. "This is really good," she says, and I just nod at her, taking a piece of pita and eating it.

"Who did you go to Greece with?" I ask her, wondering if she has someone. Usually, she flies solo. There is even a side bet going with certain players to see who will finally tame her. If Matthew found out, he would ream their asses.

"I went with my cousin from France," she says. "It was two weeks of heaven. Sunny every single day. We stayed in the little village at this little place." I raise my eyebrows. "Fine. We had our own villa, but it was beautiful. And we chartered a yacht for two days, and it was perfect."

"My father is from there," I tell her, and she looks at me. "So I visit once or twice a year, and then I go to Italy and visit some of my mother's cousins."

"That doesn't sound like a bad trip," she says, smiling, and I shake my head.

"Not a bad trip at all," I tell her. "Why didn't you call?"

"I'm not sure," she says, taking a big gulp of wine.

"Did you not want to?" I ask her, hoping this pull I feel isn't just one-sided.

"Oh, I wanted to," she finally says softly. "I just didn't want to muddy the waters."

"Meaning?" I ask her.

"Meaning, I don't know what would happen after," she answers me.

"You'll never know unless you call," I tell her. "I'm not asking for your hand in marriage, Vivienne. I'm old-fashioned," I tell her, and she raises her eyebrows, "but not that old-fashioned."

"Old-fashioned?" she questions me. "Does that mean you do all the work?"

"What fun would that be?" I tell her and lean forward softly. "Nothing sexier than watching a woman ride." And just like that, her eyes change to the darkest blue I've ever seen. I watch her swallow and see that she shifts in her chair, but I don't want to push her. "I'm sure you'll agree."

She looks at me, and I see the wicked out in her. "Personally, I like to look over my shoulder."

I nod at her. The waiter comes and places all our food on the table, but I'm not the least bit hungry. I don't even want to eat. The only thing I want to do is fuck her on the table, but I know I can't yet. She eats some lamb, and the rest of the conversation is easy.

"Are you excited for the start of the season?" she asks.

"I am," I say. "I think Matthew has done a good job putting the team together. Plus, we got a couple of rookies coming in who are impressive, and we did just get Viktor."

"I met him yesterday at the barbecue," she says. I wait for her to say something about him. "Not a talkative type, but then again, I was trying to sleep on our way home." I don't let it show that this piece of information bothers me. "Zoe spent most of the time talking to him."

"I met him today. He seems like a good guy who got a bad rap, but that's what happens when you aren't private."

"Is that so?" she says, finishing off her glass of wine and then drinking some sparkling water.

"If you don't give anyone anything to talk about, they move along," I point out, grabbing my card and putting it down in the black check folder and then waiting for him to come back. I push away from the table after I finish signing the bill and hold out my hand to help her up. She puts the linen napkin on the table, and when I see her smooth tan legs crossed, I wonder if they are soft like silk. She grabs her Chanel purse with one hand and holds out the other to me as she gets up.

"Merci." *Thank you,* she says in French, and I suddenly want her to talk French to me all night long. I make a note to learn some French words for next time. Her hand lingers in mine, and I was right. She is soft as silk, softer even. As we walk through the restaurant, her hand lingers next to mine, grazing it softly. When we finally walk out of the restaurant, the warm breeze hits us right away. She stops in the middle of the sidewalk. "Well, this was fun," she says. "We should do it again."

"Should we?" I bait her. "Maybe if you called, that could be arranged."

"Only time will tell." She laughs and leans in. I know she is going for a kiss on the cheek because I've seen this play with her many times before, but I'm not going to let her. I put my hand around her waist and bring her right up against my chest while her hands grasp my arms. Her breath hitches, and her eyes just look at me as shock fills her face. I don't let her say anything as I lower my mouth to hers, slipping my tongue into her mouth that is already open in shock. I'm not sure what I'm expecting, but I melt into her. The taste of honey from the baklava she just had lingers on her lips, and when I turn my head to the side to deepen the kiss, she is there every step of the way. As our tongues twirl and dance with each other, my cock hardens, ready to finally claim her.

Her hands move up my arms, and her arms go around my neck. I kiss her for a couple more seconds, and then I slowly let go of her lips. Her eyes slowly open, and I see the desire in them.

"Good night," I whisper, and it takes everything in me not to kiss her again. To pick her up and drag her back to my house. My arm slowly loosens on her waist, and my cock is not happy I'm walking away from her. I look down at her lips, seeing that they're plumper than before and with little spots of red from my beard. Her tongue comes out to lick the bottom lip, and I want to bite it. "Thank you for joining me," I say and then nod and walk away from her. I turn around and start to walk backward as the sound of police sirens gets closer and closer. "You should really use my number!" I shout at her, and she just shrugs.

"I'll think about it," she says, and I stop walking as she turns and walks to the edge of the sidewalk and puts up her hand to flag down a cab. A yellow cab stops right in front of her, and she opens the door and turns to me. "I mean, if I'm bored, that is." She smiles and winks at me, and just like that, she leaves me here, shaking my head as I watch the car disappear into the sea of red brake lights.

I've never been this nervous or this twisted over a woman. They usually come to me and don't really make me work for it. Not that I've never worked for it before, but this woman has had me on a string waiting for two years.

We would see each other and stare. The pull was there, and then when you would look around, it would be over. She would be gone. I'm not saying I twiddled my thumbs waiting for her. She's just always been a what-if. I unlock the door and walk into the dark apartment.

Making my way to the stairs and upstairs to my room, I turn on the lights and then dim them. I walk to the window and look out into the darkness at the sun slowly coming up, a couple of lights flicker in the distance. "I'm going to make that woman mine," I say to the universe and to whoever else is willing to listen to me. "She just doesn't know it yet."

VIVIENNE

$\mathcal{I}$ SIT DOWN in the cab, and I'm thankful my legs didn't give out after he kissed me. I take that back. He didn't just kiss me; he rocked my world. He had my stomach fluttering. I put my hand on my forehead to check to see if maybe I have a fever. Maybe the kids gave me something.

I pick up the phone and text Karrie.

Me: *Are any of the kids sick? I think I caught something.*

I put the phone down and look out of the window, my heart hammering in my chest, and the phone rings.

"Allô," *Hello,* I say into the phone, knowing it's Karrie.

"What's the matter with you?" she asks me in a quiet voice, and then I hear a door close.

"Where are you?" I ask her.

"I was in bed, but Matthew is crashed out, so I left the bedroom. Why?" she asks, and I take a deep breath in and then exhale.

"I need to tell you something, but I need you to swear to secrecy," I tell her. "Almost like I did when you told me about that time you had sex in the arena."

She hisses, "You were not supposed to ever bring that up."

"Do you promise?"

"Do I have a choice?" she asks, and her voice is getting a touch louder so I know she's probably downstairs in the kitchen.

"I just had dinner with Mark," I say the words out loud, and then I wait.

"Which Mark?" she asks.

"Dimitris," I say softly and hear a whistle. "PM, which, by the way, does not stand for private masturbation," I say, and I hear her spitting something out and then coughing. "What is wrong with everyone?"

"Oh my God," she says between heaving and coughing. "I just sprayed water all over my kitchen. I can't," she says. The cab comes to a stop, and I swipe my card in the machine and then get out. The doorman nods at me and opens the door for me. "I know that it stands for Private Mark."

"Really," I say, smiling at the security guard. "How do you know that?"

"My husband is a retired hockey player. You don't think I watch seven hours of *SportsCenter* when he's home. I pick up some things," she says. "Wait a second, didn't you guys have a thing two years ago?"

"Negative," I say into the phone, getting into the elevator. "I mean, he told me to call him, but I never did."

"And you called him today?" she asks me, confused. I get

out of the elevator and walk into my house. Not turning on any lights, I make my way to my bedroom.

"No, I ran into him literally while I was walking down Lexington," I tell her. "And he took me to dinner."

"So why do I have to keep it a secret?" she asks me.

"He kissed me," I tell her.

"Okay," she says. "You've kissed other men."

"Yes, but this one was different. My stomach did a thing." I put my hand to my stomach, and just thinking about the kiss makes the same thing happen again. "Little flutters."

"Oh my God," she says.

"I think I caught something from the kids. I'm going to check my temperature right now," I say as I go into the bathroom and get the thermometer. "Maybe I caught the bug."

"Yeah, the love bug," she says, laughing, and I roll my eyes.

"Can you be serious for a minute? I might be dying. Maybe I have a tumor," I say.

"You don't have a tumor nor are you sick. You felt like that because you like him," she points out. "I felt the same thing with Matthew."

"Karrie. Please, can we focus for one minute? I have to google what sicknesses are going around New York. Maybe it's an epidemic." I put her on speaker and open my internet browser.

"There is nothing wrong with you. You kissed a man, and you like him; it feels different when you like someone. It's not just a wham, bam, thank you, ma'am."

"Jesus, I hope I never meet a man who is wham, bam, thank you, ma'am," I say, holding my chest now. "Imagine a one-time man. What do you do with that?"

"You make the one time last longer." Karrie laughs. "You know Mark. You flirted with him, and you find him hot."

"Well, his cock is huge," I tell her and then want to take it back when she gasps.

"How would you know this if you just kissed him?" she asks me.

"Well, I was kissing him, and obviously, I'm great at it, so he sprung to action," I tell her. "Full mast and it was hard as fuck," I tell her. "Mon Dieu," *My God,* I say. "You think he's a one-time man? He can't be."

"I have no idea. I don't know anyone who's slept with him," she says, and the thought of him with other women bothers me. I mean, who am I to say anything? I am not a virgin nor do I plan to slow down. I'm just in a rut, is all.

"There is always that website that ranks the hockey guys. You know those puck bunnies love to vote on shit," Karrie says. "I can't check because I don't ever go on there. It's the devil's playground." By the time she finishes talking, I'm already on the site.

"There is nothing for him," I tell her. "I see Max's name but ..."

"Ohh, how is he rated?" she asks me, and I laugh.

"Takes his time and makes sure you finish first." I repeat what someone wrote. "It was from ten years ago. People change," I tell her, and she laughs. "I'll ask him the next time I see him."

"Can you make sure I'm there when you do?" she says. "So what are you going to do?"

"I'm going to call the doctor and see what he says," I tell

her.

"You aren't sick, Vivienne. You finally like a man who piques your interest for more than one night."

"It can be two nights. Even three. But I draw the line at four because then it becomes too much of a commitment," I tell her.

"Why are you down here?" I hear Matthew's voice.

"Vivienne called. She thinks she's sick," Karrie says, and now I hear Matthew's breathing.

"Does she have a fever?" he asks close to the phone, so I know he's hugging her.

"No, more like a stomach bug," she tells him. "What woke you up?"

"I missed you," he says, and I fake barf in the phone, making Karrie laugh.

"I'm going to let you go before I get more nauseated," I tell her. "I'll let you know what the doctor says tomorrow," I say and hang up after she says goodbye.

I put my phone down and tie my long hair on top of my head and start my bath. I need to soak in the tub. Maybe since I haven't had sex in so long, my body didn't know how to react to him. I slip into bed, and my dreams are of him all night long, and when my eyes finally flip open the next morning, it is right before he fucked me. I groan and close my eyes, hoping to be taken back to that exact moment in the dream, but instead, my bladder starts to wake up, and I have to go to the bathroom. Grabbing my silk kimono robe, I slip my arms through it and make my way to the kitchen to start coffee.

I press the button to open the shades and then turn on

the television, switching it to TF1, a French television station, then open my laptop. I grab my coffee and sit at the table while I go through my emails. Then I open my blog page and start something that I was thinking about last night.

Can one kiss give you butterflies, or does the fluttering in your stomach mean you have food poisoning? I kissed a man last night, or actually he kissed me, but I let him. I mean, there is just something about that first kiss that everyone talks about. I've had the lead in kisses many, many times before. You know the one when you spend the night eye-fucking each other and then actually kiss just so you can get naked? But that isn't the kiss I'm talking about. At least not this time.

This time, all I did was have dinner with him, flirted with him as per usual, and then at the end of the night standing in the middle of the sidewalk, he just kissed me. There was no lead-up. I mean, maybe there was, and I had no idea. But regardless, he just kisses me, one kiss. Maybe it lasted a minute, or maybe it lasted five minutes, but the only thing I knew was that my stomach had the bizarre flutter. Even on the whole ride home, my mind played it over and over again. I even thought I was sick, but Google confirmed I wasn't.

Now here is the question, can one kiss actually give you flutters?

I press send on the blog post at the same time that the doorbell rings. Getting up, I walk to the door and open it to see the doorman with a huge basket in his hands. "This was just delivered for you," he says, and I reach out to take the cellophane-wrapped basket.

"Thank you so much." I smile at him and carry it to the kitchen. A red bow on the handle of the basket but no card.

I untie the bow and open the cellophane and see that it's a French coffee press. I pick up the baby blue coffeemaker and find packs of coffee next to it—all gourmet and all French. There, tucked into the packs of coffee, is a white card. I grab it and open it, and I have to sit down.

We had dinner, so we should have breakfast.

My number hasn't changed.

Use it.

Private Mark

Oh. My. God. This man is too much. I take a picture of the basket and send it to Karrie who answers me back right away.

Karrie: ***I can't do coffee today, but I can do it tomorrow.***

Me: ***That isn't for you; that is what M just sent me.***

She doesn't answer me by text. Instead, she calls me. "What do you mean he sent it to you?"

"Exactly that," I tell her and repeat what he wrote on the card.

"Are you going to call him?" she asks.

"No, I'm not going to call him," I say, blowing out my breath. "What good is it going to do if I call him?"

"You can have sex with him, and then you can know if it's something or just an itch you need to scratch."

I look up. "That is the best thing you've said in a while. I should just call him, fuck him, then forget him." I tap my chin. "I don't know why I just didn't do that from the beginning. It's been two years."

"Or maybe you haven't done it because you know you like him," she says, and I hear the car door slam.

"Karrie, how can one person have the best idea one minute and then fall flat in the next?" I ask her. "Seriously, I'm not a woman who commits. It's just not me."

"That's what I'm saying," she says, and I'm switched to Bluetooth. "Have you not pursued him because of this thing?"

"There is no thing," I say, my voice getting loud. "Now I have to let you go so I can call him and go have sex with him."

"Notice you didn't say fuck him," she says, laughing. I hang up on her, but she gets the last laugh when she texts me

Karrie: **You hate when I'm right.**

I open my contacts and scroll down to M and click his name. My finger lingers on the call button. My heart starts to speed up, and my mouth suddenly goes dry. My leg starts to bounce up and down. I just press his number, and then hold my breath. Not one single breath. One ring, two rings, three rings. I take the phone from my ear and hold it out to make sure that I got the right number. Then I hear his voice.

"You've reached Mark, leave a message." His husky voice makes my nipples peak against the cold silk kimono. I contemplate hanging up, but then he has caller ID, so he'll know it's me anyway.

"The one time I call you, and I get your voice mail. Is this a sign that I shouldn't call you?" I laugh, looking down at the card. "I got your package," I say. "I mean, not your pack-age package, but the coffee package." I close my eyes and cringe. "Anyway, this is me calling you. Your move, Private Mark," I say and hang up.

What the fuck was that? I think to myself. Where was the

sassy girl? It's like I got stage fright. I look down at the phone and expect it to ring, but it doesn't. It also doesn't ring after lunch, and when I go to bed that night, it still hasn't rung. I check my outgoing calls to make sure I actually called, and when I see that I did, I wonder why he hasn't called me back. Should I call him again, or should I wait? I've never had to go through this, and this moment right here reminds me why I don't do these things. "Just forget him," I tell myself, turning off the light and falling asleep. Except my dreams don't forget him. Instead, they torture me.

Mark

"*Y*OU NEED TO come out more in the crease," the goalie coach, Pierre, tells me. "You can block more angles like that." I nod at him and skate back to the net, pulling my mask back down on my face. My eyes watch the puck the whole time—right, left, right, left, right—and I know he's going to shoot it. I'm expecting it, but he doesn't, and just like that, I know he's going to wind it up and try to slap it in. I move over to the other side where I see the puck aiming for, and I block it with my blocker. The sounds of it bouncing fills the arena.

I'm at practice. Everyone else already left the ice, but I stayed behind with my trainer to go over a couple of things. Getting back on the ice after four months is always a little shaky. I've kept up with weights and cardio and have skated for the past two weeks. I pick up my mask and grab the squirt bottle and squirt water into my mouth. "Want to go for a bit more?" Pierre asks. I just nod and put my mask back on, and for the next hour, I block shot after shot. Right, left, and center from behind the net—we practice every single angle.

I skate off the ice and head down to the locker room, seeing it half empty already. Viktor and Evan are sitting there talking. I walk to my corner and put my mask on my shelf above my name. I sit down and start to untie my pads. I hear them talking, but being me, I keep to myself. "I swear you look like you stayed in the sun all summer," Evan says, and I laugh at him.

"I'm European. We tan easily," I say, putting my pads to the side of my bench. Because of the size of my equipment, I have my own bench facing the doorway and everyone else. It's also the closest to the shower.

"It looks like you were on a yacht living life," Evan says, getting up, and I just shake my head. "I'm going to go do some cardio. Anyone coming?"

"I have an appointment with Zoe," Viktor says from his own bench. "Maybe another time." He takes his stuff and walks out of the room.

"What about you?" Evan asks me.

"I have to eat. Maybe I'll catch you later," I tell him as I pull off my jersey, and he walks out of the room. I grab my phone and see that I have one missed call and five emails. I open the emails first, seeing that I have to answer a couple of questions for the opening of the New Orleans store. Then I spot a weird number and press the voice mail button. Her voice comes through right away, and my face lights up with a smile immediately. She sounds nervous, and I wonder if

I should call her back. I'm dying to call her back, but I put the phone down and take a shower instead. The rest of the day goes by so fast, and I have dinner with a couple of people from the SPCA to see about doing some ads to bring awareness to animal cruelty. When I finally get home, I take out my phone and see it's way too late to call her. So I text her instead.

Me: *I just got in; the day got ahead of me. Give me a call tomorrow morning and we can talk about my package.*

I think about sending it and then just put the phone down. I turn on the television and watch the news, and then right before I'm about to drift off to sleep, I think about sending it again. Instead, I delete it.

The next morning, my alarm rings at seven, and I get out of bed, walking to the kitchen in my boxers. I turn on the television and start the coffee while I go to the bathroom. Sitting on the couch with my coffee in my hand, I watch *SportsCenter* and see that hockey is slowly coming back into the news. Since preseason starts soon, I watch it for an hour and then grab my phone and call her, not even thinking that it's early.

"You better be dead or bleeding," she mumbles, and I laugh.

"Good morning, sunshine," I tell her, and then she groans.

"It's eight a.m.," she moans.

"It's time to get up," I say. She moans again, waking my cock. "Meet me for breakfast."

"What?" she finally says, and I wonder what she wears to bed.

"Come and have breakfast with me," I say again. "My

house."

"Is that a code for come and suck my cock?" she asks, and I shake my head and laugh.

"It's code for come and eat." My voice gets soft. "If my cock is on the menu, that will be your decision."

"Now, we are talking," she says, and I hear her stretching. "I'm really hungry."

"Good. I'll have things ready when you get here," I tell her. "I'll text you my address, and you text me when you will be here."

"D'accord," she says and hangs up, and I look at the phone.

What the hell does D'accord mean? I press the button on the phone. "Siri, what does d'accord mean?"

She answers me right away. "Décor means the furnishing and decoration of a room."

"No, not décor," I say and then open my Google translate page and put in "daccord," and it tells me it means okay.

I get my shorts on and a shirt and run down to the bakery where I get an assortment of French pastries, some fruit, and grab a can of whipped cream. *Hey, you never know, right?* I'm walking in the door when my phone beeps in my pocket, and I see it's from Vivienne.

Vivienne: *I will be there in an hour. Breakfast better be ready.*

Me: *Are we still talking about my cock?*

Vivienne: *Trust me, when we talk about your cock, you'll know.*

Me: *D'accord.*

I put my phone down after I answer her. Grabbing a plate

from the cabinet, I put the pastries on it and then cut up the fruit. I start the coffee and then hear the doorbell ring. I walk to it and see that it's the delivery guy with two bags. I grab the bags and head back into the kitchen and open them. Eggs and pancakes and some French toast.

When the bell rings again twenty minutes later, I know it's her. I get up from the couch and look down at myself. Maybe I should have changed; my heart speeds up just a touch, and my hands get clammy. I walk to the door and open it with a smile on my face, and it's a good thing because she literally takes my breath away. She stands there looking like she just walked off the runway. She's wearing a light pink long flowy skirt with a brown belt and a white camisole with spaghetti straps and not a bra strap in sight. Her long black hair tucked into her tan hat that she is wearing. "Well, well, well," I finally say, and she walks in. Now I see the sexiness to the skirt, her entire legs are exposed to her thighs when she walks, exposing her tan strappy sandals.

"Well, well, well," she counters and comes to me, kissing me on the lips. "Took you long enough," she says and walks into the foyer, and I close the door behind her.

"It took me long enough?" I shake my head and see her looking around. "It took you two years to call me."

"Yet it took you a day to call me back." She crosses her arms over her chest, and her tits just push up even more.

"Someone told me that good things come to those who wait." I remind her of what she told me.

"Well, I guess the wait is finally over," she says, and I walk to her, take her hand, and bring it to my lips.

"It's a nice day. Let's eat outside," I say and pull her with me toward the kitchen. We walk out of the little door, and she gasps at the view.

"This is beautiful," she says, seeing the skyline and then walking to the railing. "We should eat outside."

"Do you want to sit on the couch?" I say, pointing to the left at the face-to-face loveseats with a table in the middle. "Or do you want to sit at the table?" I point at the other side table with two bench chairs.

"Hmm." She turns and puts her elbows on the railing, and she looks at me, but with the way her hat is I, can't really see the color of her eyes. I walk over to her and take her hat off her head.

"I want to see your eyes. They are the door to your soul," I say. "Now pick where you want to eat." I turn, walking back inside, and toss her hat on the counter, and when I walk back outside, I see that she's taken off her shoes and is sitting on one of the loveseats. With her legs outstretched, her dress hangs in the front, showing all her legs. "Couch, it is."

"Look at this view. I'm in heaven," she says to me, and I place the plates down in front of her. "Did you cook that?" she asks, pointing at the eggs and the pancakes.

"No," I tell her. "I ordered that, but I did run out and get the pastries."

"Well, look at you." She smiles, and I lean down and kiss her lips. I don't even know if I should have, but I do, and she lets me.

"Do you want coffee or orange juice?" I ask her, my hand coming up and my thumb rubbing her bottom lip.

"There better be champagne in that orange juice," she

says softly, and I nod at her, going back inside. The cold air hits me right away as I pop the bottle of champagne and make her drink. When I hear the door open, she says, "I came to help."

"I was just making your drink," I tell her, and she comes over to me, grabbing it and taking a sip. "You didn't put any champagne in it."

"I filled it halfway," I tell her, laughing.

"Halfway isn't the whole way." She winks at me and adds more champagne. "Just perfect," she says and grabs the plate of pastries, and I follow her out with the orange juice and champagne.

I place the fruit plate down and sit on the couch in front of her, grabbing a strawberry and putting it in my mouth. "Those are sweet," I tell her, and she takes one and bites into it and moans.

"Those are to die for," she says. "This whole thing is incredible." She takes a bite of the croissant. "Had I known this would happen, I definitely would have called you sooner."

I lean back on the couch and stretch my arms across the back. "Would you have?"

"Probably not," she answers honestly. "I shouldn't have called you this time."

"And why is that?" I ask her and see her eyes struggle with the answer. "If we go anywhere in this, it has to be done with one hundred percent truth. If you can't give me that, we'll chalk it up as two friends having a couple of meals together."

She downs her mimosa and then pours some more. "Where do you think this is going?"

"I have no idea," I tell her. "But I would love to find out."

"I don't do relationships, Mark," she tells me. "Ever. No exceptions."

"And why is that?" I ask, now suddenly pissed off.

She shrugs her shoulders and looks away, then looks back at me. "It's just easier that way."

"For who?" I ask her, and she just shakes her head and smiles.

"For everyone," she answers, taking another strawberry. "These strawberries really are the best."

"They are," I say, and I just watch her. Putting her drink down, she gets up, walking to me. She picks up her dress and proceeds to straddle me. My hands automatically go to her hips as she sits on top of me.

"I have an itch, Mark," she says softly. "An itch that only you can scratch."

"Is that so?" I ask her as she grinds her hips on my already hard cock.

"That is very so," she says. When she leans in closer, I take her mouth. My hand moves up her back, her tongue tasting of strawberry and orange. Her head tilts to the side in order to deepen the kiss. She wants to be in charge, and just for a minute, I'm going to let her.

When her hands go from my chest to my hair is when I take over. I wrap one arm around her waist and stand, her mouth leaving mine as she yelps. "Time to show you my bedroom." Her legs wrap around my waist.

"That sounds like a great idea." She smiles, moving her mouth close to my ear. "Besides ..." She nips my earlobe as I walk through the doorway, and I want to press her against the glass window. "It's time to show you my vagina."

SEVEN

VIVIENNE

*M*Y HANDS GO into his hair, and I slam my mouth onto his as he carries me through his house. Sitting in front of him and hearing him tell me that he doesn't know where this is going was nerve-wracking, but there is only one place for this to go. In a week, he'll move along and so will I.

His tongue rolls with mine, and the anticipation of what's to come gets all my senses going. The little flutters start again in my stomach, and this time, I know it's just because I'm eager to finally get some dick. My heart hammers in my chest, which is new, but I guess it's been a while, so every part of me is excited. I moan into his mouth when he stops moving, and I look around his bedroom. The wall of windows provides a view of the river, and the sun shines in. His king-size bed sits in the middle of the room with two chaises on one side and then a sofa on the other. His room is massive, and I'm going to fuck him on every single surface.

"This is nice," I tell him, and he just attacks my neck. He sucks in and then bites down, and it shoots straight through me. One hand wraps around my waist to hold me up, and he uses the other one to pull down my shirt, snapping the spaghetti strap. My breast suddenly feels the cool air right before he leans down and bites the pebble tip, rolling it between his teeth with just enough pressure that I throw my head back and moan. He pulls it into his mouth and then twirls his tongue around it. I'm almost feverish trying to get off him and get him naked.

"Naked," I say while he assaults my nipple, and I can't do anything except close my eyes. I'm focusing on his tongue and teeth, and I swear I'm one touch away from having an orgasm. It's at the tip of my toes, working its way up, and my breathing gets a little bit more intense. I can taste it, and just like that, he stops what he's doing.

Again, I moan, but this time in frustration. "I was so close."

"Good things come to those who wait," he tells me, and I swear I want to push him down and plant myself on his cock and take what I want. He tosses me onto the bed, and I prop myself up on my elbows and watch him. I didn't really check him out before. He grabs his shirt from the back, and I watch as he pulls it over his head. I thought he would be like this, but it's better; it's so much fucking better. Everything is defined, his pecs are perfect and round, and his abs are on fucking point. His body is tanned and his chest so wide; not one thing on his body is bad. I look down and see his cock trying to get out, and from the looks of his shorts, he's hard as a rock in every single place.

"How long are you going to make me wait?" I ask him. "I

can start without you."

"You touch yourself, and then I won't make you come the whole time," he says with his eyes focused on mine. "I'll eat your pussy so hard, and I won't make you come."

"Is that a fact?" I ask him, and I'm almost tempted to play with myself, but something about the way he looks at me stops me.

"Not a fact. It's the truth," he says with authority, and I know he'll do it. "Show me your pussy," he asks. No, he demands.

I open my legs, bending them at the knees, and the skirt falls to the sides, giving him a full view of what he wants to see. I picked this dress for just this reason, the easy access. He moves so fast; one second, he's standing by the bed, and the next, his mouth is on my pussy. His tongue slips through my folds, and I feel his tongue fuck me. I grip his head with one of my hands, and he stops. My eyes peel open to look at him, his eyes almost black. I watch him as he licks up to my clit, then sucks it in. My eyes automatically close, and I feel one of his fingers slide in me. My hips move up on their own, my legs open wider. He slips another finger in me, and my stomach dips. I feel his body moving over me, his mouth latching onto my nipple as he fucks me slowly with his fingers. His tongue moves up my chest to my neck, and then his mouth is on mine, and I taste myself on him. I kiss him frantically while my hips move with his fingers.

His thumb strums my clit, and I want to move it side to side a bit faster. I can feel the orgasm building in my toes and slowly working its way up. My pussy gets just a touch tighter, a touch wetter. I pull away from his mouth to pant out his name.

"Mark," I say, closing my eyes as I take in the orgasm just a little bit more, his finger rubbing my G-spot over and over again. And then he pulls his fingers out of me, and my legs fall to the sides. "What?" I ask, confused.

"You kept me waiting for two years," he says, and I reach out to bring his hand back. "Two years of watching you." He puts his thumb on my clit and rubs it in a small circle. "Teasing me."

"I was not," I say, frustrated, and then he lowers his mouth again. His fingers fucking me again, he nips at my clit, and I'm right back to where I was before. My hands grab my tits, twisting my nipples. "Mark." I say his name again as the feeling starts to build again. "Right there," I tell him as his fingers curl up, touching the tender spot inside. My back arches, my hips buck up, and then he stops what he's doing again. My body is shaking with need. "I need …"

"What do you need?" he asks me.

"I need …" I almost say I need him, but I catch myself. He brings his hands to his mouth and sucks me off him.

"You need to come," he says. "You come on my cock."

"Then give me your cock." I egg him on.

He pulls his shorts down over his cock, and the minute I see it, I'm sitting up and it's already in my mouth. The salty pre-cum hits my tongue first, and I take as much of his cock in my mouth as I can, stopping midway. Not only is he hung, but he is thick, and my fingers can't wrap all the way around him. I feel his hands in my hair, and he grips it and pulls my head back. "Nothing sexier than my cock in your mouth," he says. "But I think my cock in your pussy will be better."

"Then show me," I say, leaning back in the middle of the bed. He gets off the bed and pulls down his shorts the rest of the way. His thighs are so big and all muscle. "You look like a Greek god," I tell him as I watch him walk to the side table and take out a pack of condoms.

"Come here." He motions me with his finger, and I want to say no, you come here. But my head doesn't work with my body, and I'm already out of the bed. I stand in front of him, and he pulls my white camisole off my body, his hand cupping both my B cup tits in his huge hand. "I'm going to fuck you the way I want to fuck you." I watch as he almost rips my skirt off to get it over my hips. "You're going to let me fuck you the way I want to."

"Is that so?" I say, my hand gripping his cock and moving up and down. "What if I want to fuck you?"

"We'll see if you deserve it," he says, his fingers sliding through the wetness of my lips. "This is mine," he says at the same time his thumb presses down on my clit. I want to tell him to dream on, but the only thing that I can do is close my eyes and groan. I'm already halfway there, so I don't want to say anything that makes him stop.

He pulls his hands out when I get on my tippy toes and open my legs a touch more, and I open my eyes and glare at him. "You're going to take this cock," I say, my hand squeezing his cock. "And you are going to make me come, so help me." He picks me up, bringing me back to the bed.

"Legs open," he tells me. Following his command, I lie in the middle of the bed and open my legs. He rips open a condom and slowly covers himself. My heart starts to speed up, knowing at any second he is going to be in me. He climbs on the bed on his knees, moving himself between my legs. Taking his cock in his hand, he runs it down my slit one time, then moves it up. He puts the tip right there and pushes in just a bit. My eyes close, and he stops.

"Watch," he says, and my eyes slip open. "Watch my cock," he says, his words making my pussy get tighter. "See your pussy stretch to take me," he says as he stretches me to get his cock head in, and then he enters me like a fucking snail. I don't breathe until he is balls deep in me. He pulls out just a touch and then moves in me again. "You ready?" he asks me, and I nod my head, biting my lower lip. His hands grab mine and put them on either side of my head. He pulls all the way out and then thrusts back into me. If he wasn't holding my hands, I would have smashed into the headboard. He does it again and again, driving me crazy with his pounding. My legs open wider and wider. My hips tilt up to take him deeper, deeper than I've ever had before. I can't help the cry that comes out, and he stops. "Did I hurt you?"

"No," I say. "More." My mouth is dry, but my pussy pulses around him. He watches me as he pounds into me over and over again, and I move my hips with him. "Yes," I say over and over again. "I'm going to come," I tell him, and I move my legs higher and higher. His cock rubs my G-spot over and over again. I'm going to come, and it's going to be like never before. I don't know why, I just do.

"Mark," I say his name, tasting it. "Mark," I say. Just one more pump and I'll be there. And just like that, he pulls out of me, and I groan as his face sucks my pussy into his mouth.

"What is …?" I ask him, and he flips me over.

"Ass up, face down," he orders, and I'm going to do it. His hands grasp my hips as his cock slips into me slowly until he is finally in all the way. He fucks me over and over again, his speed going from slow to fast, and I grip the sheets to not fly.

"How much do you want to come?" he asks, and I'm literally a rag doll at this point. I've never been one to beg, and I've never been one to almost cry from an orgasm.

"Mark," I plead with him. "Please." He pounds in me over and over, and I move one of my hands to my clit and slowly rub it.

"Are you playing with yourself?" he asks. When I nod my head, his hands leave my hips, and he squeezes my ass and pounds in again. "I told you," he says, pounding between words. "Your pussy is mine."

"Yes," I tell him as I try to fuck him back, but I don't know how much more I can do. I look over my shoulder at him, and his eyes watch as his cock slides in and out of me. "Harder." His eyes fly to me, and he sees me watching him. He puts one thumb in his mouth and then when he pounds into me again, his finger goes in my ass, and the moan that comes out of me shocks me.

"This pussy," he says as his cock pounds my pussy and his thumb fucks my ass. "Is mine." It's there again—the orgasm I've been chasing for the last I don't know how long. My body has a sheen of sweat over it. I'm afraid to say anything or for him to stop. "This ass," he says, using his hand to smack it, making my pussy shudder, "is mine." He pounds into me, and my senses are on overload. I don't even know what's going on. All I know is that I'll agree to anything.

"Say it," he says again, smacking my ass harder this time and then rubbing it. "Or I stop fucking you."

"No," I cry out.

His cock and finger work at the same time. "Say it's mine." He teases me again and again, each time going fast until my pussy gets tighter and then slowing down.

"It's yours," I say softly, and he groans. "It's yours."

"Work your clit faster," he says, and now he's the one panting. His finger comes out of my ass, and his hands clench my hips so tight. He's pounding into me so hard my knees come off the bed, and this time, he lets me have it.

"Come on my cock," he says, and I don't wait for him to tell me twice. He lets me come, and I swear I come longer than I've ever come before. Over and over again, my pussy convulses around his cock. Every single time I think it's the end, it does it again.

"Fuck," he says and then grunts one more time before coming with a roar, prolonging my orgasm even longer. His cock grows bigger in me, and he pumps into me a little bit each time. When his fingers let go of my hips, I collapse on the bed. My legs are sore, and my body is limp as a fucking noddle. I want to get up and grab my stuff and go, but I can't move. I can't do anything. I look over at him as he takes his cock out of me, and my body screams to get it back. He walks to the bathroom, his cock still hard as a rock, and I get to check out his ass as he walks away from me.

"I'm so fucked," I say to myself. "So fucked."

EIGHT

MARK

$\mathcal{I}$ TAKE THE condom off and dispose of it and grab a cloth. My heart hammers in my chest. I haven't come that hard ever; her pussy gripped my cock so tight I thought it would suffocate. After running the warm water over the plush white hand towel and squeeze I then carry it back to my bedroom and see that she hasn't moved.

"I am trying to move," she grumbles. "But it's like my body is locked to the bed."

I walk to the side of the bed, and her head turns to look at me. "Trust me, if you were locked to my bed, you would know it," I tell her, and her eyes go from my eyes to my cock.

"How are you still locked and loaded?" she whispers, then looks up at me. "Did you take something?"

I throw my head back, and the sound of my laughter fills the room. "I don't need to take anything. I have a beautiful naked woman in front of me."

"I know how it works, Mark." She tries to turn, and I lean down and help her. She lies there naked, her nipples still pebbled, her pussy glistening. "I'm just saying usually there is a ..." She snaps her fingers, trying to think of the word. "Recovery time."

"Is that a challenge?" I ask her, and my cock is suddenly rock hard and ready. I get on the bed with her kneeling next to her. I take the cloth, and I'm about to wipe her. "How many rounds do you think we can go?"

"Considering my vagina is almost broken ..." She looks at me and grabs the cloth out of my hand before I can clean her with it. "Maybe two or three."

"Is that so?" I ask her. "Let's aim for five."

"I need to walk later," she says, and I see her eyes move to my cock in my hands, then back up to my eyes. "I mean, worst-case scenario, my doorman will carry me."

"No one touches you," I say. Reaching over, I grab another condom, tearing it open and then covering myself. "You're mine," I tell her. Moving her knees back once I get between her legs, I rub myself up and down her slit, wetting the condom. When I slide into her slowly, her back arches, and her hand reaches out to pull me closer. "You said so yourself."

She groans. "You can't take anything I say during sex seriously." I pull out of her, and her nails dig into my ass. "Mark," she hisses and looks at me.

"Is it mine?" I ask, pushing into her again and then pulling out. She doesn't say a word, so I pound into her harder. She groans and looks at me. "Mine."

"Yours," she says, and then she locks her legs around my

hips. "Now, show me why I should be yours."

"Challenge accepted," I tell her, and for the next four hours, I use her body over and over again. And when I look over, she is sleeping. I smile at her, thinking about how many times I made her beg and how many times she almost cried out in frustration. When I roll into her and take her in my arms, the way she fits is perfect.

"No more," she grumbles. "I need to sleep, and then you better feed me."

"Go to sleep, and I'll feed you when you get up," I say. She turns in my arms and puts her head in my neck, and with her legs intertwined with mine, I fall asleep.

When my eyes blink over, I look over and see the sun setting, and my arm feels like it's being crushed. I look down, and her long black hair covers my whole chest. My cock lets me know he's ready to play again, and instead of waking her up with my cock, I slowly move away from her. Going to the bathroom, I slip on my robe and then walk slowly and softly out of the room. I head straight to the kitchen and grab two prepared meals.

I set the timer on the stove according to the instructions and then walk outside where the wind is picking up. I look out over the horizon at the boats lingering on the water.

"There you are." I hear from behind me. Looking over my shoulder, I see Vivienne come outside wearing the shirt I was wearing this morning. Even with the sleep still in her eyes and her wearing my shirt that is almost like a dress, she is the most beautiful woman I have ever seen.

"Sleeping Beauty." I laugh at her, and she walks with me to the railing, the breeze blowing her hair back. I open my arms for her, and she stands in front of me, and my arms hold her. "Did you sleep well?"

"I did," she says, looking over her shoulder at me. "But then your side of the bed grew cold very fast."

I lean down and kiss her neck softly. "Did you miss me?" I whisper in her ear right before I nip it with my teeth.

"Hmm," she groans but tilts her head to give me more access to her neck. "I guess I missed a certain part of you." She turns in my arms and slides her arms around my neck.

"Is that so?" I smile and bite her lower lip and then slide my tongue into her mouth. "What part exactly?" I want to pick her up and fuck her right here against my railing. "Was it my tongue?" I twirl my tongue with hers. "My fingers?" My hands grab her hips and press her to me. "Or was it my cock?"

"All three," she says, grinding her pussy into me. "Not in any particular order." I throw my head back and laugh at this.

"I mean, I'm not going to be greedy and point out one, so I'll take them all." She smiles at me. "But I do have to get going."

"I made dinner," I tell her. "Stay for dinner."

"Well ..." She looks to the side and then at me. "I guess I should make you feed me since I lost all my energy."

"Then after, I can show you how I eat dessert." I wink at her, and she pushes me away from her. "Where do you want to eat?"

"I'm all flustered now. Are we talking about food or private parts?" she jokes with me. "Let's eat inside. It's getting just a touch windy, and well, my lady town is all open."

"Lady town? Is that what we're calling it?" I turn and walk

back inside with her following me.

"Well, Disneyland is taken, so lady town it is." She winks at me. "What can I do to help?"

"Not much. It'll be ready in about ten minutes. We can go sit on the couch until then," I tell her, and then I hear my phone ringing, the sound echoing in the house. I have the phone set up to my intercom system, so I can answer in any room. I walk over to the wall and press the button. "Hello?"

"Markos." I hear my father's voice and then look over at Vivienne who just smiles, and her eyes light up.

"Hey, Dad," I tell him. "I'm in the middle of something. Is everything okay?"

"Of course, it's okay. I was just checking in. I haven't heard from you today," he says, and I know that right after he hangs up with me, he is going to call my brother.

"I'll call you in a little while," I tell him, and then I tell him I love you in Greek.

"Markos?" Vivienne says as soon as I hang up.

"It's my full name. The only one who uses it is my father. Or my mother when she's really pissed at me," I tell her, leaning against the counter and looking at her.

"I like it." She comes to me. "A lot."

"Do you?" I push her hair behind her ears and rub her cheek with my thumb. "There's a lot that you don't know about me."

"Well," she says. "I know that from now on, I'm calling you Markos."

"Why?" I tilt my head to the side.

"Because it's original, and it's your name." She then gets really close. "And because it sounds hot." And right before

I'm about to pick her up and place her ass on the counter, the oven beeps. She claps her hands together. "Dinnertime."

I walk over to the oven, grabbing the mitts and taking the two aluminum trays out of the oven. "I hope you are good with grilled salmon."

"I am," she says, opening the cabinets to get plates. After her third try, she finally grabs two plates and comes over. "It smells divine." She places the plate down, and I fix her plate with the salmon, quinoa, and vegetables.

"You grab the plates, and I'll get something to drink," I tell her. "Wine?"

"Yes, please. White, if you have it," she says, grabbing both plates, "but red is okay also." She walks through the doorway to the dining room, and I grab the chilled bottle of white wine and bring it with me along with two water bottles. Placing the items on the table, I walk over to the china cabinet in the corner grabbing a glass for her wine.

She sits down to the right of the head of the table, and I have to say, having her here in my space means everything. Now I have to just keep her here. I uncork her wine and pour some into her glass. She waits for me to sit down and then picks up her glass. "Santé." *Health,* she says in French.

"Santé," I repeat, grabbing my bottle of water.

She takes a sip of wine and then grabs her fork. "This is really good," she says after she takes her first bite. "So you speak Greek?"

I nod. "Not as much as I did when I was in Greek school."

"You went to Greek school?" She smiles. "Talking during sex just got moved up a notch."

"Is that so?" I ask her. "I could be saying anything, and

you wouldn't know."

"That's the whole intrigue. It's mysterious," she says.

I laugh at her and take another bite of the salmon. "Should I ask you to talk dirty to me in French?"

She takes a sip of her wine. "If you like to. I usually only bring out the French when I'm annoyed or pissed." She takes another bite. "I haven't been either with you yet."

I shake my head. "There's always tomorrow," I tell her.

"Are you close to your parents?" she asks me, and I smile at her.

"I am very much so. My father calls me every single day just to say hello and find out if I'm okay."

"Every day?" she asks, a bit shocked.

"It's not like the conversations last hours. It's just an are you okay. Good. Talk to you tomorrow," I tell her.

"That's nice," she says, smiling. "Were they strict parents growing up?"

"I mean, they are very traditional," I tell her. "We had a curfew until we left for college. And I was a good kid and listened. Now, my brother, on the other hand, there were times he thought he could climb through the window and bust out in the middle of the night." I laugh. "Little did he know, my father had installed an alarm, and the minute his window went up, the blaring started."

"Mon Dieu," she says in French, laughing.

"My father came running in with a bat, only to see my brother with one foot out the window." I think back to that day. "He got grounded for a month, and he had to do all the chores around the house."

"So you never snuck out of the house?" She sits back in

her chair, looking at me.

"I didn't say that," I tell her. "I just never got caught, which is why I was the good kid." I wink at her, and her laughter fills the room. "What about you?"

"Moi?" she says, pointing at herself and shrugs. "Not much to say. I'm an only child. My family is very well-known in France, something I try to hide, so …" She motions with her fingers doing a zipper. "I came here when I was sixteen. It was supposed to be just a yearlong thing, but it turned into me going to college here."

"What about a job?" I ask her, wanting to know everything about her.

"So curious," she says, smirking.

"I am," I finally say after taking a drink of water. "You're a beautiful woman. But I want to know you." I lean back in my chair and watch her.

"You know me better than most people." She laughs and starts to stand. "In fact, I think you know me four times more than most people."

"Want to make it six?" I ask her, and she looks over at me while picking up her plate.

"What happened to five?" She puts her plate down and then drinks the rest of the wine in her glass.

"I like even numbers," I tell her, and I pounce up from the table, grabbing her over my shoulder. The shirt falls off her bare ass, giving me the perfect opportunity to slap her ass cheek. I do it with a smile on my face, but she squirms, and I don't even make it up the stairs. Instead, round number five happens against the wall on the way upstairs, and then round number six is in the shower right before she leaves me with a simple kiss.

"Why are you getting dressed?" she asks me while she slips on her shirt.

"I'm taking you home," I tell her, slipping my feet into my shoes.

"I can make it home without you," she says as she slides her feet in her shoes.

"I know you can make it home without me," I tell her, grabbing a baseball hat and putting it on my head. "But I want to take you home. That's the difference."

"Aren't you the chivalrous one?" she says, laughing as she picks up her purse.

"Call it whatever you want," I say, closing the door behind us. Then I follow her downstairs and watch her as she hails a cab.

"You know, it's silly for you to come with me and then have to come all the way back home again."

"I like being silly," I tell her when a cab finally stops and follow her instead. "It'll be two stops," I tell him right away, and he just nods. Vivienne gives him her address and sits down next to me. "Are you going to call me?"

She looks down and then up again, trying to hide a smile. "Probably."

"Or probably not," I tell her, and she just looks out the window. I don't push it anymore, and when the car stops, she turns to me.

"I had a great time."

"Just kiss me, Vivienne," I say, not wanting to hear what else she has to say. I lean in, and she kisses me just a soft little kiss on the lips and then reaches for the handle.

"Bon Nuit, Markos," she says and gets out of the car and slams the door. I watch her walk into her building and then into the elevator, disappearing from my sight.

"Where to now?" the driver asks me.

"Back to where you got me," I say, sitting back in the seat. When I walk back into my house, her smell lingers, and I wonder how I'm going to get her back. Regardless of what she says, I know one thing. She will be back.

VIVIENNE

$\mathcal{I}$ WALK INTO my lobby, pretending not to have a care in the world. I smile at the nighttime security and press the button for the elevator on shaky legs. "It's just a myth," I keep saying over and over again. When I step into the elevator and turn to look out, I see him sitting in the cab with his eyes on me. It's dark, but I would know his eyes anywhere. The door closes, and when it finally does, I lean back and put my hand up on the rail. "What the fuck?"

I unlock my door and walk in, not turning on the lights. I don't do anything but go sit down on the couch and gaze outside. I think back on the day, and what I thought would happen. I thought I would show up at his place, we'd fuck, and it would be done. The itch would be gone and the whole chase over. What I wasn't expecting was to be so properly fucked that I wanted to go back for more. Today, tonight, tomorrow—I wanted it. I rub my hands over my face, and it's the wrong thing because his smell is all around me. I need another shower to wash him off me. I get up and step into the shower, the hot water washing away all his touches. "Are you going to call me?" I still hear his voice.

I dab myself with the white plush towel and replay the dinner over in my head. I don't ever date, so I wasn't prepared for his questions about me or what I did for a living. What shocked me even more was that I wanted to know more about him. I wanted to know what he liked to eat and what his favorite color was. I was actually interested in knowing everything about him, and it freaked me out so much I had to stand and get away from him. My heart speeds up when I think about him taking me in the hallway, and the condom in his pocket as if he'd planned it all along.

Sliding into bed, I grab the cream on my night table and rub it over my hands. As I turn on the television, my body feels like it went through fifteen rounds of boxing. My arms hurt, and I didn't even use them. The second my head hits the pillow, I'm out like a light, and he's there, waiting for me in my dreams. His smile, his touch, everything is there, and when my phone rings, I feel like I'm in that movie *Groundhog Day*.

"This better be someone dead," I say, not even looking at the name on the phone.

"It's almost eleven," Karrie says, chuckling, and I hear horns in the background. "Why are you still sleeping?"

"I'm tired," I tell her and roll over. My body aches, but it's nothing like the soreness between my legs. "I can be tired."

"You can be, but only if you went out last night," she says, and I now hear sirens in the background.

"Jesus, where are you?" I ask her, peeking one eye open.

"I'm in the city. I had an OB/GYN appointment." She laughs. "I'm not pregnant."

"You know you can swallow, right?" I laugh and turn back to my side. "They like it better sometimes."

"Do they? I'll remember that. Now, do I come over, or do you want to meet me for lunch?"

"Is this a trick question?" I ask her as I try to stretch my muscles, pulling from everywhere. "Come here. I don't want to get dressed. Oh, and bring breakfast."

"It's eleven," she says again. "It's almost lunchtime."

"Karrie, I've been up for four minutes. Get coffee and some croissants, pretty please, mon amie préféré." *My favorite friend.*

"Already on it," she says, and then I hear a car door close. "Be there in ten."

"D'accord," I say. I toss my phone to the side and linger on the bed for a couple of minutes before getting up and walking to the bathroom. I'm washing my face when I hear heels clicking across the floor, coming closer and closer.

"Did you just get up?" she asks me, and I look at her while I wash my face and apply my cream. "And are those fingertip bruises?" she asks, coming closer. I look down at myself. I haven't gotten dressed yet, so I'm naked.

"Where?" I ask. When I look over my shoulder, I see what looks like a fingerprint bruise right above my ass.

"Right there," Karrie says, pressing on it and making it hurt.

"Ouch," I tell her, pushing her away and grabbing my kimono hanging behind the door. "That hurt."

97

"The question is, how did it get there?" She folds her arms over her chest.

"I can't answer these questions without coffee and a mimosa," I tell her. Walking away from her, I'm dreading what I'm going to tell her, knowing she'll see it for something more than it is. Which is nothing.

I walk to the kitchen to grab the tray of coffee and open the pink box right next to it to look at the buttery croissants placed perfectly so as not to be squished. I take one out and bite the tip off and swallow it down with a sip of my café latte. "Almost like home."

"You can keep circling around the topic, but it doesn't mean I'm going to forget," she says. Laughing, she grabs the box and walks to the couch with it. She places it on the table between the couches and then walks over to the cabinet against the wall to grab the champagne glasses. "Now, I'm assuming there is a bottle of prosecco in the fridge?"

I shrug. "If there isn't, someone will be fired." She walks away laughing and comes back out with a bottle of prosecco and a jug of freshly squeezed orange juice that I have delivered every other day. I take another bite of the flaky goodness while she pours us each a mimosa. She grabs a croissant and sits in front of me on the other couch. I curl my feet under me, getting comfortable. "I fucked Mark," I say when I finish my last bite, and then I turn to look out the window at the sun shining in the sky to avoid looking at her.

"Mark who?" she asks, and I see her kicking off her shoes and curling her feet under her.

I take another sip of my drink, draining it and then fill my glass up again. "Mark Dimitris."

I don't have to look up to see the shock on her face as her gasp fills the room.

"But," she starts to say and then stops. "I thought," she stutters out. "I don't ..."

I finish the second glass and then look at her. "But how?"

I shake my head. "After four kids, you are asking me how? Matthew isn't doing something right."

"I know how." She leans forward and puts her untouched drink down, and I grab it. "I'm asking how did it happen."

"He invited me over for breakfast." I take a big inhale. "I left after supper."

"That's ..." She starts counting on her fingers.

"It was all day long. Six rounds, to be exact." If I thought she was shocked before, her mouth hanging open now says everything. "Four almost back to back."

"Is that even possible?" she asks me. "Did he take something?"

"All natural." My answers are literally two to three words. I don't give her anything extra even though I know she's just waiting for more.

"You usually just dip and go," she points out. "I mean, three is your max." I shrug. "And then what happened between four and five?"

I shrug. "I napped," I tell her, and she throws her head back and laughs her ass off, annoying me.

"You napped? Mrs. 'I don't sleep in anyone else's bed but my own'?" She points her finger at me, mocking my words. "Mrs. 'I fuck and leave, make them wanting more.'"

"Yeah, well, he wanted more," I tell her. "So I gave him two more. He doesn't like odd numbers."

"So he has to fuck twice or what, it throws his game off?" she asks. I have no answer for her, but she doesn't let it bother her. "How was it?"

"It was fine," I say, avoiding her eyes.

"Hold on for just one second," she snaps, and I look at her. "You are never one not to boast about shit. Especially the epicness of all things related to your vagina."

"I mean, my vagina is magic," I say, laughing.

"On a scale of one to ten." She sits back and puts her arms up on the back of the couch, and I know she's just waiting for it. "How good was he?"

"Ten," I answer her honestly. "He is hands down the best I've ever had."

"Like ever?" she asks me, confused. "Since you started having sex?"

"Yes," I finally say, letting it all out. "He is the best I've ever had. Hands down the biggest I've ever had." My brain is telling my mouth to stop, but I can't. "Honestly, I thought my vagina would be bruised." I start to open my legs to show her, and she yells.

"I don't want to see your bruised vagina, woman!" she yells while she turns her head and puts her hand in front of her face.

"I've seen four human heads come out of your vagina, and you can't look at mine?" I stand, putting my hands on my hips.

"That is different," she says, getting up now. "That's a natural thing."

My hand shushes her away. "Oh, please." She turns and looks at me now.

"Is he really that good?" she asks, and I nod.

"Better, and it's a shame I won't be able to give it another go," I tell her, sitting back down. "Like really, really bad. I swear if they made vibrators out of his cock, I would buy it in bulk."

"Why can't you give it another go?" She sits back down herself and grabs another croissant.

"I have a rule, Karrie, and I stick to my rule, so there isn't anything cloudy," I tell her. "You know this."

"But what if you like him?" she asks me, and I want to tell her that I do like him. I like the way he smiles, and the way he looks at me. I like that he's private, and I like that he talks to his parents everyday.

"I like him," I answer her. "But I like a lot of people. Take Thor, for example. I like him a lot."

"Vivienne, one of these days, you are going to fall in love," she says softly, and it's my turn to gasp.

"That is the most hateful thing you have ever said to me, and now you've put that into the universe." I put my hands up, shaking. "It's like bad mojo."

"You mean karma," she corrects me.

"Whatever you want to call it," I snap at her. "Take it back."

"Okay, fine, you aren't going to fall in love." She takes it back. "Now what if he calls you to go out again?"

"He isn't going to call me," I tell her, and her eyebrows go up. "I won't answer." I really mean it; I won't answer. Or maybe I will answer but just to tell him that it's a no-go.

"This isn't like all the other ones," she says, dusting the crumbs off her shirt.

"You have to promise not to say anything to anyone," I

tell her. "He's a very private person, and I don't want people to talk about it."

"As I said, he isn't like the others. It's almost like he's a silent predator."

"And what, he's going to come out of the water and bite me?" I ask her. "He's a nice man. A great time in bed. And that's it. It was two consenting adults scratching an itch."

"Are you trying to convince me or yourself of this?" she asks me, and I just glare at her. I'm about to snap when her phone rings. "Hello, love." She looks at me and smiles. "I'm at Vivienne's, why?" I get up, grabbing another croissant, and then go to the bedroom to grab my phone. Seeing I have two missed calls from the man in question, I put the phone back down and then walk out to the living room. "Okay, come get me now," she says, hanging up the phone. "Matthew finished his meeting early, and he's going to come get me."

"Why are your cheeks all flushed?" I ask her, and she looks down. "Was he talking dirty to you to get the motor going?"

"No," she says, trying to avoid my eyes. "He's picking me up, and we are going to swing by The Plaza for lunch."

"You mean, he's booked a room, and he is going to make you scream his name over and over again?" I clap my hands together and laugh.

"You try having sex with four kids coming in all the time," she says, getting up. "Now I'm going to let my husband take me to a hotel and have his way with me, and with any luck, his parents will take them for the night, and we can do it six or seven times."

"Will he need help?" I ask her, and she glares at me. "What? He's coming up on the ladder in age. How am I supposed to know that he doesn't need it?"

"Trust me, he doesn't," she says. Grabbing her purse, she comes over to me, bending to kiss my cheeks. "Now, with any luck, *my* vagina will be bruised tomorrow."

"I will keep my fingers crossed for you." I kiss her, and she turns and walks out of the room and shuts the door with a slam. "Crazy kids," I say, thinking back to how she fought it when they first got together. I'm about to go grab my phone when there is a knock on the door, and I wonder who it could be. I walk to the door and swing it open, and my mouth hangs open.

"We just got this for you," one of the bellhops says. The huge box covers his face, and he peeks at me around the side. "Do you want me to put it in the living room?"

"Yes, please," I answer him and move out of the way so he can come in. The huge brown box is so big I don't know how he's carrying it. He places it on the dining table and then looks at me.

"It's not heavy, just big," he says, nodding and then walking out. *What in the world could it be?* I think to myself. My name is written on the top of the box, so I pick up the cover and put it aside.

A white envelope sits on the top of the white tissue paper. I turn it over in my hand and pull out the card.

Vivienne,

I went to bed with your scent on my pillow and have thought of nothing else since. Have dinner with me under the sea.

I promise not to bite unless you ask me to.

Markos

I smile and laugh at the same time and put the card to the side. Opening the white tissue paper, I laugh even louder. In the boxes are stuffed animals. A baby octopus in blue, an otter, a whale, a penguin, a sloth, and then at the bottom what looks like a huge shark. I pull it out and see a ribbon tied with a small card attached to it.

I'll pick you up at eight.

Call me now.

Markos

I sit down in the chair, looking at all of this, and I know it's a bad idea. Even getting up and walking to the phone, I know I shouldn't call him because it's just setting me up for the fall, even if it's just a little fall. But something stronger is taking over, and it's that same force that makes me pick up my phone and text him.

Me: ***I'll be ready.***

TEN

MARK

"*I* WANT TO bring the fucking cup back." Matthew sits at the head of the table during the meeting. I lean back in the chair and take a drink of my protein shake. I woke up this morning before my alarm and took advantage of it by getting to the rink early and working out before our ten a.m. meeting with the coaching staff and the top players on the team.

"I think we have all the pieces." Max was the scouting agent and is now the assistant to the GM, Matthew. My eyes go to Viktor, the newest player to be acquired and while in rehab, no less. I don't know his story, and I also will not ask him for his story. If he wants to tell me, he will. If not, then so be it.

"I agree," Evan, our captain, says. He's been our captain for the past two seasons, signing the day Matthew and Max retired. It was Matthew's first big deal. He's the best that there is, so it was no surprise that Matthew made him an offer when his contract was up with Dallas. It also helped that his sister was dating him. "Our defense is good, but it has to be better." He looks at the coaching staff, and they nod their heads at him. "We also need to be on the puck more and work on the turnovers in the neutral zone." He taps the table with his finger. "We need to work on keeping the pucks for this guy." He motions with his head.

"I need backup," I finally say, and all eyes turn to me. "Not going to lie, the last year was tough with no backup goalie you trust. I get it, the kid was young, but you need to know once you get between those pipes, you leave everything at the door." I take another drink. The kid we had last year played with his heart on his sleeve. If he came in and had a fight with his girlfriend, we knew he wouldn't play worth a shit. It sucked because I also needed a break once in a while. "A second goalie I can count on in case anything happens."

"I agree," Matthew says, and Max nods.

Coach Scott now speaks up. "That is why you aren't playing preseason games." I look at him, raising my eyebrows. "I mean, maybe a home game so the fans can get a taste, but other than that, I want to test what we have, and we need you on the sidelines to help." I just nod at him. The rest of the meeting is more of the same, and it's over by ten thirty. I get up and nod at everyone, walking out and taking my phone out of my pocket. She hasn't called, but I'm not surprised. She's going to make me work for it. My whole bed still smells like her, haunting me almost.

I pull out my contacts and start making a plan. The

phone rings twice, and then he picks up. "Mr. Dimitris." His smooth voice comes out. "What can I help you with on this beautiful day?"

"Fredrick," I say his name. "I was wondering if it would be possible to rent out the aquarium for the night?"

"What time were you thinking?" he asks.

"I was thinking maybe eight thirty," I tell him. "It would mean a great deal to me."

"It would be an honor," he says. He confirms that the aquarium will be shut down for us at eight and to come in anytime we would like. After hanging up with him, I call my florist, Amanda, except I don't order flowers, making her laugh even louder. Amanda has been a close friend since my early twenties; we ran in the same circle.

"You know that this is a flower shop, right?" She laughs.

"I know, but I have no idea who else I can call to order this from," I tell her, and she talks to someone in the back.

"Okay, but you owe me one. Do you want any flowers with this box of stuffed animals?" Amanda asks me, and now I laugh.

"Not today," I tell her. "And you know that I'm good for it."

"Yeah, yeah," she says and disconnects when she gets the address she needs. I call Vivienne, and I'm not surprised she doesn't answer my first call or my second, but when she ignores my third, I send Amanda a text with different instructions than the first.

"Hey, you're still here." I look up and see Matthew walking toward me.

"Yeah, I was going to get on the ice for an hour or so," I tell him. "What's up?"

"I'm heading out to pick up my wife, but I wanted to touch base and see if everything is okay." I watch his eyes as he asks me this. I don't think Vivienne would have told him anything, and I try to see if she did.

"What do you mean by that?" I ask him, trying to see if he knows anything or if it's all in my head.

"I know that you were beyond frustrated last year," he says, and I breathe a sigh of relief. "And I just want you to know that we are behind you one hundred percent."

"Thanks," I tell him, nodding. "Last year was not a good one, but we can do better this year, so let's do that."

"I agree." He slaps me on the shoulder. "Now I'm off."

"Have fun," I say and walk away from him. The phone beeps in my hands.

Amanda: *Everything is taken care of. Who knew so many stuffed animals could fit in one box?*

Me: *Thanks.*

I put the phone away and then walk into the changing room and see I'm the only one left. When I walk to Pierre's office, I see that he isn't in either. I can't really go on the ice and not have anyone to practice with. When I look around, I see that most of the people are heading to a meeting or taking off. Next week, things will be back to normal and more people will be in. I grab my stuff and make my way home, tackling my email as soon as I walk in. I'm about to send an email for New Orleans when my phone pings, and I see it's from Vivienne.

Vivienne: *I'll be ready.*

I smile, and I'm tempted to call her just to hear her voice, but instead, I text her back.

Me: *I can't wait.*

I put my phone down, and the day drags on. Or maybe I'm just anxious to get to her. I slip into my white jeans and my red, white, and light blue button-down shirt, leaving the top three buttons undone. I tie the cuffs and put on my Rolex and then slip into my red jacket, pulling the sleeves down. I spray my cologne on and then grab the keys to the Range Rover. I usually don't drive in the city, but I will today so I can keep this private.

I look at the time, and it's 7:59 when I finally pull up in front of her building. I leave the car at the curb when I get out, and the doorman comes over to me. "I'm picking up Ms. Paradis," I tell him. He just nods and turns to go inside at the same time the elevator doors open, and I see her. All eyes turn to her, which is no surprise since she's gorgeous. She walks out of the elevator and uses her fingers to wave at the security. I take her in before she sees me, and I want to take her back upstairs and stay in for the night. She's wearing beige and black shorts that float around her mid-thigh and show off her long, tanned legs. Legs that wrapped around my waist perfectly. Her black silk spaghetti strap top is tucked in and a silver watch and black beads wrap around her wrist. She's carrying a black hand purse in one hand, and she looks down and then to the side again, and this time, I see that her long hair is pinned at the nape of her neck. When the doorman calls her name, she looks at him. Then her eyes fly to mine, and the smile I've been thinking about all afternoon long is finally there. Her whole face lights up when he holds the door open for her.

"Well, well, well," she says. "This is curbside service, Markos," she says as she walks to me, and I immediately want to grab her by her waist and kiss her mouth. But I look around at the people on the street and stop myself. She stands in front of me, and she is the one who leans in and kisses my cheek. "Don't you look all handsome."

"Vivienne," I say and inhale her smell. "Everything pales compared to you."

She shakes her head, tucking her purse under her arm. "Very well done." She smirks at me.

I laugh and lean in and kiss her neck now. Her breath hitches when I do that. I turn, taking her hand with mine. "Shall we?" My hand reaches out to open the door, and when she steps into the truck, I close the door after her and get in a second later. "Ready?" I say, starting the truck and putting on my seat belt.

"I mean, as ready as I think I am," she says, looking at me, and I pull out into traffic. "Although I will say your invitation has me curious."

"Does it?" I look over, smirking at her, and then turn back to look at the road. "Why is that?"

"Have dinner with me under the sea." She repeats what was on the card. "What does that even mean?"

"So does that mean you thought about me all afternoon long?" I ask, grabbing her hand and bringing it to my lips. I have to touch her. Being this close to her and not touching her is torture.

"Not all afternoon," she says. "Just for a couple of minutes here and there."

I laugh at her. "What did you do today?" I ask her.

"Well, I slept longer than I thought I would," she says.

Looking outside, she tries to see if she knows where we are going. "I had a very hard workout yesterday, and my body had to recover."

"Was it?" I ask her, taking the backroads so she doesn't recognize the surroundings. I pull into the side entrance and spot Frederick there waiting. "Well, let's hope your body is ready for round two," I say, and then her door opens.

"Welcome," Frederick says. "We are so pleased you could come."

"Thank you," she says, grabbing his hand and stepping out of the truck. I grab her other hand and pull her toward me, causing Fredrick's hand to fall from hers.

"Is everything set?" I ask him, and he just nods at me. "Thank you," I say, turning to walk toward the entrance.

"Are you going to tell me where we are?" she asks with a smile, her fingers linked with mine as we walk toward the doors.

"Coney Island," I answer, the sound of our feet on the wooden bridge right at the entrance. "We are at the New York Aquarium," I tell her, and her mouth opens when we stop at the blue and white sign right in front. I open the door, and she follows me in. "The whole place is closed for us. Where do you want to start?"

She looks around and then back at me. "What do you mean?"

I walk toward the underground aquarium. "Well, I wanted to have dinner with you under the sea," I tell her and then enter the tunnel with the glass surrounding us. The lights illuminate, and you can see the fish all around us. A table with two chairs sits in the middle. "This," I tell her, letting go of her hand, "is under the sea." I shrug. "Well, as under the sea as I could get in short notice."

She turns in a circle, her mouth hanging open as she takes in where we are. "You closed down the aquarium for us to have dinner here?"

"I did," I tell her, and she walks to the glass now. Putting her hand on it, she watches fish swim by her. "This is …" she starts, turning around. "It's incredible."

"No," I tell her, not moving from my spot. "You're incredible."

She turns and looks back at the fish. The whole time, she doesn't sense the beating of my heart or the fact that I held my breath, hoping she didn't laugh at this ridiculous plan.

ELEVEN

VIVIENNE

"*No.*" HIS VOICE comes out softly, his eyes staring straight into mine. "You're incredible." I don't say anything to him. I just turn and look at the colors in the water.

When I answered his text, I picked up my phone about seventy times to cancel it. It was silly to go out on this date. The main reason was I don't date. Ever. But every time I would draft up a "sorry, something came up" text, I would erase it and go in search of an outfit. Each time, I was thinking I was stupid to even do this because I was leading him on. But the next time I picked up my phone, instead of texting him, I googled *what does one wear to a date when it's under the sea.* I got lots of floral advice, but then I went into my closet and the cheetah print shorts were the closest I came to flowers. So I went online and ordered five flower dresses.

"Thank you." I feel his hands on my arms and look over

my shoulder to see him right behind me.

"For?" I ask him, my heart speeding up. His outfit fits him like a glove, and when he got into the truck, he undid his jacket, and his arms looked like he was going to burst out of it. The need to lean over the console and just kiss him silly took over me, and I turned my head to look out the window instead of stare at him.

"Coming tonight."

"I mean …" I turn and face him. "You did have my curiosity piqued by the whole under the sea thing." My hand goes to his shirt collar and then moves down, my fingers trailing inside his shirt across his smooth skin. "I thought you would just take me back to your place and fuck me under your shower." He throws his head back and laughs, and I look to the side as the bright colors of the corals catch my attention. The yellow fish are just swinging around and around. "But this," I tell him, letting go. I walk to the wall of glass and place my hand against it, feeling the coolness right away and watching as the corals sway side to side almost peacefully. "This is so much better than being fucked in your shower."

"Really?" he says, and I turn to watch him. "Obviously, I didn't do that right."

It's my turn to throw my head back and laugh. "I have no complaints," I tell him. Someone comes out with a tray with a glass of champagne and a glass of water. Mark takes both and then the man turns and walks away. He hands me the champagne glass. "Merci."

"To not drowning." He winks at me and then clinks my glass.

"And to a redo in the shower," I counter and then take a sip of the chilled champagne. The bubbles hitting the roof of my mouth right away.

The man comes back again. "Dinner is ready," he says, and I look at Markos, who nods at him and then guides me toward the round table in the middle of the room. When he pulls out a gold chair, and I sit down, I don't expect him to lean down and kiss my shoulder. Or for his beard to make my whole body shiver. He walks to his chair, facing me, and I look down at the cream linen cloth covering the table and the white and gold plate settings. The cream-colored linen napkin in the middle is folded into the shape of a seashell. I put it in my lap and then look at the little touches on the table. What looks like sand in the middle of the table with a starfish and seashells everywhere.

"I hope that you like seafood." He leans in. "I mean, I know it's rude of us to eat some of the creatures' friends but …"

I laugh. "Badass." Then I look around. "Watch out, little fish, or else we'll eat you, too." I grab my glass of champagne and finish it, and it's quickly refilled by someone waiting in the wings. The man comes out again, this time with two plates, and places them in front of Mark and me. He explains what we are eating and then goes away.

"Where is this food from?" I ask him, and he looks at me. "Is it a secret?"

"My friend, Eric, likes to cook," he tells me, "so I asked him to cook for us." The food melts in my mouth. Every single bite is better than the last one, and plate after plate comes out until finally, the dessert comes out.

"This is the best meal I've ever had," I say as I finish off the warm chocolate fondant with smoked chocolate and a marshmallow on top.

"I hope everything was to your liking," the man says, and I look up. "Chef Eric sends his regards and says next time he hopes you will come in so he can cook for you there."

"It was amazing as always," Mark says, and then the man leaves.

"Why do I feel like Chef Eric is a big deal?" I tell him, taking the last sip of my champagne while Markos shrugs. "You aren't going to tell me?" I watch Mark get up from his chair and come to my side, and my head tilts back to look at him. "What if I'm craving his food?"

One of his hand wraps around the back of my neck, and he bends down so his lips are close to mine. I watch him the whole time, expecting him to kiss me, waiting for him to kiss me, wanting him to kiss me, but he doesn't. Instead, he moves his mouth to my ear, and he whispers, "Then you call me, and I'll take you there." His breath on my ear makes me shiver.

"You are obsessed with me calling you," I tell him, and his face comes back to hover over me.

"I'm obsessed with you, Vivienne," he tells me and then finally kisses me with the taste of chocolate on his lips. The kiss leaves me breathless, making my whole body want his touch, but then he pulls away from my lips. He holds out his hand for me, and I grab it, putting my napkin on the table and picking up my purse. "Let go see the sharks."

"Or," I say, "you can take me back to your house and show me that shower again." His eyes twinkle in the darkness. "I somehow seem to have forgotten about that one. So technically, we only had sex five times."

He comes close to me now. "I don't do odd numbers." He pushes the hair that came loose from my bun behind my ear. "Always even."

"Well, then we better go and rectify that. We don't want the universe to do something crazy." I smile at him. "The whole world can come to an end, and we'll be stuck at five."

"We can't have that happening," he says while we walk out of the door, and he makes his way back to the truck. The wind blowing makes me shiver, and he stops and takes off his jacket, putting it around my shoulder. The heat from his body suddenly envelops me, and I hear the truck door being unlocked. He opens the door for me, and I turn to him.

"You know, if this is going to mess up anything, we should maybe just have a quick one in the truck and then do double at your place," I tell him, rubbing my ass against his cock before getting into the car. I expect him to close the door, but he doesn't. Instead, he leans in close to me.

"If there weren't five cameras watching us, I'd fuck you bent over this truck," he says, and my pussy contracts. "If it was later in the night, I would let you suck my cock while I drove, but instead, you're going to sit in your seat, and I'm going to tell you all about what I plan to do to you." I have the sudden urge to grab his head and push it down to my pussy because he didn't mention anything about that. He doesn't say anything as he gets in and starts the truck. My body is on full alert, having his smell all around me, and the drive to his house is agony as he tells me how he is going to take me, how he's going to please me, and how I'm going to come over and over again. I swear to Christ, if it was later and there weren't people driving by, I would totally have given him head.

My eyes blink open, and I look over at Mark lying on his back with the sheet pushed down to his stomach. One arm is above his head, and the other across his chest by my teeth marks under his nipple. That was after the shower when he teased me to the point of exhaustion. I didn't plan to fall asleep, just wanted to rest my eyes, or at least, that is what I told myself, and now I look over at the clock and read the time. It's 4:17, so I've been sleeping for three hours. I slowly get up, the sheet falling from my chest, and I look down and I have my own set of teeth marks from when I rode him. I get out of the bed and tippy toe around to see where my panties ended up and then remember he tore them off. I look over at him as my body feels so relaxed. I bend and pick up my bra and my shirt and then grab a shoe that he tossed over his shoulder. I finally find my shorts at the front door, and I'm shimmying myself into them when I hear him behind me. "Where do you think you're going?" His voice is thick with sleep, and I look over at him standing there naked. The light from outside shows me all of him, and his body is sculpted like a god.

"I was going to go home," I tell him, and then I see him walking toward me.

"It's four a.m.," he says and stops in front of me.

"I was trying not to wake you." My hand goes to his chest.

"Do you know what would have happened if I woke up and found you gone?" he asks, and I tilt my head, waiting for his answer. "You know what? It's better if I show you," he says and picks me up, and I gasp. "Definitely more fun to show you," he says, putting me over his shoulder like I weigh nothing. His palm meets my ass right away, and the sting shoots through me, and three hours later, I'm a sweaty mess. My ass still stings from all the times he's smacked me, and then he brought me to the brink of orgasm so many times, I thought I was going to pass out. Even if I wanted to leave right now, I don't think I would have the energy.

"I can't move," I tell him, looking at him as he comes out of the bathroom. "My arm feels like it weighs a hundred pounds." He picks me up and carries me to the bathroom. "Where are you taking me? I swear, Markos, I don't think I could go another round," I tell him and then look up at his face. "Okay, maybe one more, but it would have to be quick and not like an hour."

He laughs and steps into his tub with me and sets me down. The warm water washes over me, and the ends of my hair float around me. "Did you want to wet your hair?" He sits facing me; the tub big enough for him to stretch out his legs.

"I don't even care," I tell him. "Honestly, I feel like I'm high," I tell him. "Maybe your cock is laced with some sort of drug, and every time I lick it or you stick it in me, the drug wears off." He puts his head back and laughs, and I rest my head on the side of the tub. "I'm going to have to google that when I get home."

"How is it you can get me all hot and bothered one minute, and the next, I'm laughing so much my stomach hurts?" He wets his face with water.

"It's a gift." I put my hand under my head, closing my eyes but then opening them and gazing out his window. "This view is crazy."

"It's the whole reason I bought the place," he tells me. "Wall-to-wall windows."

"Where else do you have houses?" He looks at me confused. "Well, Matthew and Max all have houses in Canada, so I don't know. I was just assuming ..."

"I have houses in Canada and in Los Angeles," he tells me, and I look up. "I also have condos in Florida, San Francisco, Chicago, Greece, and Italy, and a house that I'm looking at in Montana."

"Which is your favorite?"

"Greece or Italy. I love them both the same," he says.

"Why?" I wonder to myself, not realizing I asked it out loud.

"It's where I can be me. Where I can walk to the corner restaurant, sit down at a table outside, order a coffee, and just watch life pass by." He smiles while he describes it.

"That sounds amazing." I smile back at him, then look outside again. We sit in the tub until the water turns a touch cold. He gets up first and wraps a towel around his waist and then comes back, holding open another towel for me. I stand and walk into the towel and smile up at him. "Thank you, Markos."

"For you, Vivienne, anything," he says, and my stomach feels like it just flipped. I look down, ignoring the moment. Refusing to acknowledge what just happened, I tell myself this is getting out of hand and this will be the last time I see him. I walk to the front door dressed in last night's outfit and kiss him twenty-five minutes later. I let the kiss linger just a bit longer than it should, knowing it'll be our last. My lips are still tingling when I press the elevator button for down.

I look over my shoulder when the elevator gets here. "Take care, Markos."

TWELVE

MARKOS

*A*S SOON AS the elevator door closes, I want to call her and tell her to come back and share breakfast with me. When I opened my eyes and saw that the bed next to me was empty, I had a semi-heart attack. Surely, she wouldn't just bail in the middle of the night. When I heard little footsteps going down the stairs, I knew she was planning to do exactly that.

I close the door softly and walk to the kitchen to start my coffee. Looking over at the clock, I see it's a little after eight a.m. *I got maybe two hours of sleep*, I think while I rub my neck with my hand and wait for my coffee to brew. I take my shot of espresso black, sipping it, and then hear the front door slam and heels click on the tiles. "Morning," Tracy says, putting all her bags on the table in the middle of the room. "Did you just wake up?"

"More or less," I tell her while she opens the bag of food

she brought with her. If she would have gotten here five minutes earlier, she would have come face-to-face with Vivienne, and although I don't hide that I date, I also don't flaunt it.

"You look like shit," she says, going to get her own cup of coffee and starting the machine. "Was it a late night?"

"More or less," I tell her, grabbing a strawberry from one of the trays she brought. "I'm going to go get dressed. I'll be back."

"Want to work outside?" she asks, and I look out and see that it's another sunny day. "We might have to come inside, though, because the wind is picking up."

"Yeah, that sounds good," I say as I walk upstairs and go to my room. Closing the door behind me, I see the bedding on the floor and the sheet lying to the side. I walk to the bed and can still see where she held the sheets in her hands. I walk to the closet, and slipping off the robe, I hang it up and then grab boxers and a pair of khaki slacks with a white linen button-down shirt. Grabbing my phone, I open my texts and send her one.

Me: *Let me know if you made it home*.

I see the three dots come up.

Vivienne: *Home and going to bed.*

I smile, and then I call Amanda, and she answers on the first ring. "Are you sending flowers today?"

I chuckle. "Not exactly but I was wondering if you could help me."

"You know I say this with much love, but you're the biggest pain in my ass," she says, and I hear her take a sip. "What now?"

"I was wondering if you can maybe get a fish or a little aquarium," I tell her.

"A fish?" she asks. ""Like in a bowl or with a huge machine?"

"I have no idea," I tell her. "What do you suggest?"

"Flowers," she says right away. "Always flowers."

"Besides that, smartass." I laugh and walk back downstairs.

"I have no idea. Let me google and I'll text you. I'm assuming you want this delivered to the same person?"

"Yes," I tell her, walking to the outside door. "Let me know what you do, and I'll send you something for the card."

"Oh, how about 'do you want to hook up'," Amanda says, laughing, and I smile, shaking my head. "You get it, right?"

"I do, and I'll get back to you," I tell her and then disconnect, seeing Tracy walk back inside. "What happened?"

"It's too windy. I just chased the same paper five times," she says, carrying everything in her hands to my office. "Go eat while I set up." I walk to the kitchen, opening my container with my name on it and grabbing a fork. I eat standing up while I check my emails and a message from Amanda comes through.

Amanda: ***I got her a betta fish in a big bowl with different colored plants from a friend of mine. What do you want on the card?***

Me: ***Under the Sea***

Amanda: ***That's it? Nothing swoony or panty melting?***

Me: ***Nope. Just under the sea.***

Amanda: ***Boring but you are the boss. I'll bill you.***

Me: ***Perfect.***

I finish my meal and walk to the office with a water bottle. "Let's get started," I say as I sit behind my desk and open my schedule. Five hours later, I close my schedule. "With hockey and the new stores, it's going to be a crazy six months."

"I think in the next six months, you only have Christmas off," Tracy says, laughing. "And that's just because things are closed that day."

"Let's hope nothing changes," I say, and she grabs her stuff.

"Your dinner will be delivered soon," she says with a nod and walks out. I finally have time to check my phone.

There is a picture from Amanda sent at noon of the fishbowl. Rocks and a starfish cover the bottom, and then there are blue, pink, purple, and white plants scattered all around the bowl, and in the middle, is the purple and white betta fish.

Amanda: ***The fish has been delivered.***

I smile and then walk to the kitchen, grabbing another bottle of water. I'm about to call Vivienne when the phone rings, and I see it's my father.

"Markos," he says the minute I press speakerphone.

"Hey, Dad." I grab the phone and walk outside to get some fresh air. The wind has definitely picked up, and it looks like it's going to rain. "How are you doing?"

"I'm okay." He exhales. "I spent the day picking tomatoes for your mother."

"It's that time again." I sit down and think about the summers when my mother would round us up and make us pick tomatoes. Then she would spend the next week making homemade sauce with her cousins. I always remember that as a time for us to get together with our cousins. It's a memory that always makes me smile.

"Yes, your mother is already washing the canning jars," he says. "You know she'll send you some."

"I still have some from last year," I tell him, thinking of the jars in my pantry. I open them only on Sunday. Another tradition that I get from my mother—pasta Sunday. Every single Sunday, we would go over to my nonna's house and have lunch. All of us would gather around the two tables while she made meatballs, sausage, and braciole stuffed with prosciutto and cheese. As the family kept getting bigger and bigger, the tables stayed the same, but we just didn't have as much room. When Nonna passed away, my mother took over the tradition, so every Sunday, the smell of sauce would linger in the house starting at six a.m.

"You know your mom," he says, and I just nod. "She wants to make sure you have it. How is hockey going?"

"Good," I say, leaning back in my chair. "I'm sitting out for the preseason, but I will send you guys tickets for the opening game."

"You know we would never miss it," my father says, and I smile. He was there for every single game with his jacket zipped up and his hands nervously tapping his leg the whole time. My mother shrieked every single time the puck came to me. "You sound tired."

"Yeah, I didn't get much sleep last night," I tell him, my mind going back to Vivienne, and I wonder what she's doing.

"You do too much, Markos. You need to find a woman who can take care of you," he says, the traditionalist in him.

131

"I can take care of myself." I laugh. "I haven't starved yet."

"Yeah, but you need a woman," he says, and I close my eyes. "You know, to keep you warm."

I groan. "And that is how we are going to end this conversation," I tell him. "I love you. Kiss Mom for me."

"I will speak with you tomorrow," he says, and I hang up, putting the phone down. Feeling a water drop on my hand, I look up and see gray clouds rolling in.

The door closes behind me right as the sky opens, and it begins to pour. I see the lightning strike in the distance and listen to the thunder. I pick up my phone and call Vivienne; it goes to voice mail after four rings.

"Bonjour laissez-moi un message."

Her French makes my whole face light up.

"Hey there, it's me. Just wondering how you are doing. Call me back."

As soon as I hang up the phone, the door buzzes. I walk over, expecting it to be my food. Instead, Vivienne's standing there soaking wet, and she's holding the fish tank in her hands. "Are you crazy?" she shrieks, and all I can do is look at her. "You sent me a pet."

"It's a fish. I don't think it qualifies as a pet," I tell her, and she shoves the bowl lightly into my stomach.

"Why would you do that?" she hisses as I hold the bowl. "Why would you throw that responsibility at me?" she shrieks.

"It's a fish," I say slowly. "An easy fish."

"Good," she says, throwing up her hands. "Then you keep it. Send me pictures." She turns and walks back toward the elevator, all the time talking to herself in French.

"Wait a second, don't you want to come in?" I ask, looking down at the fish.

"No," she answers, pressing the button and then the sound of lightning rocks through the walls.

I put the fishbowl down by my feet and run to her, grabbing her hand. "Please come in."

"You sent me a pet," she says. "A pet that I need to feed and make sure that it doesn't die."

"It was supposed to be cute," I say, trying to hide my amusement.

"If you want to be cute, send me a pair of shoes!" she yells. "A purse."

"Fine," I say. "I promise to never send you anything alive again." The elevator comes up, and I watch to see if she gets in, but she doesn't move.

"I walked here, fuming." She starts to say and crosses her arms over her chest. "Thank God, I put on this jacket." She looks down at the jacket and so do I. It's down to her knees, a trench coat of sorts, and it's tied at her waist.

"Do you want to come in and dry off?" I ask her.

"I'm not wearing anything under this," she says, and I tilt my head. "Well, I'm wearing my bra and panties."

"Are you telling me that you walked here naked to return a fishbowl to me?" I ask her, putting my hands in my hair.

"You sent me a pet. A pet." She points at me, and I take her finger now and pull her into my house, picking up the fishbowl and putting it on the table. "I think it's even dead."

I close the door behind her. "Where is the food?"

"How would I know?" she tells me, throwing her hands up and down.

"Did it come with a box?" I ask her, and she nods. "Did you open the box?"

"Briefly," she says, crossing her arms over her head. "I read the note and then came here."

"Naked," I say, my eyes roaming up and down, wondering what she's wearing under there. My heart speeds up, thinking about it.

"It's like a bikini." She puts her hands on her hips now. "And don't change the subject."

"Let me see." I don't know if I'm asking or telling her, and she glares at me. "Show me."

She looks at me, and I wonder what's going through her mind. I expect her to tell me to fuck off, but she doesn't. She unties the jacket and stands there in a light pink totally see-through bra, her nipples pebbled, and an equally transparent thong.

"Happy now?" she says and ties it back again.

"Come on, let's get some dry clothes on you and let me feed you before I take you home," I say, holding out my hand. I don't know why, but I'm suddenly scared she is going to bail on me.

THIRTEEN

VIVIENNE

"COME ON, LET'S get some dry clothes on you and let me feed you before I take you home." He holds out his hand to me, his voice soft. I was so angry coming here. I had a plan to return the fish and leave and never see him again. I spent the day sleeping, and when I got up, I had a package waiting for me. I went ballistic when I saw the fish.

"I'm fine like this," I tell him. "I came to return that." I point at the fishbowl. That really is pretty with the different colors.

"I was going to make myself something to eat," he says and comes closer to me. "Let me feed you, and then I can take you home."

"Fine," I say, although everything in me is saying to run. "What are you having?"

"My dinner should be here soon, but I can make you pasta with my mother's homemade sauce," he says to me, turning and walking to the kitchen.

"You know how to cook?" I ask while I slip off my Louboutins and then untie my jacket. Slipping it off my shoulders, I toss it on the floor next to my shoes. "Who taught you how to cook?" I hear a pot bang and walk into the room. "What can I do to help?"

He looks up at me, and my heart speeds up a touch. How can I still want sex? It's been a two-day almost marathon. "You can help by putting something on," he says, opening the fridge and grabbing something. He's dressed casual today, and the sight of his ass makes me want to go over and bite it. "Then come back, and I'll have a glass of wine waiting for you."

"Does me naked make you uncomfortable?" I ask him, my stomach suddenly getting weird.

"No, it's making my cock uncomfortable trying to burst out of my pants, and I'm trying to cook you dinner," he says and then opens a cabinet, taking the oil out.

"Fine, when you say it like that, I'll go put something on," I tell him and walk to the stairs going up to his bedroom. I step into his walk-in closet, rolling my hand over his suits, and then I spot his robe in the middle of the room. The same robe he wore this morning when I left with every intention of never coming back. I pick it up to hang it up and then go to his drawers and find a pair of shorts and a T-shirt. Both are five sizes too big for me, so I tie the shirt in a knot on the side and roll the waist of the shorts five times. Then I walk to the bathroom and wrap my hair in a white towel.

When I make my way downstairs, the smell of garlic fills the house, and my stomach rumbles. I walk back into the kitchen, and he's filling a pot with water. "It smells divine," I say, walking to the stove and seeing tomato sauce simmering in the pan with fresh basil on top. I pick up the wooden spoon and stir the sauce. "Almost smells like Italy." I look at him from the side, and he smiles as he puts the pot of water on the stove and turns it on.

"Your wine is on the counter," he says and leans down, kissing my neck. It's the first time he's kissed me since I came in. I walk to the counter, grabbing my glass of wine, and a clap of thunder sounds outside, the wind howling. I walk to the window and look out. It got dark so fast. "So how was your day?" I hear him ask and turn back around to see him slicing fresh mozzarella on a cutting board.

"I spent most of it sleeping," I tell him as I sit on one of the chairs at the little table in the kitchen.

"That sounds relaxing," he says, placing the mozzarella on a plate and drizzling something over it.

"It was until I woke up," I tell him, now sitting up. "Imagine my surprise." I tap my finger on the wine glass. "They called to tell me I got something. I was expecting maybe flowers, but then I open the door and they hand me that thing."

"It's a fishbowl," he says, smiling, and I glare at him.

"It was a pet, which, in turn, means I have to take care of it, which means I'm going to go crazy and then it's going to die and then who knows," I tell him, my voice getting higher and higher. "I called Karrie, but she didn't answer, and I didn't know what to do."

"It's a fish," he says, placing the plate of mozzarella in front of me, but it's with sliced tomato and pieces of fresh basil.

"I almost dropped it off at the fire station," I say. When he

139

throws his head back and laughs, I want to kick him suddenly. He goes back to the kitchen and comes back with two plates and two forks and knives.

"What do you think the fire station would have done?" he asks, placing a plate and fork in front of me and then turning to go and stir the sauce.

"I don't know what they would have done. They have to take it, no questions asked." I take a piece of cheese and cut some of it up.

"It's not a child," he says, laughing.

"Really?" I say, taking a sip of wine. "Does it not have to be fed daily?" I ask him, and he doesn't answer. "Will I not have to change the water and clean the bowl?" Again, he doesn't answer. "Will I have to make sure it doesn't die?" My voice goes higher. "It's like a child." He sits in front of me, and then I smell fresh bread. "Are you cooking bread?"

"Yeah, I threw in some bread that my mother made the last time she was here," he says like it's a natural thing. "Did you name the fish?"

"Why would I name the fish?" I ask. He takes a piece of the cheese and chews it, and even though I have the sudden urge to kiss him, I remind myself he just gave me a fish.

"I'm just wondering if I'm going to have to change the name," he says and then gets up when the oven beeps. "Nemo," he says, taking the bread out of the oven and then pouring the pasta into the pot and stirring it. He sets the timer and then turns to look at me. "Dori."

"That's so cliché," I say. "I mean, at least come up with something original. Is it a girl or a boy?" I ask him, and he shrugs. "Bubbles. Elsa," I finally say. "I saw it with Allison last time. She's a kick-ass girl."

"So I guess her name will be Elsa," he says, and then I see him take something else out of the oven. "I made some salmon also." Instead of answering him, I get up and walk over to him.

"I can't believe you did all this," I tell him, and he rubs my face.

"Well, I had to make it up to you since I sent you a fish." He laughs and then leans down and softly kisses my lips. No tongue, just a small peck. "Now, let's talk about you walking here naked."

"I wasn't naked," I huff out, rolling my eyes. "I had a jacket on."

"Let's say something happened to you, and you fell," he says. The oven beeps, and he grabs his gloves and moves me aside as he drains the pasta. "Then you're lying in the middle of the street naked."

"With a dead fish," I point out. "So you see how this is all your fault. It's the six degrees of Markos buying me a fish."

He laughs now, a full-on belly laugh. His eyes crinkle on the sides. "Go sit down. I'll bring the food out." Shaking my head, I walk to the table and wait for him. He comes over with a round big bowl and I swear it's the best thing I have ever smelled. He scoops some pasta and places it on my plate and then does the same for him. Putting the bowl with the remaining pasta in the middle of the table.

"Bon appetite," he says in French, and I smile at him.

"Bon appetite," I tell him and grab my own fork. The minute the pasta hits my tongue, I moan. "How did you make this?"

"It's my mother," he says while he takes his own bite. "She makes the sauce homemade."

"Like boils them and peels them and all that?" I ask him.

"Yes." He nods. "They do it every year."

"That is so cool and amazing," I tell him, and he nods, telling me about all the times he had to pick tomatoes. I laugh at his stories while I finish my whole plate, and when I get up, I push him down. "You cook, I clean," I tell him. "It's the least I can do." I put the plates in the dishwasher, and when I finally finish the pots, I look over and see him yawning. "Did you go back to bed when I left?"

"No." He rubs his face. "Tracy got here as soon as you left."

"Who's Tracy?" I ask but don't look at him, my heart hammering in my chest. It never even occurred to me that he could be dating other women, and I am just a number.

"She's my assistant, and she takes care of the business part of things for me," he says, getting up. "I'm going to go get my keys."

"You don't have to drive me home. I can take a cab," I tell him, but he just walks away from me and comes back. "Well, then, let me get my shoes on," I tell him, walking to the door and seeing the fishbowl.

"Where are you going to put it?" I slip on my shoes asking him, and he shrugs. I grab my jacket and the fish food in the pocket makes it heavy. "Not so easy." Reaching into my pocket, I take out the food. "You'll need this." I hand him the small fish food, and he grabs it and puts it beside the bowl.

We walk out of the door, and the door clicks locked behind us. I look down, seeing my hand hanging right next to his, but he hasn't tried to grab it once. When we step into the elevator, he presses the button that takes us down to the underground garage, and I follow him to his truck. The only sound is the click of my heels echoing. He opens the truck door for me and helps me in, and his touch lingers long after he closes the door and walks over to the driver's side. He gets in and makes his way to my house, pulling up to the front door. I spot the doorman running over to help me out. "Thank you for dinner." I look at him, and he puts his head back on the headrest.

"Thank you for not killing the fish." He smiles at me, and I want to lean over and kiss him, but I just shake my head and laugh.

"Night, Markos," I say, grabbing the handle, but the door is pulled open by the bellman.

"Welcome home, Ms. Paradis," he says, holding out his hand to help me step out.

"Thank you," I say and walk into the building, never once turning back to look at him. I don't have to turn around because I can feel his stare. When I finally walk into the elevator and turn around, my eyes land on his, and when I raise my hand up to wave goodbye, the door closes, and I let out a sigh. I unlock the door, slipping off the damp jacket and hanging it up. I hear my phone ringing somewhere in the house and realize I didn't even grab it when I left in a huff. I run to my bedroom, seeing Karrie's face fill the screen.

"Allo," I say out of breath.

"Where the fuck have you been? We've been calling you for three hours," she snaps.

"I left and forgot my phone." Sitting on the bed and taking off the shoes, I walk into my closet and put them away on the shelf.

"You never leave the house without your phone." And I know she's stopped what she is doing to tell me this. I have actually been at a diner and left to go home and get my phone.

"I didn't even know I didn't have it," I tell her, taking off his shorts and folding them.

"But you eat with it at the side of your plate," she reminds me, and I roll my eyes. "When you shower, it's on the sink. When you sleep, you usually either put it on the side table or under the pillow next to you."

"Wow, you sound like a stalker." I try to change the subject "Why have you been calling me?"

"Vivienne and Allison wanted you to sing the French song to them," she says, and I smile. "'Clair de lune.'" She mentions the song I used to sing to them when they were babies, and my face fills with a smile.

"Aww, do they miss their ma tante?" I use the French word for aunt.

"They do," she tells me, and I hear the water turn on in the background.

"Why don't I come over tomorrow and spend a couple of days with the rug rats?" I tell her. I think this is what I need—some space from the city and from Markos.

"They would love that," she says. "Me, too."

"Good. Arrange for movie night and I'll take them to get their nails done and buy the boys some dirt or something." Karrie and I laugh at the same time.

"Matthew is going in tomorrow, so he can pick you up on

his way home."

"That sounds like a plan. I'm headed to bed, and I have a couple of things to get off to my editor tomorrow. So I'll text him when I get up and plan it with him," I tell her and hang up with kisses. I go into the bathroom and look at myself, debating whether to take a shower. Then I look down at his shirt I'm wearing, wondering when the last time he wore this was. I untie the knot in it and walk to the bed, turning off all the lights and slipping into bed.

I look out the window because I forgot to close the shade, and I'm too lazy to get up and close them, and then my phone beeps, and I grab it. It's from Mark, and it's a picture of the fishbowl.

Markos: *I've fed him, and he's still alive.*

I laugh and reply right away.

Me: *He's a she.*

Markos: *You can't just assume it's a girl.*

Me: *I can assume that just like you can assume sending me a pet was a good idea.*

Markos: *I will never do that again. Good night.*

Me: *Bonne Nuit.*

I turn and smile, thinking of him, and then slowly my eyes get heavy as I play that night over and over.

FOURTEEN

MARK

"*Y*OU NEED TO stick to the corners better," Pierre tells me, coming over to me while I drink some water. "Your skate has to touch the bar, or it will give even that little space, and if you move, it's enough for a puck to go in."

I nod, then pull my mask down and get into position. Stick down blocking my two skates, glove out to the side and crouched down. I watch the puck going back and forth on the blade of his stick. I don't just look at the puck; I look at his hands, and I look at the way his body moves. Even with the most sudden movement, I know which way he will be going.

When it looks like he is going to shoot, I see the sudden flick of his wrist to pass it to the other guy across the ice, and I slide just in time to catch it with my glove.

"Fuck." I hear Viktor hiss. "Thought I would get it past you," he says, hitting my pad with his stick. "Good call."

I toss the puck up with my glove and let it fall to the ice, and then I pass it back to the coach. The team spends two hours on the ice, and I get another hour in with Pierre, and when I skate off, my whole body is wet with sweat. I walk to the back room and undress without a word to anyone. I stand in the shower and let the water wash over me, and then I get dressed and head off to the gym to run on the treadmill for a while. By the time I'm done, I need another shower, and the room is mostly empty. The only ones remaining are the rookies excited to play this year. You see it all the time. They're eager to become a superstar and happy to be a part of the team, so they stay longer and work harder. It's always a hard fall when they fuck up, and even though we all fuck up and have bad games, the rookies take it the worst.

"Later, boys," I say, grabbing my baseball hat and putting it on backward. My keys, wallet, and phone are the last things I pick up. Sliding my wallet in my shorts pocket, I then see my phone with notifications. I scroll down while I walk to the truck and I really look to see if Vivienne texted me and see she hasn't.

Getting in the car, I'm tempted to call her and ask her to have coffee with me, but I don't. Instead, I call my brother, and we discuss our New Orleans trip next weekend. "It works out perfect," I tell him, turning onto my street. "The preseason starts two days after that, so I'll be back in time to fly to Philly with the team."

"I've got a dinner in Silicon Valley the same night, and I have to be there," Chris says, and I nod.

"It's fine. It's pretty much me showing up and cutting the

ribbon. I plan to just fly in Saturday morning and out Sunday," I tell him and then pull into my parking spot. "I'll keep you in the loop."

"Okay," my brother says and disconnects. He's in the middle of creating another app. When he does that, he goes into his own mind.

I get out of the car and walk to the elevator, and my fingers move faster than my brain does, and I text Vivienne.

Me: *Want to go to New Orleans for the day?*

I press send, and then I spot the three bubbles appear and I smile.

Vivienne: *I'm in Long Island until Sunday. Maybe next time.*

Me: *Promise?*

Vivienne: *Cross my heart.*

Me: *Good it's for the 15th, clear your schedule.*

Vivienne: *Oh, smooth.*

I get tired of texting and call her instead, and she answers laughing. "Well, there goes that message." The sound of her voice has me smiling. "What can I do for you?"

"That has to be a trick question." I think of her standing in front of me holding the fishbowl and then sitting at the table and not dragging her chair beside me to have her close by. To kiss her neck when I want to. To pick her up and take her to bed with me. "So are you free on the fifteenth?"

"Ma tante." I hear a small voice in the background, and then I hear her speaking French.

"Oui, ma chérie," she says, and the way her French comes out and the tone, I stop breathing.

"Vivienne breaks this," the little voice says again, and I

149

look down, ignoring everything at the moment. I ignore the elevator getting there and closing without me.

"Give me a minute, and I'll fix it for you," she says softly, and then I hear her kiss her. "Go get ready for the movie." She then comes back to me. "Sorry, I'm in the middle of girls' day."

"Where are you?" The question comes out right away.

"I'm at Matthew's house," she tells me, and I hear her moving. "They left to take Mini Cooper to the rink, so I'm staying with my favorite girls while the smelly boy went to hockey," she says.

"What time are you coming back?" I ask her, knowing it's none of my business. "I mean, the fish was asking about you this morning." Her laughter rips through her.

"Tell Elsa I'll be back Sunday afternoon." She chuckles.

"Want to come over for lunch or dinner?" I pinch the bridge of my nose and close my eyes, wanting to kick myself for sounding so needy, or maybe it's just me. "If anything, just to make sure the fish is okay."

"What am I going to do with you, Markos?" she says softly, and I want to tell her nothing. Just be here with me.

"I can think of a few things," I say.

"I can think of a few things also," she says and then whispers, "and all of them end with us naked."

"Funny you say that because that is what I was going to say," I tell her, opening my door now. "Message me when you get back to town, and I'll come and get you."

"D'accord," she says again in her French. "I'll see you then, and we can maybe discuss New Orleans."

"Have a great night," I tell her and hang up. Setting my

phone on the counter, I walk outside, something I do all the time. It doesn't matter what the weather is outside. I always come out if just for a minute. I spent the night going over the things I want to do with her in New Orleans.

I walk into the rink the next day wearing almost the same thing I wore yesterday—shorts and a sweater with the team logo on it and my baseball hat backward. Carrying a shake in my hand, I bump into Matthew while I walk to the changing room.

"You're here early," I tell him. "I mean, earlier than usual."

"I got kicked out of my bed," he says, rubbing his face, and I look at him. "Vivienne is over visiting, and she spent the whole night on the couch with the girls and then decided it was a good idea to let them watch *Toy Story*." I laugh. "Of terror. I got kicked in the balls twice."

"Ouch," I say, shaking my head and trying not to laugh.

"Then this morning, she comes upstairs all refreshed and speaking in French," he says, and I'm jealous suddenly. "But what can I do? I love her." I don't say anything. "You doing okay? How are the backups?"

"Good," I say to him. "I think one is going to work out, but I don't want to say anything yet."

"Yeah, I think you're right," he says. "I'm going to enjoy sitting in the box with you and watching you freak out because you don't have a say in how the game is played."

I shake my head. "I think I'll be okay."

"You say that. I still remember my first game as GM, and we were losing, and I swear I wanted to run downstairs and suit up." I laugh. "Anyway, I have a meeting to get to." I nod at him as he walks away. Going into the room, I listen to everyone talk about what they did last night. I've never participated, and I'm not going to start now. The day is almost the same as yesterday except when I get home, I have boxes waiting for me. All with merchandise I need to sign for the upcoming season.

I get out of bed on Sunday morning earlier than expected, and I wonder if I'm going to see Vivienne. She hasn't called or texted since our last conversation, and I have to wonder if she will even show up. Maybe her plans have changed. When I start my espresso, my phone rings, and I press the button. "Hello," I mumble.

"Hey, were you sleeping?" she whispers.

"No," I tell her. "I just got up." As soon as I say the words, I hear a soft knock on the door almost like an echo. I walk to the door and open it, and there she is, standing as if she just walked off the runway.

"Bonjour," she says, dangling a white box from her fingers, but I don't notice the box. I just notice her blue eyes shining bright. I don't even know who lunges for who first, but she's in my arms and the white box is on the floor. "Good thing they put the string on that," she says and wraps her legs around my waist. Her arms go around my neck, and her mouth crashes down on mine. One hand holds her ass while the other grips her hair, pulling it back, but she won't leave my lips. "Didn't think this through," she says. "Should have worn a skirt." She grinds herself over my covered cock that is ready to come out and play.

I push her against the wall right next to the stairs, and I press her back into the wall, pushing my cock into her pussy. "I want you," I tell her, and she nods. "Naked." I look at her silky bronze shirt that is practically see-through. My hands go to the sash around her neck tied into a bow. I pull it loose, and I see that it's open to show her lace bra under it. Her back arches against the wall, and with my cock pushing into her, holding her against the wall, I rip her shirt open, and a couple of the buttons fall to the floor. She gasps, but all I can see is her semi-covered tit. The nipple is showing, and I lean down and bite it until she moans and starts to move her pussy up and down. "Naked," I tell her, moving to the other nipple. "Naked on my couch spread eagle waiting for me." I twirl her nipple with my touch. "To eat your pussy."

"Yes," she says, and I put her down. Her legs are a little unsteady while she holds one hand.

My hand goes to the button on her blue jeans. "I'm going to eat your pussy until you come on my face." My hand slips inside her jeans, and I find her soaking, my middle finger slipping inside her. "Twice." My mouth crashes on hers as my finger fucks her, and I swallow her moan. Her jeans don't give my hand room to move, so I take my hand out of her pants and lick my finger clean while she watches me. Once I'm done, her eyes never leave my fingers as she watches me grab her jeans and pull them off her hips, ripping her lace thong along the way.

"That's two pair you owe me," she says and stops talking when I lick up her slit and suck her clit into my mouth. I open her lips with two fingers and see her pink clit waiting for me to suck it. Instead, I bite down on it and slip two fingers in her. I suck in once I stop biting her, and her pussy swallows my fingers tighter and tighter, almost dripping on my hand.

"Fuck," she says as one hand goes into my hair while she tries to keep me in one place so she can come.

"Right there," she says of my finger touching her G-spot, and I know she's going to take off any minute. Her panting picks up, and her moans get louder. And right before I know she's going to come, I take my fingers out of her and my mouth covers hers. Her tongue fights mine as her hand slips into my robe, and she takes my cock in her hand.

I pick her up, her arms going around my neck, and I carry her upstairs to my bedroom. My room is so big I have chaises on both sides of the room. The open shades display the wall-to-wall windows and the view of the water. "I told you," I say, putting her on one of the chaises, "that I want you spread out." She shocks me when she leans back and opens her legs almost doing the splits with her arms going behind her head.

"Like this?" she asks. When I look down at her, my mouth falls on her, and I bring her to the edge over and over again. Her hands claw the chaise, and finally, I know she can't go on anymore.

"You want to come?" I ask her, my fingers moving in her slowly, and she looks at me, almost in a daze. "How badly?"

"Markos, please," she pleads and lifts her ass to get my fingers in her faster. Taking my finger out of her, I slide my pinky in her and then when I come out, I slide two fingers in her pussy and my pinky in her ass. Her eyes open just a bit wider when she feels me. My thumb continues circling her clit in small little circles.

"Yes," she whispers. My fingers play her over and over, and I know she's going to come. I look down at her, seeing sweat over her. "I'm …"

"You're going to come?" I ask her, bending and sucking in her clit and then nipping it. "Come for me," I tell her, and she does. She comes over and over again. One leads into another, and when she is finished, I get up and walk over to the side table to grab a condom. I open my robe and slip the condom on, letting the robe fall to the floor around my feet. She hasn't moved from her position; her eyes are glazed over, and she licks her lips.

"Ready?" I ask her, getting on my knees in front of her. She nods, and I rub my cock up and down her slit and then sink in. "Fuck," I hiss as her pussy squeezes me so hard I can hardly move. My hand goes to her waist, and I slowly move her on the chaise onto my cock. I pound into her over and over again, and each time, she gets tighter and tighter. I watch my cock disappear into her, and then I pull out, and she moans again. "Bend over," I tell her, getting up, and she gets up and turns herself over the chaise. Her hands going to the back of the chaise as she leans over. "Put your knees on the chaise," I tell her, keeping my cock in my hand as I watch her get into position, her pussy so wet it glistens. I don't take my time with her; I just ram into her over and over again. "Play with your clit," I tell her. "I need to come," I say, and she does. I feel her fingers grab my balls and squeeze, and I ravish her over and over again until we both come.

FIFTEEN

VIVIENNE

"SEE, I TOLD you the croissants would be great in the bath," Mark tells me while he grabs another one from the crushed white box and hands it to me. I smile at him; we just spent the past six hours lost in each other. Just knowing I was going to see him today, I tossed and turned, and then finally at six thirty, I got a car to take me here. I grab the glass of champagne that he brought me when he went down to retrieve the croissants.

"Champagne and croissants," I say, taking a sip of my champagne. "And a lukewarm bath. Perfect combination." I laugh and then look back at him. His bronze chest sports a few more bite marks to the one I left the last time. Something about that just turns me on even more.

"What do you want to eat for dinner?" he asks me, and I just shrug. I don't let on that I was going to leave as soon we got out of the bath. I don't tell him that I wasn't even going to take a bath. When he left the room, I thought about getting up and getting dressed, but then the other side of my head said just lie there in his bed.

"I was going to head ..." I start to say, and he looks at me with a weird face. "What?"

"You didn't even visit with Elsa," he says, and I put my head back and laugh out loud, something I am always doing with him.

"Well, then, if I have to visit with Elsa," I tell him, "then I have to stay for dinner."

"Chinese," he tells me, and I nod, grabbing the champagne and sipping the cool bubbly. "Or pizza."

"God, no more pizza," I tell him. "I had to babysit for three days, and we ate pizza every single day."

"Why?" he asks softly, taking a foot in his hand and rubbing it.

"Well, because, according to the kids, it's the best food on earth. Ever and ever." I tell him what the kids told me.

"Well, Chinese it is," he says, leaning over and kissing my lips. "I'll go order it." When he stands, I look at his thick legs, and then my eyes go to my favorite place. Even hanging, it's the biggest I've ever had. Then my eyes travel up his six-pack to his perfect pecs and that beard. "You keep looking at me like that, and we may flood the bathroom." And just like that, I'm not hungry anymore.

He steps out of the tub and grabs his plush white robe with an M monogrammed on it. He turns and walks into his dressing area attached to his walk-in closet and comes back with a box. "What is that?"

"I got you something," he says, and I glare at him. "Nothing alive," he says, and I smile.

"I'll leave it here for you." He puts it beside the tub, and I get up and grab the white box.

I open the top and then see the white tissue with blue under it. I open it, and I have no choice but to laugh. It's a baby blue plush robe with all kinds of fish over it. "Figured that would be okay."

"This is more than okay," I tell him, getting out of the tub. He kisses me and then walks out of the room to go order the Chinese, leaving me to dry off. I slip into the robe and then walk downstairs to find him. He's sitting in the living room. I walk in and see the same view as in his bedroom, wall-to-wall windows showcasing the beautiful sunset. It's such a big living room that it's divided into three. I walk past the fireplace in the middle of the room with two chairs in front of it and then toward the L-shaped gray couch that faces the water. "It's so pretty," I say, going to sit next to him in the middle of the couch and curling my feet under me. "Did you order?"

"I did. It should be here in about thirty minutes. I didn't know what you wanted, so I ordered more food than we will eat." He looks over at me.

"So tell me about New Orleans." I'm still not sure if I want to go.

"It's a place I'm opening, and I have to go for the ribbon cutting." He pushes the robe from my legs and puts his arm over them and rubs them. "So I am flying in on the fifteenth and coming back the next day."

"Wow," I say, smiling. "That's amazing and sounds so formal. Ribbon cutting." Leaning in, I kiss his lips. "I would love to."

"I'm going to get us a jet early morning," he tells me.

"Or we can go down on the Friday night and walk Bourbon Street," I tell him. "I might even flash the boobs to get some beads." I laugh when he glares at me. "I can do it privately." Leaning in, I kiss his neck.

"If you really want to flash your boobs, we can eat naked." He rubs my legs. "I can get some melted chocolate."

I laugh now. "Cherie ..." I swallow, wanting to kick myself for calling him that. "If you want to eat chocolate off me, all you have to do is ask." He laughs, and the doorbell rings.

"Stay here," he says, and I shake my head.

"I'm wearing my good robe," I tell him. "I'll meet you in the kitchen." I smack his ass and walk to the kitchen and take a deep breath. I called him cherie. *Fuck. I need to reel this shit in*, I think to myself and then look at the end of the counter and there sits the fishbowl. "Well, hello there, Elsa," I say, going over and tapping the fishbowl. "I told you I would find you a good home."

"Hope you're hungry," he says, coming in the kitchen with two huge bags in a cardboard box. He puts it on the counter and starts taking things out.

"What did you order?" I laugh, grabbing the other bag.

"Pretty much anything he suggested," he says, grabbing an egg roll and taking a bite, then holding it to my lips and offering me a bite.

"Thank you," I say, opening the chopsticks that came in the bag and pulling them apart and taking a piece of beef.

"I guess we're eating here," he says, going to get plates and spoons. I open all the containers and place them together. "Almost like a buffet."

"Bien sur," I say, grabbing a plate and filling it. "I'm starving."

We sit at the table, and I tell him about the movies I watched with the girls, and he tells me about Matthew complaining about being kicked in the balls. He tells me stories that make me laugh until my stomach hurts. And when I finally look around, the sun is setting. "I should get going." I pick up my plate and take it to the dishwasher.

"Why?" he asks me. "Let's watch a movie." He gets up, rinsing off his plate and putting it in the dishwasher. "You choose."

"Wow," I say, drying my hands. "You want me to stay so badly, you are willing to watch a French movie?"

He shrugs. "Can't be that bad," he says, and I shake my head. "I mean, we can always binge watch a show on Netflix."

"*Mad Men*," I tell him. "Matthew and Karrie started watching it, and apparently, it's my kind of show."

"Then *Mad Men* it is," he says, and we put the food away. He grabs the fish food and throws a little bit in the bowl. "See, it's super easy." I roll my eyes, and he grabs us two water bottles, grabbing my hand and leading me to his media room.

"This is so nice," I say, seeing one wall with the projection screen on it. Eight big leather seats, four in the back and four in the front, have steps on the side of them. He dims the lights, and I look in the corner and see the snack table. "You have this whole setup."

I look at him, and he goes to sit in the middle chair in the front and turns on the television. He looks over at me. "Eight seasons."

I walk and sit next to him in the big chair, curling my feet under me. "No idea. Let's start with the first show and work from there." He leans over and kisses me, and my hand comes up and holds his face.

"If you want, the chair turns into a bed," he tells me, leaning his own chair back, and I suddenly want to lie next to him. I nod, and then he is the one who says something. "Come lie with me."

"I'm right here," I tell him, trying to show him that I don't really want to lie with him. He holds his hand out and grabs mine, pulling me over the armrest in the middle. He moves over to the edge, and I lie on my side next to him, and it's a perfect fit.

"See, a perfect fit." I lay my head on his arm, and he presses play. The surround sound comes on, and the screen fills with Jon Hamm. I try to keep my eyes open, but as the time goes on, I slowly rest them longer and longer until I feel myself being lifted. "Shh," Markos whispers, and I'm gently placed on the bed.

"What time is it?" I mumble, thinking I really need to get going.

"Midnight," he says and then gets into bed next to me. "We fell asleep."

"I'm going to go," I tell him, getting up, and he wraps his arm around my waist, pulling me to him.

"Shh," he says, and I lay my head on the soft pillow, my head sinking in. "Night," he says, and I turn to see that his eyes are closed. I'm going to wait until he's sleeping and then slip out. That was the plan. I tried twice, and each time, he just tightened his grip around me when I moved. My plan got aborted after the second time when I gave in and closed my eyes.

"Hmm." I hear humming, and then I feel a tongue, and my dream suddenly gets better. The warm, wet tongue is licking me. "Fuck." I hear him hiss out and slowly open my eyes and look down at him licking me. I watch him take his hand and open my lips to find my clit and stick his tongue out to flick it. I look down to see I'm still wearing the robe, except it's now loosely tied around my waist. One breast is out, and I feel a wind on it, so I know he licked it. He stops licking me and gets on his knees, and I watch him. I'm not sure if he knows I'm awake yet. The sun gives the room a little light. His teeth rip open the condom wrapper, and he sheaths himself, and I open my legs wider when he crawls closer to me. His eyes meet mine. "Morning," he says right before he slides into me. He lowers himself onto me and buries his head into my neck. My legs wrap around his waist, and he places his hands by my head. One of my hands wraps around his shoulder while the other holds his head. "Woke up," he says between soft thrusts. "The sheet was off you," he pants, picking up the speed of his thrust. "One breast was out." I close my eyes. "Asking me to suck it." He kisses my neck. "Then you opened your legs." His thrusts get short when he pulls out and slams back home. "I was just going to lick it once." My hips shift a bit to get him deeper. "I lied," he says, burying himself all the way in and rotating his hips to give my clit some friction.

"So tight," he says, and then he starts moving again. I slip my hand between us, rubbing my clit. "Help me, baby," he says softly. "Help me make you come." It's all I needed, and I'm pushed over the edge. His palms hold him up, and I look down, watching him fuck me, and just like that, I go off again, and this time, he joins me. I feel his cock get bigger and bigger in me, my pussy getting wetter and wetter, and then I feel him come. He collapses on the side and pulls me with him. His cock still in me. "Morning," he says softly, his voice thick.

"Morning," I say and kiss his neck, his arms wrapping around me. "That was one hell of a wake-up call."

"Hmm," he mumbles. I move my leg, and he slips out of me, his cock still semi-hard. I get out of bed, the sash around the robe falling open. I walk to the bathroom and clean myself, then bring a wet cloth with me to the bed. His cock now without the condom, and I look over at the side table, seeing he discarded it. He holds out his hand for the cloth, and I hand it to him.

"I'll go make coffee," I tell him, and he cleans himself, nodding. I walk to the kitchen and see the sun slowly coming up. I start his coffee and put it aside while I do mine, and I'm about to bring it to him when he comes in wearing loose gym shorts and all you see is his cock bouncing while he walks. "I was bringing it back to you." He doesn't say anything; he just comes in and kisses my neck, and I move my head to the side to give him better access.

"Thank you," he says, picking up his espresso cup and taking a sip. Grabbing my hand, he walks to the living room and sits on the same couch we did yesterday. This time, he puts his arm around me. "Watch the sun rise with me," he says, kissing my temple, and I don't say anything. I just sit here watching the sun rise with him.

"Thank you," he says when he pulls up in front of my apartment an hour after we watched the sun rise. "Yesterday was the best Sunday I've had in a long time."

"Thank you for the multiple orgasms and the Chinese food." I laugh and lean over, pecking his lips. "Have fun at practice."

"Have fun I don't even know what you're going to do," he says, and I grab the door handle of the truck.

"I have a couple of things to do today." I don't mention that I have an article due or that I also have to publish my blog post. "Be safe," I tell him and get out of the car, the doorman holding open the glass door for me to walk into. I look over my shoulder and wave at him as I walk inside, avoiding the eyes that look at me. They usually see the walk of shame at around four in the morning, never at nine.

I walk into my apartment and see the bag that I brought back from Karrie's when I dumped it off yesterday and raced to Mark's. I slip off my shoes, and I'm about to walk to the kitchen to make myself another coffee when I hear a knock on the door. I smile to myself and walk to the door. "You just can't get enough of me, can you?" I say when I open the door. My smile disappears when I see that it's Matthew standing there looking at me weird. "Hey."

"Didn't you wear that yesterday?" He points at me, and I

look down at my outfit. Luckily, the sash in the front tied in a bow hides the fact that two buttons are missing.

"Um, yeah," I say. "I just got dressed, and I was lazy, so I put the same thing on."

"You aren't wearing makeup either," he points out, smiling as he walks in.

"Are you Sherlock Holmes now?" I say, closing the door.

"You had sex," he says out loud like it's a big aha moment.

I roll my eyes. "What are you doing here?"

"You forgot this." He holds up my backpack that has my laptop in it. "We called you all day yesterday, but you didn't answer."

"I was taking a break from the phone." I reach for the bag, and he throws his head back and laughs. "It's Sunday. It's a holy day."

"Holy day," he repeats. "This from the woman who thought the church would burn down if she walked into it when we baptized the kids."

"I was just being cautious," I tell him, folding my arms over my chest.

"You kept looking back every time you heard a noise." He laughs. "And you practically ran out of there at the end."

"This is fun," I say sarcastically. "This trip down memory lane," I say, grabbing the bag. "Now, if you're done, I need a coffee."

"Always a pleasure," he says, walking to me and kissing my cheek. I met him through Karrie, but he is the closest thing I have to a brother, and no matter how many times I get on his nerves, or make the vein in his head pulse, he has

166

my back with no questions asked. "The kids loved spending time with you."

"Obviously," I say to him, smiling. "I'm pretty fucking awesome." He nods his head at me, walking to the door.

"Call Karrie, would you? She almost called the NYPD to make a wellness check," he says, walking out.

"You're obviously not keeping her busy enough." I wink at him while he glares. "She was mentioning that you haven't been, you know." He puts his hands on his hips, and I know he's getting aggravated. I put my hands up. "Don't shoot the messenger," I say. The elevator arrives, and he walks into it and presses the button.

"She did mention that she wants more ass play." I try not to laugh. "You just have to push through the barrier." I say the last words loudly as the elevator closes. I laugh at myself, walking to the kitchen and making me a coffee and then carrying it to my bedroom. I am getting undressed when my phone rings, and I run to my purse in the hallway.

"Bonjour," I say to Karrie when I answer.

"Don't you Bonjour me," she says, and I chuckle. "I'm mad at you."

"Why are you mad at me?" I put the phone on speaker and take off my shirt.

"One, what did you tell Matthew?" she asks me, and I can't hide my laughter anymore.

"Rien pourquoi?" *Nothing why*, I answer her in French, taking off my pants. Grabbing the phone, I walk to my walk-in closet and go to my drawer, getting another pair of panties.

"He was all foaming at the mouth, asking me if I'm satisfied sexually," she says. "He went on and on about what he's going to do to me tonight."

"Really?" I say, shocked.

"He even asked me if I wanted ass play." She finally laughs out loud. "You have to stop poking him."

"But it's so much fun. I swear when I told him that, the vein in his head was throbbing. I even saw his heartbeat each time." I laugh now out loud and so does she. "I mean, tonight you are going to get fucked good, so I don't know why you would be mad about that. You should be thanking me."

"Yeah, yeah," she says, taking a drink of something. "But seriously, where the fuck where you? I called you all day, and I mean, all day—at least twice an hour and sometimes four."

"I was with a friend." I grab a pair of yoga pants and slip them on.

"A friend," she repeats. "Does this friend have a name?" I don't answer her. Instead, I grab a sweater and slip it on. "Does this friend have a huge penis?"

"Good God, Karrie," I say, grabbing the phone and coffee and walking to my office.

"Is this the same friend who left your vagina bruised?" she says, and I exhale deeply. "Oh my God, you went back for round two."

"I think it's round three." I close my eyes when she shrieks.

"When was round two?" she asks me, and although we spent four days together, she never really asked, and I never really told her.

"When he took me to the aquarium," I tell her, sitting

down in my office chair and turning my computer on. "We had dinner under the sea."

"I don't even know what that means. Is that code for he fucked you in a pool?" Karrie asks.

"No, he rented the aquarium, and we had dinner in the glass tunnel under the sea," I say, leaning back in my chair.

"Oh my God," she whispers.

"Anyway, after that, we went back to his place, and I rode the horse," I tell her, and I'm suddenly uneasy about sharing this information. "Then he sent me a fish."

"I can't," she says, and I hear her slapping the table or counter. The phone rings, and I see she is sending me a FaceTime request. Her face comes through, and I see that her hair is wet and piled on her head, and she is sitting on her bed. "You were here for four days. For four days, you didn't tell me any of this."

"There isn't anything to tell." I look at her, grabbing my coffee. "He sent me a fish." I roll my eyes. "A fucking pet. I got so aggravated I didn't even get dressed. I put on a raincoat and took him the fucking thing."

"Oh my God." Her hand goes to her mouth, and she tries not to show me that she's hiding her laughter.

"Don't fucking laugh, Karrie. He sent me a fish that was alive," I say angrily. "Do you know the commitment that would take from me?"

"It's a fish." She rolls her eyes. "They are literally the easiest pets to have."

"Really? How many fish do you have?" I ask her, and she just opens her mouth and then shuts it. "Exactly." I point at her. "Anyway, I went to his house and returned his fish."

"So then what?" she asks, taking a sip of her coffee.

"Then nothing. When I was at your house, he called to tell me that the fish was okay. And he asked me over for lunch ..." I trail off the last words.

"Lunch." She shakes her head.

"Well, I went over at eight, and well ..." I trail off. "I got home this morning."

She sits up and grabs the phone, bringing it closer to her. "Are you telling me you went back for more, and you spent the night?"

I roll my eyes. "It's really not a big deal. I dozed off watching *Mad Men,* and well, I got to wake up to sex, so I win."

"I'm coming into the city on Friday," she tells me. "Want to do lunch?"

"Sure," I tell her, and put it on my calendar at the same time I block off the following Friday and Saturday and even Sunday. "Now, if you are done with all the questions, I have to get to work. Have fun tonight," I say and then smile, and she starts to say goodbye. "Oh, and, Karrie, enjoy the ass play." She gives me the finger, and I hang up on her.

I open my blog and start my post.

Is a fish considered a pet? Here are my reasons.

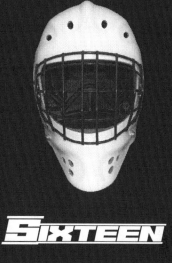

SIXTEEN

MARK

SITTING DOWN AT the table by myself with my plate for lunch, I hear the chattering all around but don't really pay attention. I grab my phone and check my emails, then shoot off a couple to Tracy about New Orleans and one to my brother.

"I swear to God." I look up and see the chair in front of me being pulled out, and Matthew sitting down with his own plate. "I can't believe I'm going to say this, but I can't wait to go on the road." I shake my head and take a bite of my chicken. "I'm going to sleep in the middle of the bed like a starfish," he says, taking a bite of his meal.

"Rough night?" I ask, being polite.

"Yeah, the kids are having nightmares, so they pile into the bed with us. Woke up with the biggest hard-on of my life, and then when I went to reach for my wife, I got my daughter's head. Do you know how fast it takes a boner to go down?" He looks at me. "A millisecond."

I laugh at him. "Good to know." The other chair is pulled out, and I look over to see Evan sitting down now with his plate.

"Hey," he says, opening his bottle of water. "What are you guys talking about?" he asks, taking a bite of his pasta.

"Matthew is going to sleep like a starfish," I inform him of the half conversation we just had, and Evan looks at him. For the rest of the meal, I only contribute a couple of comments, and only when it has to do with hockey.

"I can't wait to get back on the ice again and start playing," Evan says, leaning back in his chair. "I like to practice, but I'm getting antsy."

"I'll remind you of that in January when you're bitching that you can't wait to take a vacation," I point out and then start to get up.

"Buzzkill PM," Evan says, using my nickname. "Are you giving any interviews this year?"

I laugh. "They don't want to talk to me. They want the pretty boys." I wink at him, and Matthew laughs.

"Two years ago, there was this female reporter who came in and made a beeline for him." Matthew starts to laugh while I shake my head, thinking of the story he is going to tell. "She was wearing a tight skirt, and I think she even opened a button on her shirt. She walked up to him, and he was already scowling." He holds his stomach, trying not to laugh. "She started off with a question about the game and then said they call you PM, is there a reason."

"Oh my God," Evan says, putting his hand to his mouth in shock. "I mean, it's not a secret, but …"

Matthew slaps the table, laughing. "He looked at her and said it stands for postmortem. Like this interview." Now Evan laughs, slapping the table. "Her face dropped, and then every time she came back in the room, she would stay away from him. She transferred the month after."

"Postmortem," Evan says between his pants while he laughs. "I mean, they call you Private Mark, but postmortem? Savage." He gets up now. "I have to go work out. You coming?"

"Yeah, I'm doing weights today," I tell him, grabbing another bottle of water. I walk to the gym with him, and it's crowded. "Got to love back-to-work week." I laugh and go to the treadmill to warm up a bit.

Two hours later, I'm slipping into my track suit and grabbing my phone as I walk out to the garage. I get into the truck and stop at the butcher on my way home. I call Vivienne, and she picks up after two rings. "Hey," I say when I hear her voice.

"Well, hello there," she says, her voice going soft.

"I am going to stop at the butcher. Did you want to come over?" I ask her before I get out of the truck.

"I'm making Coq au vin," she says, and I laugh.

"Is that where you suck my cock with wine?" I ask her, and now she laughs.

"I don't need wine to suck your cock," she counters. "Why don't you come over for dinner?"

"Sure, what can I bring?" I ask her.

"Nothing. I have everything. Just bring yourself," she tells me.

"When do you want me to come over?" I ask her nervously.

"Whenever you want," she says softly.

"I'll be there within the hour. I have to go home and feed Elsa," I joke with her and hang up. I don't go home. Instead, I go to Amanda's store. When I walk in, the bell over the wooden door rings, and the smell of fresh flowers hits me right away. I look around at the pots of flowers everywhere with a clear path to the counter.

"Welcome," Amanda says, coming to the front from the back and then smiling when she sees me. "Well, well, well, if it isn't the stuffed animal lover," she says, and I walk to the wooden counter and lean over it to kiss her on her cheek. "What can I do for you? I'm even afraid to ask."

I laugh at her. "I was wondering if you could make me a bouquet quickly?" I ask her, looking around at some of her flowers. I point at the pink flowers by the door.

"Peonies, that is a good choice. I have them in pink, a light purple, and a burgundy wine. That is stunning," she says, walking over to one of the containers and picking up the flower that looks exactly like red wine.

"That sounds good. I love that color," I tell her, and she picks the bucket up and carries it into the back.

"I'm assuming you want a big bouquet?" She winks at me. "In a vase."

"Yes." I nod at her. "Do you know what France's flower is?" I ask her.

"It's the iris." She points over at the blue flowers in one of the pots. "You want one with those also?"

"Yes, please," I tell her, and in twenty minutes, I walk out of there with two vases of flowers, and I set them on the floor in my back seat, hoping to fuck they don't fall over.

When I pull up to her apartment building, I get out and motion to the doorman. "Is it possible to leave these with you while I go park the car?" He looks at me weirdly. "I'm visiting Vivienne Paradis."

"Oh, of course," he says. "I can take your keys and have your car parked if you like."

"That sounds great," I tell him, and he grabs the keys while I take the flowers with me and head in.

"May I help you?" the security man asks me.

"I'm here for Vivienne Paradis," I tell him, and he picks up his phone. I'm assuming he calls her, his voice going low, and I'm suddenly nervous and annoyed.

"Very well," he says into the phone. "Let me help you," he says, walking into the elevator with me and pressing the button to her floor. When the door opens on her floor, she is standing there waiting for me. Her black hair is piled on her head, and her blue eyes bright. I am always shocked by her beauty, but now that I see her in her space looking just as comfortable as she is at my house, she just pushes her beauty a touch more. She stands there in a one-piece pink button-down shirt, but it's long to her mid-thigh, and the sleeves are rolled up to her elbows. She spots me and then the flowers and laughs.

"I know that you don't like living things, but ..." I tell her. Walking to her, I bend my head to kiss her. "Hi," I whisper to her.

"Hi," she whispers back and puts her hand on my cheek. The smell of the food hits me right away.

"It smells amazing," I tell her, and she takes a vase from

me, bringing it to her nose.

"Welcome," she says. Moving aside, she turns to walk down her long hallway lined with art. Totally Vivienne. I see the kitchen as we walk down to the huge room at the end of the hall. Two windows provide a view of Central Park at the end of the room with a long couch facing the room. With the same couch on the right and two double couches facing it. She walks toward the glass table in the middle of the couches and places the red peonies down. "Let's put the purple ones on the dining table." She motions to the table to my left, which is a marble table with six white chairs—clean, sleek, elegant, and totally her. She grabs the vase from me and places it in the middle of the table. "These are beautiful," she says, leaning in and smelling them. As I watch her dress riding higher, I've had enough of not touching her. I walk to her, my hands going to her hips, and she looks over her shoulder at me, then turns and faces me.

My hand comes up, and my thumb brushes her cheek. "Your eyes get crystal blue when you smile," I say softly, and she looks down and then back up, licking her lips "They turn just a touch darker when you are unsure, like right now."

She laughs. "Let me show you around," she says, and her fingers link with mine. "That is the kitchen." She points at the doorway off the side. She takes me back down the hallway and turns down another hallway, pointing at the closed door. "That's my office," she says and then we pass another bedroom door that is open. "That is the guest room," she says, and I spot the stuffed animals on the bed. "The girls are going to love those stuffed animals." She walks me to the door at the end of the hallway. "This is my bedroom," she says, winking at me. We pass her walk-in closet and the bathroom and then it opens to her bedroom, and I have to smile.

The room is white with gray border and wallpaper. Drapes fall over the white headboard and are pinned up to the side. The big king-size bed has a white plush embroidered cover and about twenty pillows. The side tables look like they have a cloth on them. A white bench sits in front of the bed. But what makes this even more Vivienne is the crystal chandelier hanging over the bed. "This is so you," I say. Going to the bed, I sit on it. She comes over, and I open my legs for her to step between them. Her hands go on my shoulders before she takes off my baseball hat and runs her hands through my damp hair. My hands rub her legs and then roam up the back of her legs, going under her shirt to cup her bare ass. "You aren't wearing panties."

"They keep getting in the way, and you keep ripping them off," she says, leaning down and kissing me, my mouth opening for her tongue. She moves her knees to either side of me and straddles me, her bare pussy sitting right on my cock. My hands move up and find her not wearing a bra, and I pinch her nipples.

"How much time do we have before the food is ready?" I ask her.

"Enough time for me to ride you." She moves her hips. "Then take you down my throat." I groan.

———

"Fuck. I'm going to come," I say, looking down at her as she tries to take me all the way down, my hips thrusting more into her mouth. I try to pull out of her, but she just sucks me harder as she swallows my cum. My eyes close as I come; she lets go of my cock, and the timer on the oven dings.

"Right on time," she says, getting up, and I spot her pussy glistening. My hands come out and grab her hand, knowing she was playing with herself. I bring her fingers to my mouth, and I was right.

"After dinner, I'm having dessert," I tell her, sucking her fingers. "Chocolate pussy."

"In some cultures, they eat dessert before the main course," she groans, and I laugh, and the beeping sounds again. She turns and walks out of the room naked, going to the kitchen. I walk to the bathroom and clean myself off. "We have about thirty minutes," she tells me, walking to the closet and grabbing another shirt-like dress. She goes to put panties on, but then she looks over at me. "What are the chances these don't get torn?"

"On a scale of one to ten?" I ask her, folding my arms over my chest. "Ten."

"So that's a no to panties, I guess," she says, putting them back in her drawer, and my phone starts to ring from her bedroom. I walk out and go to the pile of my clothes, getting my phone from my pants.

"Hey, Dad," I say, spotting his name before answering it. I sit down on the bed and look at Vivienne as she quietly leaves the room.

"Just checking in," he says, and I look at the time, exactly five thirty. "Everything okay?"

"Yeah, just fine," I tell him, and he spends five minutes telling me about his day and then lets me go. I put my pants back on and find her in the kitchen taking the pan out of the oven.

"Just in time," she says and grabs two plates. She fills up my plate more than hers and tells me to grab the basket of bread on the counter. When we walk to the dining table, she puts down the plates.

"Sit," she tells me and then goes back to the kitchen. I sit down, waiting for her. She comes back with three water bottles and then walks to the cabinet by the wall and grabs a bottle of wine, pouring herself a glass. She sits in front of me, raising her glass. "To your coq with my vin." She winks while I laugh and know I'll remember this moment forever.

Seventeen

Vivienne

"*I*'M DOWNSTAIRS," KARRIE says once I answer the phone.

"Coming," I say, slipping into my black blazer and tying the button. Grabbing my black Gucci purse, I head out of the apartment. I try to walk properly, but I'm still sore from the sex we had last night and followed up this morning. For the past four days, he's been picking me up after his day, and we've been spending it at his house watching *Mad Men*. That is what I'm telling myself.

The door opens, and I spot Karrie smiling as I get into the car. "Bonjour," I say, leaning over and kissing her.

"You look like you're glowing," she says, and I roll my eyes as she pulls off into traffic, heading to our lunch spot.

"It's getting colder and colder," I say to her. "Which means one thing. I need to go to Mexico or something soon."

"You say that all the time, and you're the first one to clap when it snows," she points out, and I shrug. When we get to restaurant, the valet opens my door, and I step out, smiling at him, then wait for Karrie to walk around the truck. We are dressed almost identical, only she's wearing black heels with her jeans, and I'm wearing a pair of greenish booties. We walk in and are seated right away to a booth in the corner.

"I'm starved," I say to her, looking at the menu. "I didn't have breakfast."

"So tell me," Karrie says, grabbing the glass of water in front of her while she looks at me. The menu opened in her lap. "How are things?"

I don't answer because the waiter comes over, and we order a bottle of champagne with a pitcher of orange juice. "Matthew is going to drive home," she tells me. "Now spill."

"There is nothing to spill," I tell her. "We bang." It suddenly tastes weird.

"You bang?" she repeats, leaning in, and then stops talking when the waiter comes back and pours our drinks. "To banging." She mocks me, and I click her glass. "So that is all you do? Just bang?"

"Well, we eat, too," I tell her. "God, I'm not a savage, Karrie."

"Does he cook for you?" she asks, grabbing a piece of bread and eating a piece.

"Mostly," I tell her, then look down at my menu. "I cooked once."

"Hold on a second," Karrie says, closing her menu and putting it I don't even know where. "You cooked for him?"

"I didn't really cook for him." I grab my drink and finish

it, then pour myself another. "I cooked for myself, and he called, so he came over."

"I'm sorry," she says, looking around. "You cooked for him *and* had him come to your house?"

"I was cooking there, so yeah." I take another drink, ignoring the hammering in my chest.

"The same place you call sacred and never have anyone over in," she says, looking at me. "The same place you said would never be tarnished by any dicks." She hits the table, laughing. "This is too good. Did you"—she looks at me, and my eyebrows pinch together—"you know?"

"If you're talking about sex, yes, I had sex with him before and after," I tell her and then pretend I'm reading the menu, but I can't concentrate on anything.

"When was the last time you saw him?" she asks me, and I know full well that she's waiting to laugh.

"This morning," I tell her, and she laughs. "Karrie, I go over and visit the fish, okay?"

"The fish?" She puts her hand in front of her face. "The same fish you were going to give to the fire station?"

"Well, I didn't, and I go visit her," I tell her, and it sounds ridiculous even to me.

"How many visitations have you had?" she asks me, and I finish another glass and pour myself another one.

"Daily," I tell her, and she gasps out in shock.

"We are just, you know," I say, motioning with my hands. "Banging."

"Holy shit," she says. "You like him."

"Don't be absurd. Of course, I like him. I wouldn't be going to pound town five times a day if I didn't like him. I for sure like his cock," I say, motioning with my hands.

We order our food, and I change the subject to her, and just like that, we've finished two bottles of champagne, and it's almost four o'clock. "Is that ringing?" she asks, looking around.

"Did you put in a plug and forget about it?" I ask her, and she gasps out loud. I lift my hand to get the waiter's attention.

"Can we have cake?" I ask him, and he looks just a tiny bit annoyed. "Chocolate."

Then I look at Karrie as she answers the phone. "Hello, lover." She then laughs at herself. "I'm having lunch." She winks at me as she listens. "At the restaurant. Where else would we have lunch, Matthew?" She rolls her eyes. When the guy puts the plate of chocolate cake down, she grabs a fork and puts it in her mouth and moans. "Cake," she says and spits out just a bit.

I take my own piece. "This is so good."

"Are you coming to get me?" she asks him. "Okay, fine." She hangs up. "Matthew is coming to get me, and he said to tone it down and something about something, and I don't know what else."

"You know what you should do," I say, pointing the fork at her. "You need to go home and do anal. It's the perfect time," I say, grabbing another piece of cake. "You're relaxed and drunk. Spend the hour in the car telling him all the dirty things you want to do with him."

I'm about to say something else when I look over and see Matthew coming into the restaurant, but I'm not looking at him. I'm looking at Mark who follows him. "Oh, shit," Karrie says when her eyes follow mine. "Do I look okay?"

I'm about to answer her when Matthew gets to our table. "You've been here since eleven," he says and looks at the two bottles face down. I look at him and then at Mark, and I don't know what to do.

"Matthew," Karrie says to him, and he looks at her. "Why don't you eat chocolate off my …" she says, pointing down at her vagina, and I have to put a hand in front of my mouth to stop the laughter and so does Mark. "Do you not like my vagina?"

"Oh, good God," Matthew says, looking at me. "You," he says, "stop telling her about all your sex."

"Matthew, it's not my fault you aren't satisfying your woman." I mock him. "Have you spoken to the doctor?"

"About what?" he asks, putting his hands on his hips.

"Karrie said the most you can go is three times." I look down. "She's in her prime. If you can't, you know, you should at least give her the vibrators back."

"Oh, for the love of God," he says, now looking up and then at Mark. "We have sex a lot."

Mark just puts his hands up, not saying anything, because Karrie starts talking. "Matthew, I'm going to be filthy in the car."

"Are you going to barf?" he says to her.

"No, not that filthy," she says, getting up and then falling back down, but Matthew catches her. "I mean, I'm going to tell you all the ways we are going to do butt play."

"Ass play," I correct her, and then Matthew looks over at Mark.

"Do you think you can take that one home while I get

this one in the truck?" He motions to Karrie, who is licking his neck like a dog.

"Oh, you trust me with Mark?" I ask him, knowing he doesn't let any of the guys next to me.

"He's not going to fall for your spell," Matthew says, and I just roll my lips. "Stop licking me," he tells Karrie, who now is licking his lips.

"Lick my tongue," she tells him. "Let's go to the car and have sex," she says to him not quietly.

"She is going to be sleeping by the time I walk around the truck," he says, putting a hand around her waist.

"We are going to have butt sex," she tells him. "Vivienne says I'm relaxed enough."

"Please stop talking," he tells her and carries her out, and then I look at Mark whose eyes are trained only on me.

"How are you feeling?" he asks me, and my eyes don't leave his.

"Fine," I tell him, trying not to sound like Karrie, but the giggle that I do after makes it hard. "Why?"

"Figured if you are giving Karrie advice about her ass …" he says and looks at me.

"I'm listening," I tell him, squeezing my legs together.

"I'm going to pay the bill." He looks around and motions for the bill from the waiter. "Then we are going to go home, and I'm going to work that ass," he says. "Any objections?"

"I have an account here. It's already paid," I say, getting up and steadying myself, then winking at him. "Where are you parked?"

"Morning." His voice is chipper when I walk into the kitchen. "You're walking funny." He looks over at me as he sits on his chair reading the newspaper. Who reads the newspaper anymore, anyway?

"Well, you would be walking funny, too, if you got fucked by a baseball bat," I tell him and wince when I sit down.

"You were the one who begged for more," he reminds me. "I'll make you coffee." He gets up. "Then I'll run a bath for you."

"It's really annoying when I'm trying to be pissed at you, and you are all sweet and shit," I point out to him. He shakes his head and makes me a coffee.

"It's nice outside. Do you want to sit outside?" he asks, and I look out the window and see the sun's out. He holds out his hand, and I take it, walking with him outside, and he's right; it is nice. There is no wind, and the sun is shining. "Let's sit on that couch." He points at the couch on the other side, and I walk with him, wearing my robe he got me.

"It's a really nice day," I say, going to sit down, but he pulls me down on him instead. His arms go around my waist, and he buries his face in my neck, and he fits perfect-ly. "We should go for a walk," I tell him, and he just hums. "In Central Park."

"That sounds good," he says, and then he turns to me. "Want to have a picnic there?"

"Yes," I say with a smile. "That sounds like fun." I finish my coffee, walking inside and heading to the bath while he orders us a picnic basket. "I have to go to my place and get some comfy clothes," I tell him, starting the water and getting in.

"Or you can pack a bag and leave stuff here?" he says, and I smile at him. "Just a thought."

"I'll keep it in mind," I tell him as the hot water pours around me. "You can look all you want, Markos, but your cock is on hiatus until Monday."

"That's three days." He gasps, then shrugs. "We can do other things."

"Yeah, like what?" I ask him, almost glaring.

"Better if I show you." He winks at me, and I suddenly want to stay in today and make him show me.

EIGHTEEN

MARK

"I'M PULLING UP right now, Vivienne," I say into the phone. "Do you want me to come up and help you?"

"No," she says, out of breath. "I'm in the lobby." I get out of the truck and look at her walking toward me. Her smile is huge when she sees me. She's wearing jeans and a white shirt with a cream-colored jacket that goes to her knees and the same colored heels on her feet. Her black hair loose with a gray hat on. Her purse in one hand, her phone in the other, and the bellhop wheeling her Louis luggage to me. He puts it in the trunk next to my own luggage, and she is already in the truck. I get inside and lean over to give her a kiss. For the past two weeks, we've been with each other every single night. We usually just stay at my place, and I drive her home in the morning.

"Morning. You look handsome," she says, looking at my blue jeans and white polo. I put my aviators back on and take off toward the private airstrip. I park the car and get the luggage out. The plane is waiting, so we board as soon as we check in.

She stands in front of me, taking off her jacket. "You should have worn the skirt," I tell her, grabbing her ass, and she looks around. "Mile high club."

"I didn't know that was an option?" She winks at me. "There is always the flight back home."

I clap my hands together. "Now we're talking."

"Welcome back, Mr. Dimitris," the blonde flight attendant says with a smile. "We will be leaving as soon as you're seated."

The flight takes three hours, and we spend it sitting on the couch going over the things she wants to do while we are there. We step off the plane, and the mugginess hits us right away. "Well, I don't need this jacket." She folds the jacket over her arm. I let her step off first, and there is a car waiting for us. She slides into the back seat and waits for me. "Will you tell me where we are staying now?" she asks, turning her body toward me. I've kept pretty much the whole trip a surprise to her.

"I was going to rent us a house, but then I decided to stay in the French quarter." I grab her hand and bring it to my lips. "We are staying at the Ritz-Carlton."

Her eyes light up with a smile. "It really doesn't matter where we stay." She looks outside and then turns back. "But, just for the record, I approve."

I shake my head and laugh, looking out the window as the car takes us to the hotel, and when we pull up to the front door, someone is there to open the car door for us. I watch her get out and then I get out on my own side. Walking around the car, I look around, and a man comes out in a Ritz-Carlton uniform. "Mr. Dimitris, welcome," he says, coming to me and shaking my hand. "It's an honor to have you."

"Thank you," I say, shaking his hand.

"Right this way. Your suite is waiting," he says, turning around, and I hold out my hand to gesture Vivienne ahead, then put my hand on the small of her back. He takes us into the marble lobby and straight to a private elevator. "This is exclusive for you during your stay." He turns and puts his key in, and it takes us straight to our floor. We walk out, following him, and he takes us to the end of the hall. "Welcome to the Ritz-Carlton suite," he says, opening both doors. He gives us tour of the room, and I look over at Vivienne who doesn't say anything. He leaves us on the outside terrace with a view of New Orleans and the sound of a saxophone off in the distance. I walk to the concrete railing and look down at Bourbon Street, turning to see her sitting on the outside couch.

Her shoes already off, she's tossed her hat on the table right next to the champagne she's already drinking. "Santé," she says, holding her glass up and taking a sip. "We definitely have to have sex out here."

I laugh and lean back on the railing, crossing my ankles and then my arms over my chest. "Is that right?"

"Yeah," she says, looking at me, and I can't get over her beauty. It's always like the first time when she's around, always making my heart speed up. "Nighttime. Us up here, quiet while the party roars down there."

"Shall we get out and do some sightseeing?" I ask. "I also

want to stop by the shop and see how it's coming along."

"All I have to do is get my sneakers, and I'm good to go," she says. Getting up, she finishes her drink and then comes over to me. "Laissez les bon temps rouler." She smiles and put her hands around my waist, my arms opening for her. I pull her to me and kiss the top of her head. We stand like this for a couple of minutes, and then she lets me go to grab her shoes and her hat to go inside and open her luggage. "I have to hang up my outfit for tomorrow," she says, and I nod, watching her take out the pink jacket and skirt and hanging it in the empty closet.

"The butler can do all that. Just get your shoes," I tell her, and she grabs a pair of white sneakers and puts them on. "How do you make everything you wear sexy?"

She looks at me. "I'm just all that and a piece of cake." She winks at me. I grab her hand, and she links her fingers with mine. She never does this in New York. I tried once, and she let me go as soon as someone came up to me and asked for a picture.

"I was reading that one of the top ten things to do in New Orleans was shop for lingerie," she says and puts on her sunglasses. Just like that, she looks like a supermodel. Her plump lips are nude, and I can't help but lean down and kiss her. She smiles and puts her free hand on my cheek. "You do owe me panties."

"And I always pay my debts," I tell her and take out my phone and put the address in. "It's about an hour walk." I look at her. "Do you want to take a cab?"

"No," she says, looking around. "Let's walk and explore along the way," she says, and I couldn't agree with her more.

We walk down the street just like the other people. No one approaches us like they do in New York, which makes her a little bit freer in a way. The sound of jazz music filters out from the stores as we walk down the street. From one street to the other, we both point out things the other would like. "Oh, look, Café Du Monde." She stops walking. "We have to stop there."

I lead the way to the green and white awning that reads Café Du Monde in white. The tables under the awning are mostly all taken as people sit and eat. "Do you want to sit in or out?" I ask her, and she leads me to a table in the corner and sits down facing the street. "I guess out it is."

The waitress comes over dressed in a white shirt with black bow tie and hands us the menu. "They speak French here," I tell her.

"No." She shakes her head. "They speak creole. Totally different."

The waitress comes back, and we order some coffee with beignets. I let Vivienne order it to hear her French come out when she says the word. Once the waitress leaves, I pull her chair closer to mine, leaning in and speaking softly. "You're sexy as fuck when you speak French."

She smiles and raises her eyebrows. "Really?" I put my arm around her chair and pull her even closer. "If you move me any closer, I'll be sitting in your lap."

"Don't tempt me," I tell her. "I didn't get my fix this morning."

"What fix is this?" she asks, putting her leg on mine.

"My Vivienne fix," I tell her. Looking around, I see people come and go, but no one is watching us. Everyone is in their own little world. "My cock, your mouth," I tell her, looking at her, then looking out again. "My cock, your pussy." I pretend I'm looking around, but I can feel her hand on my lap now. "My mouth, your pussy."

"Well," she says, looking around but sneaking her hand under her leg right on my cock. "We should maybe find someplace where we can remedy this." She looks up, and my tongue slides into her mouth, and I get lost in her like always. She lets go of my lips faster than I want her to.

"Voila," the waitress says, putting down our coffees in front of us and then the plate of beignets in the middle of us with two glasses of water.

Grabbing a beignet, she tears a piece off and puts it in her mouth and moans, closing her eyes. "So good," she says and then tears a piece off and offers it to me. The powder sugar falls all over her legs while she feeds it to me. She laughs when she almost misses my mouth and leaves a big dot of white power. She leans in and wipes my lips with her thumb, and then she kisses me. "It tastes even better on you," she says and then tells me about the almond crois-sants from Paris that are her absolute favorites. Her hands going nuts when she describes them to me.

We get up after I pay the bill, and she holds out her hand for me. I grab it as we walk to Washington Square Park. "Let's walk through the park," she says, pulling me through the path, and at this moment with her here, I know I would follow her anywhere she wanted to go. I would give her anything she wants just to see her smile. We walk down the paved road, and she stops at an empty bench in the middle of three elm trees that hang down. "Sit with me," she says, sitting down and watching the grassy area where people are going about their day. I sit next to her and stretch my arm across the back of the cast-iron bench. She leans into me, sitting back and crossing her legs as my thumb rubs her arm. "Do you ever people watch and make up stories in your head about them?"

"No," I say, looking at her. Her hand comes up and holds the hand I'm rubbing her arm with. Our fingers linked together.

"See that woman over there with the stroller?" She points at a woman walking down the path with a baby sleeping in the stroller. "She woke up to her husband going down on her, and her screams of ecstasy woke the baby."

I laugh. "Or she was up all night because the baby is teething, and she just wants to sit down and cry." She shrugs.

"I like my story better," she says. "What about that couple?" She points at a couple sitting in the middle of the park with the sun shining on them. The man is wearing a suit, but his jacket is folded on the grass beside him. The lady is also dressed in office attire, her shoes off as she lies with her head in his lap.

"They are making plans for the weekend, and he's going to give her all the orgasms she wants," I say, laughing.

"Or," she starts, "he's married to his high school sweetheart who is pregnant with his child and he is having an affair." Her voice trails off. "And he keeps promising to leave his wife, but we both know he never will." She gets quiet as her eyes stay fixated on the couple. The man leans down and kisses the woman's lips. She doesn't say anything else, and I don't press it.

"See that dog over there with the guy?" I point at a white little dog being walked by a guy who isn't paying attention. "He's hoping that his owner steps in shit." She throws her head back and laughs. After that, her smile comes back, and we get up and continue our way to the shop. When we get there, I see my sign hanging, and I smile. Who would have thought that with just an idea, it could be this?

"There it is," she says, excitedly pointing, and I walk up the one step, opening the glass door and looking around.

"There he is," Tracy says from the side, and she walks over to us, smiling. When she spots Vivienne, though, her smile becomes forced. "You found it."

"I did," I tell her, and then I introduce Vivienne. "Tracy, this is Vivienne. Vivienne, this is Tracy, my right hand." Vivienne's smile is as forced as Tracy's.

"Nice to meet you." Vivienne lets go of my hand to shake Tracy's. "This looks amazing," she says. Looking around, I see that the store's walls are painted purple with a mural of dogs and the bottom half of the wall is lined with hydrants like a fence. It was something I thought up while designing. There is a bed by the window where the dogs could go and sleep or see outside.

"Come see the back," Tracy says to me. She turns to walk toward the back, and I follow her. There is a place where you can give them a bath and cut their hair, and then on the other side, she walks in and there are six rooms with a bed and toys. "This will be for the boarders," she says, and each room has cameras so you can check in. We also had the intercom put in so they can talk to their pets.

I look back and see that Vivienne didn't follow me, so I

walk back, and she is standing there reading the wall where I have all the rules and regulations. "There you are," I tell her, and she looks back at me.

"Some of these rules make me laugh." She points out the one about dogs in heat. "So if I'm in heat, I can't come?" She shakes her head. "That defeats the purpose of being in heat."

I shake my head, and I'm about to kiss her when Tracy comes back into the room. "Okay, so for tomorrow, it starts at one. You should get here maybe by twelve thirty to mingle. There will be little appetizers," she says, looking from me to Vivienne. "It's going to last until maybe four or five, depending. The ribbon cutting will be at three. The press will be here, so you can expect pictures." Her phone rings, making her stop talking, and she answers it right away. "Hello, one second." She turns back to me. "Dinner tomorrow, do you have any plans?"

"I do," I tell her. "I'll be available for the afternoon, but I have plans after that." She nods at me and then walks away.

"You really don't have to," Vivienne says, looking at me. "I can stay at the hotel while you do your thing."

"I have you all to myself for three days. Do you really think I'm going to give up that time?" I say, and she smiles. "Now, shall we go back and rest?"

"If that is code for let's go back so you can eat me"—she winks—"then yes please."

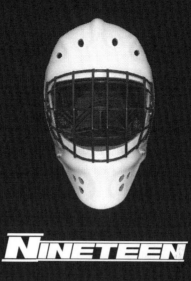

NINETEEN

VIVIENNE

"*W*E ARE GOING to be late." I hear him from the bedroom while I slip on my metallic pink heels. I look in the mirror and put a hand to my stomach. Suddenly, I'm nervous as hell. It's his big day, and I want to support him in any way I can. After we left his store, we came back to the room and got lost in each other over and over again. So much that we didn't leave the room. We ate on the terrace with my legs over his, and then I climbed into his lap, and we had sex while the jazz band played on in the distance.

I apply my nude-colored lipstick and gloss. My eyes are sparling blue today, and I put on my diamond earrings. And then look at my outfit in the full-length mirror. It's a light jacket and skirt. The skirt hugs my every curve and stops just after my knees. But it's the jacket that makes the outfit. It goes low in the front and then crosses over tight around the waist and then flares out. "Baby," he says the nickname he sometimes calls me, and I haven't told him to stop yet. I keep reminding myself that I should say something, but it hasn't come up yet. He knocks at the door. "The car is downstairs."

"Hold your cock, Markos," I joke, opening the door and seeing him standing there. I stop breathing, but I smile and try not to let him see. He's standing there in a light gray suit that molds to his whole body with a white button-down shirt underneath and a dark blue tie around his neck. "I'm ready."

"You aren't wearing that?" he says, looking at me up and down, and I put on hand on my hip.

"What's wrong with this outfit? Is it the color?" I ask him, looking down. "I didn't pack another one."

"One, it's too low in the front." He points at the jacket that goes down a little, but it's tight fitting so nothing is coming out. "Two, we know you aren't wearing a bra, so that's a no."

"The bra is built in," I tell him, picking up his hand so he can feel the little pads.

"Three, I want you to change," he continues, and then I shake my head.

"Well, this is the only outfit I brought," I tell him, annoyed now. "So either I go like this or I stay here and get a massage. Ball's in your court," I say, walking away from him and going to grab my light pink Hermes purse I brought.

I feel him right behind me, his hands now on my hips pushing me into him. "Your ass looks so fuckable," he whispers in my ear, and I know he means it because his hands are holding my hips the same way he does when he takes my ass.

"Well, if you behave …" I turn in his arms, his hands finding my hips again. "When we come back, I can grant you access to said ass."

"Fuck," he hisses, throwing his head back. "How am I supposed to walk around aroused the whole time?"

I shrug my shoulder. "I have no idea, but if it helps, I'm wet just thinking about it."

"You're wearing something, right?" he asks, glaring at me. "Like there is a barrier covering lady town."

Now it's my turn to throw my head back and laugh. "Lady town is fully covered." I kiss his chin, his beard tickling me. "Now shall we go, or you'll be late." He grabs my hand, and as we walk through the lobby, I'm aware of all the eyes on us. The truck is waiting for us, and he helps me in and then slides in. He sits there and closes his eyes. "What's wrong?"

"My cock feels like it's being choked to death," he says, opening his eyes and looking at me. "Watching your ass get into the truck did not fucking help!" he says, rearranging his cock.

"Do you want help?" I ask him, trying not to laugh when he just looks at me. When we finally get to the store, I'm shocked by how different it is today. There are purple and white balloons outside with a red carpet leading inside. The driver opens the door, and Mark walks out and then holds his hand out for me. He walks inside holding my hand, and then I let it go when I see Tracy coming to him. She's dressed in her own outfit, and I smile, seeing that her dress matches his tie color. I swallow down instead of laughing out loud. It's a tight little lace number that shows off her body, her blond hair tied up at the nape of her neck.

"You're here," she says to Mark with a huge smile on her face. "See, I told you that tie matched." And my stomach suddenly burns, and I wonder if I'm hungry or maybe I need a drink.

"You were right," he tells her, and I have to wonder if he really doesn't see it, or he's just ignoring the fact she wants him. I look at how easy they are with each other and wonder if they ever dated. I never really asked him about his other women because frankly, I didn't care. It had nothing to do with me or with us. Or whatever it is we're doing. As long as we are exclusive while we are together, I don't really care.

"The press is already starting to arrive, and I'd love to introduce you to the staff members," she says, and I stand here, and he looks at me.

"I'll be here," I say to him with a smile, and then he nods, following Tracy. I look around and see that there are high tables now with purple flowers on them. A waiter who comes over with a tray of champagne.

"Merci," I say, my French slipping out.

"Èske ou pale fransè." He asks me if I speak French, but in creole, which is really different.

"De France pas de Louisiana." *From France*, I say, *not Louisiana*. He smiles at me and walks away. People slowly start arriving, most of them dressed in their Sunday best, and I stand in the corner the whole time watching him do his thing. He meets with everyone, shaking their hands and smiling while he talks. Everyone smiles when he talks to them, also probably under his spell. He finally finds me a little while later.

"I'm so sorry. I was trying to get over here, and it was

always something," he says to me, his hands in his pockets.

"Don't worry about me," I tell him. "I have champagne." He laughs and now turns when Tracy calls his name. "Would you go and do your thing?" I push him, and he looks down and then up again at me.

His voice goes low, and he looks at me. "Come with me." He holds out his hand, and I know I should let him go socialize without me, but instead, my hand goes out to his. He introduces me to everyone who he meets, never giving me a title. And when he has to pose with the press, I opt out and use the bathroom as an excuse.

When I come back, I see that he is still taking pictures and now Tracy is the one standing beside him. I look at her, and I wonder if one day he'll see her in that light. My hand goes to my stomach as the burning comes back again. I really have to eat; I look around to see if any of the waiters have food, and then I hear Tracy's voice fill the room as she knocks a crystal glass.

"If I can get everyone's attention," she says, smiling, and I pretty much hate her face. "On behalf of Walk 'N' Licks, Mark and I would like to thank you all for coming down for our opening ceremony," she says. I grab a glass of champagne from a passing waiter, drinking it down in one gulp. She hands the speaking over to Mark, who thanks everyone for coming and hoping to come back many more times, and I wonder if I'll come with him the next time he comes here. Will he come alone, or will he come with someone else? I exhale suddenly, and then Tracy asks everyone to step outside for the official cutting of the ribbon. I walk out of the shop and grab my phone, standing with everyone else facing them. He stands in the middle of the group with the mayor on one side and Tracy on the other side of him.

I take four pictures of the group and then take one of just Mark while he smiles and talks to the mayor. I stand here as everyone mingles and then start to walk to the sidewalk, and he calls my name. "Vivienne." I walk to him, and he smiles, taking my hand.

"This is the mayor," he says, introducing us. "He speaks French," he says, smiling, and now he puts his hand on the small of my back. I speak French to him, and he actually answers me. I joke with him for thirty minutes until he excuses himself to leave. "Are you having fun?" he asks me, pushing the hair over my shoulder and tucking it behind my ear.

"It's been nice," I tell him, and then Tracy comes back, and I swear she is worse than a fruit fly. Her fake niceness when she smiles at me irritates me.

"If I could just steal him," she says with a smile, and I wonder how it would be to throat punch someone. I'm assuming it would hurt.

"Have at it," I tell her, smiling, and then turn to Mark. "I'll be here," I tell him, and he kisses my cheek and walks away with her. I take out my phone and text Karrie.

Me: *Does it hurt when you throat punch a person?*

Karrie: *Um, I've never been throat punched before, but I'm assuming it would, why?*

Me: *Nothing. Just asking for a friend.*

Karrie: *I'm heading into the arena for Cooper's game, and the service is spotty.*

Me: *I'll be back home on Sunday night.*

I put my phone away and look at the pink and green

shop with knickknacks in the store window next to Mark's. I walk over to the next store that has candles in the window, and I open the door, walking in. The woman stands up from behind the cash register counter. I smile at her and look at the two round tables when you walk in. Different baskets with different colored crystals. My hands reach for a pretty rose-colored one.

"You picked the one that holds the strongest love energy." The woman smiles, and I see her close up. Her eyes are crystal blue almost like mine. She walks over to another table and comes back with a bracelet that is the same as the crystal I picked up. She grabs my hand and puts it on me. "Don't take it off," she tells me, and I look down at it.

I look back at the baskets and pick up another one that is pink and black, and she laughs. "You have to pull down the walls if you want love to come in."

"Is this table just about love?" I ask her, and she laughs and then turns to walk away.

"Come, ma cher," she says, and I follow her through the beads hanging in the doorway into a small room with a table and two chairs in the middle. She sits in one and points at the other chair, so I walk in and sit in front of her. She puts her hands on the table palms up, and I don't know if I should do what she does or not. I don't have a chance to think about it because she then puts her hands down on the table. "Ca fais mal." *It hurts to say*, she says, pointing at her chest. My heart starts to speed up as she closes her eyes. "You suffered a broken heart," she says. I need to swallow, but my mouth is suddenly dry. "Closed your heart off," she continues. "Now it's open."

209

"What?" I ask, shocked.

"You will break his heart," she says, and I want to get up and walk away. "But not as much as your own." She looks at me. "He's the one you've been waiting for."

"I don't." My voice comes out in a whisper.

"The one who broke your heart; he's not finished with you." I gasp. "But you are the one who will finish with him, and then you'll see what love is." My mouth goes dry, so dry like a desert. "He's the one that was for you all along. The one you've been looking for was right in front of you, but you ran." I look at her confused. "You are still running." She looks down and then looks up. "He's going to run with you; as long as you run, he'll be there waiting for you. You can run from love, and you can run from him, but he runs faster." I'm about to laugh when the bells ring. "He's here for you," she says, getting up.

"Who is?" I ask her, suddenly not sure.

"Love," she says she walks out, and I follow her. I walk through the beads, and I'm shocked to see Mark there.

"I was looking everywhere for you," he says when he sees me.

I walk to him, my legs shaking just a touch. "I was looking in the shops and stopped here," I tell him, and he kisses me for the first time this afternoon. "Look at how pretty this is." I show him the bracelet that I put on.

"It matches your dress," he says, smiling, and I laugh.

"It does match, doesn't it?" I say and then go to the counter to pay for it. "How much?" I ask the woman. Looking up at her, I see her eyes are now brown, and I take a step back.

"Accept the gift in front of you," she says, smiling, and

then walks through the beads and disappears.

"That was so freaky," I tell him when we walk out. "I swear her eyes were blue when we met almost like mine."

"Are you done?" he asks me. "I would like to get out of here and take off this suit."

"I'm ready when you are," I tell him, and he grabs my hand and walks toward the truck that brought us here. He opens the door for me and helps me in. "Don't you have to go and say goodbye?" I ask him when he closes the door.

"No," he says and reaches for me, pulling me to him. "Stay near me," he says, his voice soft, and just like that, I nestle next to him perfectly. His hand hangs on my shoulder, and I fold my arm up and hold his hand in mine, and I kiss it softly. The whole time, I'm trying to forget the words she just told me.

TWENTY

MARK

"*I*'M FLYING BACK home tomorrow," I tell her while we FaceTime. It's been a week since New Orleans, and I've been on the road for the past two days. The preseason has kicked off, and I am not going to admit it, but Matthew was right.

Sitting in the box watching the game is nothing like I've ever experienced before. Knowing that I have to sit back and watch my team lose is the worst feeling.

"Well, I'm sure Elsa will be happy," she says, smiling at me, her face filling the phone. New Orleans was a dream. Then we got back, and I had to leave. I already hated the traveling part, but now it was even worse.

"I should arrive in the morning. Do you want to come to my place, or I come there?" I ask her, and she laughs.

"What if I had plans?" she says, turning on her side.

"You do have plans." I wink at her. "With me."

"Smooth, Markos," she says, laughing. Besides my parents, she is the only one who calls me that. "Why don't you come here? I can cook."

"That sounds good," I tell her, and she tells me about what she wants to do this weekend, and we make plans to have dinner after the game on Saturday. I'll be in the box with Matthew that weekend. It'll be interesting to see how we act.

"Okay, baby," I say, using the little nickname I call her sometimes and wondering if she likes it. "I'm going to bed."

"D'accord," she says in French. "Je te verrai demain."

"I have no idea what you just said, but it was sexy as fuck," I tell her.

"I said I'll see you tomorrow." She laughs. "Go to bed."

"A demain," I say in the French she taught me in New Orleans.

She smiles at me "A demain." And then she hangs up. I put the phone down on the side table and turn off the light. I turn on my side, and it takes me a while to fall asleep, yet I still get up before my alarm.

"Excited to get home?" Matthew asks me when he sees me in the lobby.

"I guess so. I'm the first one here," I tell him, looking around. "Where is everybody?"

"You're ten minutes early," Matthew says, looking at his watch. "It's travel day. You know everyone drags their feet." He laughs. "Plus, it's the beginning of the season, so the newness of being away is still there."

"I hate it," I tell him. "If we could play home games year-round, I would not complain."

"You aren't the only one," he says, and then I hear some of the guys as they walk toward us.

"The bus just got here," Oliver, the PR for the team, says.

"Let's go home, boys," Matthew says, and I follow him out to the bus. The plane ride isn't that bad, and when we land, I get in my truck and make my way to Vivienne's. The bell guy knows me now, and I toss him my keys and walk in. I wonder if I should call her and tell her that we landed early. Too late now.

I press the elevator button and knock on her door and then I hear her footsteps coming to the door. She swings open the door, and I know she's surprised right away when her mouth opens. Then her eyes go big, and it lasts two seconds before she lunges at me, and I catch her in my arms. "Good catch," she says, wrapping her arms around my neck and then bending her head down to mine and kissing me. I slip my tongue into her mouth, and I feel like I just won the lottery.

Her hair is all over me, but we don't stop kissing the whole time I walk to her bedroom. "Did you miss me?" I ask her when she lets me go and rips her shirt over her head.

"I plan to show you how much I missed you," she says, and she does just that. For the next three hours, we get lost in each other.

She lies on her stomach beside me, the sheet covering her ass, but one foot has come out. "So good," she says, her eyes blinking slowly.

"Good to know." I lean over and kiss her. "I'm going to shower. Are you coming with me?"

"Are you going to do that thing again?" she asks me,

looking over her shoulder.

"What thing?" I ask her because God knows we've tried everything you could think of.

"That thing with your tongue and then your fingers." She smiles and rolls over, a faint hickey forming right next to her nipple.

"I can be talked into it," I tell her and make my way to the bathroom. "You'll just have to come and find out," I taunt. I don't even have the water on before I feel her behind me.

"I came just in case," she tells me, and I get her in the shower and give her what she wants. I stay in until the water starts turning cold, then get out before her as she rinses out her conditioner.

"Should I order some food?" I ask her, and she laughs.

"I was going to cook!" she yells from the shower. "But I got sidetracked by cock."

"I guess since I'm the cock that benefited from that, I forgive you." I walk into the bedroom and slip back into my pants and my shirt. I get my phone out and order us a pizza since it's easier.

She comes out of the shower ten minutes later with her hair wrapped up in a towel and wearing one of my shirts. "Did you order?" she asks me, and I nod, taking a drink from the water bottle I just opened.

"I did. I ordered pizza," I tell her, and there is a knock on the door. "I'll get it." I walk to the door, grabbing the pizza, and walk back into the kitchen where she is sitting at the dining room table.

"I got everything," she says, and I walk out to see she has two plates and some water.

I open the pizza box and give her a piece and bite into mine. "How was the road trip?" she asks while she takes a bite of her own slice.

"Good," I tell her, wiping my hand on the napkin. "I just can't wait for next Saturday when I can get on the ice."

"Is that the season opener?" she asks me, and I nod.

"My parents are coming in," I tell her, and she stops chewing. "We'll meet up with them after the game."

"Um ..." she says, and I look over at her. "How about I pass this time?" She looks down at her pizza and then up at me.

"What does that mean?" I ask.

"It means that I'll meet them another time," she says, and I push away from the table to get some water. I grab a bottle of water and take a drink and then look at her.

"Does this mean you aren't going to be there to support me?" I ask. My heart is hammering in my chest, and I'm trying not to squeeze the shit out of the water bottle.

"Of course, I'm going to support you," she says. "It'll just be on the down low."

"What is going on right now?"

"I have no idea," she says, her eyes watching mine.

"We are together," I tell her. "And I want you to meet my parents."

"I don't do relationships," she says softly, and my heart stops pounding or beating, or perhaps, I just stop breathing. "You know this."

"What the fuck do you think we're doing?" I yell louder than I want to. "Honestly, Vivienne, what the fuck do you think we are doing?"

"We are having fun," she says calmly, her face not showing anything.

"I don't do fun," I tell her. "I don't do this"—I point at her and me—"unless I'm in a relationship."

She slaps her hand on the table. "What? The first time we slept together, we were not."

"And I gave in to you, knowing that if I said anything, you would freak out," I tell her finally. "We went on dates." I point at her. "We spend all our time together."

"I know that, Mark," she says, not using Markos, and I know that no matter what I say, she will never change her mind.

"Well, then," I say, putting the bottle down on the table. "I guess this …" I want to say that it's over, but the words get stuck in my throat. "I'm going to go."

"Oh, come on." She stands up now. "You've never just had fun?"

"No," I tell her. "I've never fucked just to fuck, Vivienne. Not before and not now." I shrug. "It's just not who I am."

"Well, it's me," she says, folding her arms over her chest. "It's who I am." I just nod at her and block out the sound of my heart echoing in my ears.

"You deserve better," I tell her softly. "I deserve better." I walk back to her bedroom and get my shoes and my jacket. I don't look at the bed that I just lay with her in, the bed that still has my head print on the pillow.

"What are you doing?" she says from the doorway.

"I'm getting my stuff," I tell her, sitting on the bench in front of her bed.

"You're just going to leave?" she says, throwing up her hands. "I told you I didn't do relationships." Her voice gets louder. "I never hid that from you."

"Yeah, you did," I say, slipping my shoe on. "I also told you that I want a relationship." I stand, slipping on my jacket. "I don't do casual. I don't have just anyone in my life. I don't have anyone ever come into my home like that. They call me Private Mark because I'm private. I want someone who is going to grow with me, someone I can turn to when I have a bad day. I want someone to share my future with." I look down. "I thought that was where we were going." She shakes her head, looking at me. "But I guess I was the only one in this," I tell her. I walk to her, and I want to kiss her one last time. I want to hold her one last time. I want to beg her on my knees to give us a chance. I want to tell her all the ways I pictured us together. I want to tell her there is no other person I want to be with but her. But I don't. Instead, I walk past her, and whisper, "Goodbye Vivienne."

TWENTYONE

VIVIENNE

"*G*OODBYE, VIVIENNE," HE says, and my heart stops beating; it flatlines. The sound of the door slamming and the click of the lock make it final.

He doesn't do casual. I hear his words over and over again in my head, and I run to the bathroom, making it just in time before the pizza rises and fills the toilet. I flush and sit down on the floor, the cold tile shooting through me, but I don't feel anything. I feel nothing, just as I always do. "It'll be okay," I tell myself. "It's better now and not later."

I get up on shaky legs and walk to my office, grabbing my cell phone and sitting down on my chair at my desk. My finger dials the only person who I want right now.

"Hello," she answers. I hear the commotion in the background, and I almost hang up. "Vi." Her voice goes soft, and then I don't hear the commotion anymore. "Hey, you there?"

"Yeah," I say out loud, but it comes out low and high at

the same time. "Just checking in," I say, clearing my throat.

"The guys just got back." She points out something I already know. "Wait," she says. "Where are you?"

"Home," I say one word. "Go back to the gang and call me later," I say, hanging up before she has a chance to answer. I lean back in my chair and look out the window at the darkness outside. I don't know how long I sit here staring off into the distance. Getting up, I finally walk to the living room and pick up the leftover pizza sitting in the open box. The two plates both with the uneaten pieces of pizza just sitting there. I shut the box when I hear a knock on the door. My eyes fly up, and my heart speeds up. I stand here, wondering if I should answer it when the knock comes again. This time a bit harder and then harder right after. My feet take off before my brain, and I swing the door open, holding my breath and expecting to see a tall guy with my brown eyes and black hair. Except it's not. She has blond hair and tears in her eyes almost like she's afraid.

"Oh my God," Karrie says, running in to take me in her arms. "I got so scared." She wraps me into her arms, and the first tear slips out. She moves out of my arms and puts her hands on my arms and looks at me. "What happened?"

"What are you doing here?" I ask her as another tear slips out, and I swing my hand so fast it flies off my face before it even falls.

"You called me, and I knew something was wrong," she says, coming in and closing the door. Walking to the living room, she sees the box of pizza there. "Where's Mark?"

"Gone," I tell her, standing here. Not sure what to do, I wring my hands together, and she doesn't ask anything else because her phone rings.

"Hello," she says, answering it and putting it in front of her face.

"Hey, did you get there?" Matthew says. "Is she okay?"

Her eyes fly to mine, and I stand here wide-eyed as I look at her. "Yeah, she's okay. She just has the ball stuck." I look at her confused.

"How does a ball get stuck in your vagina, Vivi?" Matthew says, and my mouth goes wide.

"Matthew, I told you that in secret, and it's for Kegels so the vagina stays tighter," she tells him, and I put my hand to my mouth.

"You need to get a magnet and put it in there, and it'll just zap it down," he says, and in the middle of all this, I laugh. "I'll see you tomorrow night at the game," he says.

"Thank you for being the best husband," Karrie says, looking at him and then hanging up.

"A ball stuck in my vagina?" I shriek, and she lifts her hands.

"What the fuck was I supposed to tell him?" she shouts.

"I have no idea, but you couldn't be like she thinks she broke her foot?" I put my hand on my forehead.

"Oh, that's a good idea," she says, tapping her finger on her lips. "Shit, I should have said that."

I shake my head. "Now, where's Mark?"

"I told you, he's gone," I tell her, and she walks over to the liquor cabinet. Opening the fridge that is built in, she grabs the bottle of tequila and pours a shot.

"You are going to need this," she says and hands it to me. I'm not sure I want to take it, but I do. The cool liquid goes down smooth, and then the burn comes right after.

"I'm going to need one more," I tell her. She pours another one, and it goes down pretty much the same. "He wanted me to meet his parents," I say, looking at her, and she now takes off her jacket and pulls me to the couch with her. The bottle of tequila in her hand and the lone shot glass in mine.

"Sit," she tells me, pouring another shot. I take it, and this time, there is no burning.

"He expected me to meet his parents when they came down for the season opener," I tell her. Looking at her, my voice gets just a touch louder. "His parents."

"Okay," she says, pouring me another shot, and I look down at it, seeing the liquid in the glass.

"He thought we were in a relationship," I tell her, his words suddenly playing in my head. "A relationship," I say the words and take another shot. "Me," I say, pointing at myself, and I get up, putting the shot glass on the table in front of me. I look at her, and she sits back and watches me, giving me the time to talk, but I don't need time because it all comes out.

"I don't do relationships, you know this. Fuck, everyone knows this. I'm a one and done." She nods her head. "Okay, so maybe with him, I bent the rules by going back time and time again, but I …" I say, walking back and forth now. "He knew. It was just fun." The words suddenly making the tequila in my stomach gurgle. "So we spent the night with each other, and we spent every day together." I stop watching and then sit on the couch in front of her. "Oh my God."

"Did you get it yet?" Karrie says, looking at me. "You were in a relationship with him."

"I don't do relationships," I tell her softly. "Not since ..."

"Not since that," she starts saying, and I look at her.

"I never told you," I tell her softly. "I was embarrassed and then ashamed." The words come out.

"He was married," I say, and she gasps.

"Mark?" she asks, shocked. I never fully told her what happened. I just said we parted ways and then I just stuck to I don't want to ever fall in love.

I shake my head. "I didn't know when we met. Scott was so smooth. I fell in love with him after one week, and when I found out that he was married, I was so distraught, but he assured me he was leaving her and that I was the only one for him." I close my eyes and shake my head. "I believed every single word he said until I came face-to-face with them," I say, putting my hand to my stomach. "It was my birthday. We had just left the restaurant, and from across the street, I saw them."

"Vivi," she says softly, and I laugh bitterly.

"Oh, wait, it gets so much better," I say. "She was walking ahead of him. They had just got out of his car, and then she turned to him with a huge smile on her face, and I saw." I take a huge inhale. "She was pregnant."

"Oh my God," she whispers, putting her hand to her mouth.

"Yup." I nod. "Imagine that. He was supposed to be leaving her, and she's now pregnant. Two years after he told me he was leaving. Two fucking years I wasted in love with him."

"You believed him." She tries to make it sound better.

"I was so stupid," I tell her, the tears coming now, but they aren't for Scott. They are for Mark. "I swore I would never be that vulnerable again. I saw you fall in love, and I knew it would never happen for me."

"But …" she says, and I shake my head.

"But nothing, Karrie. I won't ever let myself hurt like that again," I say. "Ever. It went on too long, and I know this. I should have stopped it."

"You l—"

I put out my hand. "I liked him, and now it's over," I tell her, and then I look at her. "Will you help me change my sheets?" I look down.

"I'll change the sheets. You just sit there." She gets up and leaves the room by herself.

"I shouldn't have gone back for round two," I tell myself, rubbing my hands over my face, but it smells like him. His smell is still all over me, and when I look down, I see I'm wearing his shirt. "I shouldn't have gone back." I lean over and lie down on the couch, then close my eyes, and all I can do is see him. Smiling at me, leaning in and kissing me, hugging me, over me. The memories replaying over and over again.

I feel the blanket on my legs, and I open my eyes to see Karrie sit by me with her own blanket. "I need to get rid of that bed," I tell her. "And this couch." Then I close my eyes. "My shower, the table. The kitchen."

"I think it's easier if you just move," she says, then looks at me. "Was it where I'm sitting?"

"Probably," I answer her, and she closes her eyes. "Please, like I haven't sat on your couch before."

"This is true," she says.

"I might have to replace that window also." I point at the

window.

"The window?" she asks me.

"Well, I was looking outside, and he came up behind me," I tell her.

"And his dick fell into you?" she asks.

"I may have bent over." I roll onto my back. "I need to move. This is why I don't bring it home."

"He isn't just a one-night stand," she tells me.

"Merde." *Shit,* I say in French. "Merde, merde, merde."

"It'll be okay," she says, and she lays by me the whole night. When the morning comes, I feel as if I'm suffering from a hangover or a truck running me over. I'm not sure I've ever felt this bad before.

"I really hope I'm not coming down with something," I tell her, sitting in joggers and a shirt that is not Mark's with my hair piled on my head. "My bones ache."

"It's called heartbreak," she tells me, sipping her own coffee.

"Yeah, that's what I was afraid of," I say into my own cup. "I can't go to the game tonight."

"I know," she says, and she doesn't push me. She doesn't tell me that I have no choice; she just accepts it.

"I hope he's okay," I whisper and look over at her.

"Me, too," she says. "Me, too."

I turn to look out the window, and I wonder where he is right now. I wonder if he's sitting on his terrace looking at the water or if he's just lying on the couch like me.

TWENTYTWO

MARK

"*T*HERE HE IS." I hear my mother's voice when I walk into my apartment door. She comes to me with her arms open. "My baby boy," she says, and I bend down to hug her. Her brown hair curled as always. I hug her like I always do, and she presses her cheek to my chest.

"You know he's in his thirties," my brother says from behind her. My eyes fly to him, and I smile at him. It's been one week since the huge blowup at Vivienne's house. One week since I've seen her, spoken to her, felt her, hugged her, or kissed her. It's been a week since I've been able to breathe.

My mother's hands still around my waist while she tells my brother. "Shush and stop being jealous." I smirk at him as she shuts him up, and that smirk lasts for maybe a second before the next part comes out of her. "You look skinny," my mother says, and I roll my eyes.

"He does not look skinny," my brother says, and now it's his turn to smirk at me. "He looks exactly as he did when we saw him last." He stands there now, putting his chin in his hand. "Actually, Mom, he does look skinnier."

"Fuck you," I mouth to him over my mother's head, and he laughs at me.

"Where is Dad?" I ask them. They got here today for the season opener tomorrow. A day I usually enjoy, but now I dread it. I wonder if she is going to be there. For the past few home games, I've opted to sit in the press box instead of with Matthew in the lodge with his family. No matter how many times I told myself not to look, I did anyway, but I never saw her.

"He's outside wondering why you don't have a garden," my brother says, and I just shake my head. My mother lets go of me and walks ahead of me straight to the kitchen.

"What is that smell?" I ask, following her into the kitchen and then looking at the four pots on the stove and the fan going as steam comes out of all four pots.

"I'm making some food for you for when I'm not here," my mother says, going to the stove and stirring something, then replacing the cover on it.

"For a year," my brother says, going to the counter and taking a piece of bread that she cut up. "And for a village." He pops the piece in his mouth.

"You," she says, pointing at my brother. "Get away from that bread. It's for dinner."

"Mom, there are seven other loaves right there," he says, pointing at the bread cooling on the rack.

"I need to go to the store and pick up a couple of things,"

she says, taking off her apron and putting it on the counter. "Christos, drive me."

"Mom, you know that we can have everything delivered. It's the city," he says, groaning and then she gives him one look. The same look she gave us when we were in high school that used to make us stop in our tracks. He holds up his hand. "Fine, fine. Let's go." He looks at me and holds his hand out for my car keys.

"Go see your father." She grabs my face and brings it down to her, turning and kissing me on the cheek. "I'll be back soon, and we can eat all together."

She picks up her purse and smiles up at my brother as he puts his arm around her shoulders. I turn and walk out to the terrace, seeing him sitting on the couch. His black hair now a salt and pepper color, and he turns to look at me, his face beaming with a smile. "Markos," he says, getting up, and he's almost as tall as me. "How are you doing?" he says, hugging me and then squeezing my shoulder. He's wearing jeans and a long-sleeved polo shirt.

"I'm good," I tell him, looking down and not at his eyes, knowing he would probably see everything that I haven't told him. There is just something about my father; he knows just by looking at us if we need help or not.

"Come sit with me," he says, turning to go back to the couch. I walk with him and take off my hat, throwing it on the table and running my hands through my hair. "What's wrong?" he asks, and I look over at him, seeing him sitting there with his ankle on his knee.

"What do you mean?" I ask him, mimicking his stance and turning to him.

"You look …" He starts to say it, and I just laugh. "You look like …"

"Shit." I fill in the words for him. I knew he would see it. I even tried to hide it, and I thought it was going to be okay, but I knew he would take one look at me and see.

"Not shit," he says. "But …"

I take a deep inhale and hold the breath for a minute before exhaling. "I fell in love," I tell him. My stomach starts to hurt again, and my chest feels a sudden pressure. His face fills with happiness, and I put my hand up. "Before you start making plans, it's over."

"What?" he asks, shocked. "Why?"

"She doesn't do relationships." I tell him the reason that I keep repeating over and over in my mind. "She just isn't that girl."

"But you fell in love with her?" He looks at me, and I nod my head. "How did you feel?"

"What do you mean?" I ask him, confused by the question.

"How do you know you're in love with her?" I now lean forward and put my elbows on my knees, letting my hands fall between my legs.

"She just made everything so much better," I say. "Her smile, her sassiness …" I start to smile and laugh, thinking about it. "She made everything an adventure; she made waking up that much better."

"Okay," he says, and I look at him.

"I wanted to grow old with her, and I wanted to have kids with her. Lots of kids." His eyebrows shoot up. "As many as she would give me." I laugh now. "I wanted to hold her hand.

I wanted to listen to her tell me stories or just sit by my side saying nothing. Just knowing she was there made everything okay."

"So what did you do?" He smirks at me.

"What do you mean what did I do?" I ask him. "She told me that she doesn't do relationships."

"And?" he asks again.

"And what, Dad?" I say, getting up now. Walking to the railing, I look down, her smile running through my mind. I turn around to see he hasn't moved.

"So she said she doesn't do relationship, and you what ...?" he asks me, shaking his head.

"You just left?"

"What else was I supposed to do?" I ask, my voice going louder as frustration sets in.

"Well, for one, you fight for her," he tells me.

"Dad, she doesn't want me," I tell him, the pain hurting even more than when she said it. Having it out there in the universe and telling my father just makes it even more real. When I got home that night, I sat in the dark the whole night. I didn't know what to do, so I just sat there, hoping she would come to me even though I knew she wouldn't. I wondered what she was doing or if it even affected her. Fuck, for all I knew, she really didn't care, and I was just another guy.

"She doesn't want you," my father says, almost laughing out loud. "Do you know how many times your mother tells me to get out of the house and never come back?" he says, rolling his eyes. "How many times she told me she hated me? At the beginning and even now, more so now."

"Dad, it's not the same thing." I look up at the sky.

"Do you think she loves you?" he asks me, and I look at him.

"I don't know," I tell him, and he pffts out.

"You know," he says, getting up. "You know in your heart."

"I thought she did," I tell him the truth.

"So what are you going to do about it?" he asks me.

"I can't do anything about it," I tell him and he laughs.

"You're just going to let her go?" he asks me. "Just like that? So you don't really love her."

"I do," I tell him, running my hands through my hair. "More than I thought was possible."

"Then you fight," he tells me. "You make her see what it is to love. You make her believe in love. You make her know that whatever she says, you just aren't going to go away."

"But ..." I start to say, and he stops me

"But nothing!" he shouts. "If you love her the way you say you do, you don't just walk away from that. It's a once-in-a-lifetime thing, Markos. If this is the woman who you want to do all that with, you don't just let her walk away."

"Dad, I don't know what else to do," I tell him, looking at him.

"You show her why you love her," he says softly. "Every single day that goes by, you never make her question that you love her." He puts his hands in his pockets. "Even when she throws her shoe at you for telling her that she doesn't look good in a certain pair of pants."

"Oh my God," I say, laughing now.

"Son," he says softly. "Love isn't easy, but it's so worth it. To stand there with your woman by your side," he says, slapping me on the shoulder and squeezing. "It's everything."

I'm about to say something when I hear the door. "Mom said we eat in ten minutes," Chris says and shuts the door, turning and walking away with his head down while his fingers go crazy on his phone.

"What if she really doesn't want me, Dad?" I ask him.

"Then she isn't worth it," he says and then looks through the window at my mother in the kitchen laughing with Chris. "But ..." He smiles at me. "But when you know in here," he says, pointing at my chest, "you know."

"Thanks, Dad," I tell him, and he turns to walk inside. Going straight for my mother, he puts his hands on her hips as she stands at the stove finishing what she's doing. He leans in and kisses her neck, and she looks at him over her shoulder. It's a look I've seen before, and it's the same look she used to give me right before her face lit up with a big smile.

I turn and look out into the darkness, and I wonder what it would be like if she was here. I turn and look back inside and see my mother now standing by the stove with her hand on her hip while she says something to my father, and she does not look amused. It's then the decision is made for me. "Vivienne Paradis," I say to the universe, "I hope you're ready because nothing is going to stop me from making you mine." I say the words out loud, and I'm smiling now. "Let the games begin."

TWENTY THREE

VIVIENNE

I SLIP ON my heels and look in the mirror, my stomach flipping and flopping around like a fish out of water. I pick up my phone and call Karrie who answers on the second ring. "Yeah," she says breathlessly.

"Are you having sex?" I whisper.

"Would I answer the phone?" she in turn asks me, and I grab my watch, putting it on.

"How am I supposed to know? Maybe you're not into it." I shrug.

"I was running after Chase, who took off with my phone," she says. "I'm on my way out the door now. Why did I think it was a good idea to stay in a hotel?"

"Because you're crazy," I tell her. "Would it be bad if I passed on tonight's festivities?" I ask her, looking at my reflection in the mirror. I know I have to show up, and I'm half okay with that, but I'm not sure I can be the nonchalant Vivienne everyone knows. "I don't even know."

"Vivienne," she says softly. "Remember the advice you give all the girls." I roll my eyes at this. "To get over him, one must get under someone else."

I close my eyes because the thought of sleeping with someone else makes me ill, but the thought of Mark sleeping with someone makes me dizzy, and I have to sit down. "You're right," I say, opening my eyes. "I'll meet you guys there."

"We can swing by and get you," she says, and then I hear crashing in the background. "Okay, meeting us there sounds great." She disconnects. I get up and look at my outfit of dark blue jeans that used to hug me perfectly but are now just a touch loose on me and a matching button-up shirt with puffy sleeves and a huge bow tied around the neck.

"You can do this," I tell myself. "You are the queen of being single." I hold my head high and then turn around and grab my black Chanel purse. The wind blows my hair back as I walk out of the door to the waiting car. The driver opens the door, and I sit in the back and look out the window. My stomach is a mess as the driver zigzags through traffic, and when he drops me off at the players' entrance, I get out, and my eyes make a quick sweep of the area. My stomach dips when I see some players arriving, and I reach into my purse for the pass that Matthew gets me every year. Walking with my head down for the first time ever, I don't look around and see who is there. I just make a beeline inside and go straight to the stairs that take you to the arena instead of down the carpet to the dressing rooms. I walk in, and a lot of people are already standing around. The season opener has always been a big deal, but ever since Allison did the public relations, she's made it bigger and better. When Oliver took over for her, it just went over the top. I spot Cooper and Parker right away as Cooper posts for pictures with the fans.

"Hello," I say to them, and Parker turns around and smiles at me. She has accepted me as Karrie's friend with open arms and always invites me to whatever events she plans.

"Vivienne," Parker says softly and comes to hug me. "You look amazing."

"Thank you," I tell her, and then spot Matthew coming over; his whole walk is a swagger. I almost roll my eyes with the way he walks.

"Hey there," Matthew says, giving his mother a kiss on the cheek and then giving his father a side hug. "Hey there," he says, kissing my cheek. "Where have you been hiding?"

I roll my eyes. "I haven't been hiding." I have been hiding, but he doesn't need to know this, so I ignore it. "I've been busy that is all."

"I haven't seen you in two weeks." He puts his hands in his pockets as he watches me, and luckily, I'm let off the hook when Chase runs to him and head-butts him in the balls. "Jesus," he hisses, then bends to grab his son. "How is my big guy?" he asks him, but the little boy flies out of his arms when he sees Parker there. She takes him in her arms, and he lays his head on her shoulder. Cooper puts his arm around her shoulder, and the little boy pushes his hand off, making Parker laugh and Cooper frown.

He leans into Chase, and whispers, "She's mine, buddy," making us all laugh.

I take a deep breath when Karrie comes over, and then I see Zara and Zoe behind her. "Hello." We exchange hugs and kisses, and I look around, trying to pretend I'm not looking for him. I spot him right away, but he doesn't see me as he poses for a picture with a fan. His smile makes his eyes bright, and I look away as fast as I did when I saw him.

"I have to go get something to drink. I think I'm going to head to the lodge," I tell Karrie, and she looks around and just nods her head at me.

"I'll come with you," Parker says. We walk away from everyone and make our way to the private lodge. We walk in, and Chase squirms out of Parker's arms to go down to the playroom where the kids hang out.

I walk to the bar and pour myself a glass of white wine. "Would you like a glass of wine?" I ask Parker, and she smiles and nods. I hand her the glass I poured for myself and then fill another one for me.

"To not being thirsty today." She holds her glass to me, and I have to throw my head back and laugh.

"How long did it take you to figure out?" I say, clinking her glass and then taking a sip.

"Five seconds," she says, taking a sip, and before she answers, she hears Chase call her. She puts her glass down and walks to the adjoining room, and I look at the ice, seeing it clean and empty. I look at the seats that are still empty and wonder if Mark's parents are here and where they are sitting. Before I have time to dwell on it, the door opens, and everyone starts to walk in. The kids go straight to the other room, and the food arrives.

"I need wine," Zoe says, and I look over at her going

straight to the bar. "I'll have one for Zara also." She smiles at Zara. "Don't say I never did anything for you."

Zara walks to the couch and sits down with her hand resting on her small baby bump. I walk over and sit next to her. "Did you lose weight?" Zara looks at me, and I just shrug.

"I don't think so," I tell her, taking a long gulp of wine. Zoe comes over with her wine glass filled almost to the rim.

"You look like you have," Zara says and then looks over at Zoe. "I need food," she says, getting up. "I'll bring you something," she says to me, and I just nod.

"Are you on a diet?" Zoe asks, and I roll my eyes.

"No," I say, looking at Karrie, who now comes over with her full plate of food. I grab a piece of pizza from her and bite into it. "I was just working last week, and time would run away from me."

"Are you dating?" Zoe asks, and I smile big.

"You know me, I like to dabble," I say, and the pizza suddenly feels like lead in my stomach.

"Oh, we know," Zoe says, laughing, and I look toward the ice when I hear the cheering start. "Well, guess that means the guys took the ice," she says, getting up. "I need a refill," she says then looks at me.

"I'll take another one," I say, handing her my empty glass, and she walks away.

"Dabble, my ass," Karrie says under her breath. "How many dabbles have you had?" She looks over at me, and then Zara calls us.

"Come sit down and watch the guys," she says, going to the seats right outside the lodge.

I get up and walk to Zoe, grabbing my wine glass, and then walk to the seats. I take a seat, leaving the seat next to me open, and Zoe sits in it. Karrie and Zara sit behind us. Looking at the ice, I see the guys skating shooting at the empty net. I brace myself for when he skates out. I am ready for anything and everything, I tell myself. Then I see him walking to the ice and then skating onto the ice. He's wearing his helmet, and I thought I was ready. I. Was. Not. My heart speeds up just a touch, and my stomach dips as I see him nod to the kids watching and then skate to the goal. He puts his mask on his face and then gets down into position. I spend the whole time trying not to look at him but failing miserably while I listen to the chatter around me. The noise almost drowned out by the beating of my heart echoing in my ears. The team skates off the ice, and I turn to the girls to see Zara and Zoe chatting away while Karrie just looks at me. I smile at her and bring my wine to my lips, taking another sip.

The lights turn off, and they start introducing the players. One by one, they skate on the ice, number by number. When they show his picture on the jumbotron, the crowd goes wild. They show clips of his saves from last season, and there is a cool shot of him going down and then doing a glove save. Then it switches back to him standing in the back waiting to go out. He walks to the ice and then glides on, holding his hand up to wave to the crowd. Looking from right to left, he skates with his hand in the air, going toward center ice where everyone else is lined up. He doesn't smile, and he doesn't talk to the person next to him. He just stares ahead as the rest of the team is introduced. The crowd goes equally crazy for Viktor, the new player on the team, and when Evan comes out, you can't even hear anything because the cheering is so loud. I look over at Zara who stands there proudly with a smile on her face.

After the national anthem, the crown settles down as the players take their place on the ice, and the girls settle down in the seats. Allison joins us. "I need more than just a glass of wine. I need the bottle with a straw."

I laugh at her. "Forget the straw. Just drink it like a beer." I hand her my glass of wine and get up to grab another one, and she hands me back my empty glass even before I take a step. "Don't judge me, okay? Michael walked in on Max and me." Karrie rolls her lips, and Zara laughs while Zoe hits her leg. "It isn't funny. He walked in while I was on my hands and knees."

"Oh my God," I say, putting a hand to my mouth "Doggy style? Were you facing the door or was it from the side?"

"What difference does that make?" Karrie hisses.

"Well, if she is facing the door, he walked in on her tits going nuts. If it's by the side, at least she's semi-covered." I lift my hands.

"It is even worse than that," Allison says. "Max's back was facing the door, so I'm sure all he saw was him thrusting into me while I begged him for more." Zoe now laughs out loud. "It might get worse."

"I don't think it can get worse than that," Karrie says.

"I told him to put his thumb back in," Allison says, her face going red, and she covers it with her hands.

"See," I say, pointing at her. "Ass play."

"When did you realize that your son was there and that

he would need therapy?" Zara asks.

"When the door slammed," she says softly. "I went to see him, and he was crying in his bed." She puts her hand on her chest, and now Karrie hands her, her wine glass. She gulps it down right away. "He was crying, and then he asked me, 'What was Daddy doing to you?'"

"Plowing you." I point at her. "Good, I hope." Karrie slaps my leg. "What?"

"I told him that he was rubbing my back." Now we all throw our heads back and laugh. "It's not funny. What if he tells people?"

"You have sex," I tell her. "I think everyone knows this."

"I might die. I swear to God, imagine if he tells his teacher," Allison says.

"Then you should not have Max go to the school. Bitches will pounce on that. Hockey players are the way to go," Zara says and then looks over at Zoe. "In case you want to have sex with one."

"I don't bang hockey players," Zoe tells Zara. "Unlike someone I know."

"Please," I say to them. "I'm still so thirsty, you have no idea. It's like I'm a camel in the desert. Dry. Sèche ," I say, using the French word for dry. "I swear, I went to the gyno the other day, and he had to use extra lube."

"Dryness comes with age," Karrie says, and I gasp in shock offended.

"Bitch, I'm as old as you are," I tell her. "How much lube do you have to use?" And the minute I ask that, Allison, Zara, and Zoe all groan. "Please, all this sex talk has got me hot and bothered. I'm going back for more wine." Then I look at

Allison. "I'll bring you something stronger."

I walk away and smile at Matthew and Cooper who are sitting on the stool watching the game. "Do you want something to drink?" I ask them when I pass by them, and they both shake their heads at me.

I walk to the bar and then look up at the television screen when I hear booing and see that the other team scored. Mark picks up his mask and grabs the water bottle on top of the net and squirts some into his mouth while he watches the replay on the jumbotron. "Okay, maybe next week I'll stop thinking of him," I tell myself. "Maybe, just maybe."

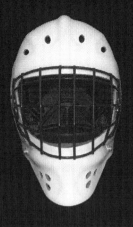

TwentyFour

Mark

"*T*HAT WAS A nice win," my brother says to me when I walk out of the locker room an hour after the game. It was a clusterfuck at the beginning, almost like I had shaky legs. Luckily, I got back into the zone, and we pulled off a win. "I was afraid I would have to take off my jersey," he jokes, and my mother hits him in the stomach.

"Hush, would you? He was under enough stress," she hisses, then hugs me. "You were great."

"Oh, please," Chris says, rolling his eyes. My father shoves him, and he laughs.

"You were shaky," my father says, "in the beginning, but then you got better." He was never the dad who told me that everything I did was perfect. No, he pointed out what I did wrong and then what I did good.

"Are you hungry?" my mother asks, and I look behind to see Evan, Matthew, and Max walk out together.

"Hey," Matthew says, coming to us. He walks over to my mother and kisses her on the cheeks, then shakes hands with my father and my brother. "Are you guys coming to the party?"

Chris laughs now. "Private Mark doesn't do parties. He does the quiet supper after the game."

"See you tomorrow," Matthew says to me. "Good game out there." I nod to them, and they take off toward the party.

"So where do you want to go eat?" I ask them, and we make our way over to the little Italian restaurant where we went the last time. I sit in the corner and never make eye contact with anyone. But it doesn't stop a couple of people from coming over and asking for a picture. I smile at them and take the picture. "This is why I go straight home after the games," I tell my parents when we walk out of the restaurant. "It's just easier."

My mother puts her arm around me and hugs me close. "Mark, you need a woman who will be there waiting for you," she says, and Chris groans. "It's not healthy to be alone all the time."

"How do you know he's alone all the time?" my father asks her as we slowly walk toward my house. "Maybe he has someone." My mother stops walking in the middle of the sidewalk, and she puts her hands on her hips. She stands there in jeans and my jersey, and I swear she looks like she is thirty.

"Markos Stefano Dimitris," she says my full name.

"Shit just got real," Chris says besides me. "It's never a good thing when she uses the middle name."

"You." She points at my brother. "Stay out of this or else."

She glares, and just like that, I feel like I'm in high school again when she found my *Playboy* stash.

"Do you have a someone?" my mother asks me. "Surely, if you had someone, you would introduce us. I mean, I'm your mother." She puts her hands on her chest, and now it's my father who rolls his eyes.

"Mom," I say, going to her. "I don't have anyone." I try to smile, but the burning in the pit of my stomach stops me from doing it. "And the minute that I do have that person in my life, you will be the first one to meet her."

"You promise?" she asks with tears in her eyes. "I just worry about you." She puts her hand on my cheek. "All alone in the big city."

"Jesus, he's thirty," my brother says and throws up his hands.

"I worry about you, too," my mother says now, crossing her arms over her chest. "Do you have someone?"

"Mom," he says. "I have many, which is why you will meet none."

"You know, your dick can fall off," my mother tells him, and now my father groans. "If you use it too much, it can fall off. The skin is very thin."

"Can someone please stop her?" Chris looks at my father, then back at my mother "My dick is not going to fall off."

"I saw it on *Dr. Phil* once. It can be caused by unlubricated sex," my mother says, looking at all three of us.

"I will pay you money if you never say unlubricated sex again for the rest of my life," Chris says to her and then looks at my father. "Do something, please."

My father smiles and walks to her, taking her in his arms.

I have no idea what he is saying to her, but she just nods her head. "They are grown men, and they will do what they need to do, and you need to stop watching *Dr. Phil*." We hear him say, and then he kisses her cheek. "Now let's get back home. We have an early flight tomorrow." She nods and takes his hand, and we walk quietly back to my place.

The next morning, I get up and drive them to the airport, and then when I get back home, I toss my keys on the counter right next to the fishbowl. I take the food out and put some in her bowl, then I grab my phone and take a picture and send it to Vivienne

Me: ***She misses you.***

I press send and then put my phone down, not even thinking about whether it's a good idea. I miss her, I miss her laugh, and I miss her swearing in French when she messes up something. I miss her just being here in her robe while she drinks her coffee and shows me animal videos on Instagram.

I grab something to eat and then start packing. We are on the road for the next five days, going first to San Jose and then up to Edmonton. When I'm finished packing, I take a shower, hanging my robe right over hers in my closet. I also see that she left a pair of jeans and also some yoga pants. She was really good about leaving no traces of herself when she came over, and I pick them up and tuck them into my drawer next to my stuff. When I slip on my suit jacket, I grab my bag and head out to the rink where we are meeting everyone.

Checking my phone in the elevator, I see she hasn't responded, but it doesn't surprise me because she's probably still sleeping. When I walk into the arena thirty-five minutes later and enter the room, I see some of the ones who have arrived all look like they got dragged out of bed.

"I swear, I don't think I slept more than two hours," one of the rookies says. They always party the most. First time out there. "Maybe three but max four."

"I told you to pace yourself," Matthew says, coming into the room with his own coffee in his hand. "Hope you guys enjoyed last night because the next time will be Halloween. Oliver and Zara are planning a huge haunted house, so keep your eyes open for that email." I sit down on the bench in front of my name, putting my bag in front of me when Viktor comes in, and he just nods at me and sits next to me.

"Late night?" I ask him, and he shakes his head.

"Not really," he says. "I didn't see you at the after-party."

"He doesn't do after-parties," Evan says, coming in and sitting next to Viktor. "Or any parties."

"That you know of," I tell him, smiling. "Besides, been there, done that."

"There were so many women last night," a rookie says, coming into the room with sunglasses on. "I haven't even slept yet."

"This should be fun," I say to Evan, and he just shakes his head.

"Six-hour flight. I bet he sleeps the whole way." Viktor laughs.

"Okay, people," Oliver says, coming into the room. "Bus is here and ready to be loaded. I have made some hard copies for you guys about the upcoming season and the activities I am in the process of planning. Any encouragement or time would be greatly appreciated."

"Does he ever relax?" Viktor asks, and Evan and I both answer at the same time. "No."

I get up, and I'm the last one out of the room, grabbing a seat in the front of the bus right next to Viktor. "Last one on, first one off."

"Then I get on the plane first, and I'm off first. It's just goes round and round," I tell him, and he laughs, taking out his phone. I wait to get onto the plane before I take out my computer and do work for Walk 'N' Licks. I also RSVP to the SPCA gala in a month, putting the address in my calendar so I don't forget. The flight goes faster than I thought it would go, and when I finally open my hotel room door, I toss my bag on the desk and kick off my shoes.

Turning on the television, I switch it to *SportsCenter* and listen to the news from last night's game. When my phone rings, my heart speeds up just a touch at the thought it could be Vivienne, but I see it's Matthew. He calls to invite me to dinner, and I pass, opting to order room service instead.

I wait for her to text me all night long, but nothing comes through. When I get up the next day for practice, I send her another text.

Me: *I think we should talk.*

I put the phone away and then go to practice. The boys are a bit peppier this morning after a good night's rest. "How was dinner?" I ask Evan.

"It was just the three of us." He laughs. "Everyone was either sleeping or ate in their room."

I nod at him and get my gear on. For two hours, I lose

myself in my job, and then I hit the gym. When I pick up my phone, I see that she hasn't messaged me back, and the messages both say delivered.

I don't text her that night or the day after. Instead, I send her Greek food from the first restaurant we went to. I wait for the phone to ring or for a text to come through and nothing. I shake my head when we land in Edmonton after taking the win in San Jose. When we finally get on the plane to head home, I send her one last text.

Me: **I'm on my way home. I'll swing by when I land so we can talk.**

I don't know if it's the threat of going to see her or the fact that she actually is ignoring me, but I smile, thinking about the ways I'm going to drive her crazy.

I'm answering an email when my phone beeps, and when I see it's her, I smile right away.

Vivienne: **There is nothing to talk about. Please stop.**

I grab my phone and smile while I answer her.

Me: **Hey there, nice to hear from you. I'm free tonight after seven, does coffee work?**

I put the phone down and see the three dots bubble come up and then disappear, and I have a picture of her freaking out about it, so I send her another text.

Me: **Do you want me to bring you something specific, or do you want to come to my place? I'm good with either.**

This time, the bubble comes up, and then it beeps.

Vivienne: **I don't want either, and I'm not meeting you anywhere.**

God, I missed her. I smile to myself as I finally start to breathe easier knowing that I'll see her tonight. It doesn't mean anything, but just knowing I get to see her is every-thing.

Me: ***Your place it is. See you at seven. I'll bring Elsa.***

She sends me five texts in a row.

Vivienne: ***I'm not home.***

Vivienne: ***Don't come over.***

Vivienne: ***I won't be home.***

Vivienne: ***There is nothing to talk about.***

Vivienne: ***Merde.***

I don't answer her. Instead, I get home and dump my bag, and I actually grab the fishbowl and walk out toward the car. I stop at Starbucks on my way to her house, and the doorman smiles when he sees me. "Hey, Mr. Dimitris, long time, no see."

"Yeah," I say, grabbing the fish in one hand and the tray of coffee and tea in the other hand. "Season's started." I walk into the lobby, and when the elevator door opens, I am so nervous. But the minute I knock on the door, I hear her heels clicking on the floor and then she swings open the door. Her hair flies with the wind of the door opening, and I know at that moment that I'm never going to let her go. That no matter how I have to fight, it'll be worth it. I smile big at her, not even noticing that she looks like she's going out. "Hey," I say, walking in, and she closes the door behind me.

"Mark, this isn't a good time," she says, and I turn to look at her. She's wearing black leather pants with a cream-col-ored turtleneck that is tucked in and leopard high-heel booties.

"You look nice. Were you going out?" I ask her and act like it's not killing me, but it is.

"I am," she says, and I can't tell if she's bluffing.

"Well, I won't keep you long," I tell her and then hand her the tray of coffee and tea. She walks over and grabs the tray from me. "Have a hot date?" I ask her, and she just walks down the corridor to the kitchen, the same kitchen we had sex in. She places the coffee on the counter and then turns to look at me.

"I have a date in twenty minutes, so you have five minutes," she says, and she crosses her arms over her chest. I have to wonder if I'm doing all this for nothing.

TwentyFive

VIVIENNE

$\mathcal{M}$Y PLAN WAS to get all dressed up and look fabulous, then lie about a date, and it was going perfectly. Wearing my best pants shows all my curves, and the lace bra under my cashmere top pushed the girls up. It was almost like I was gearing up for war, and then the knock came on the door, and I braced myself. Except nothing could have prepared me for when I pulled opened the door and there he stood. Wearing blue jeans and a black jacket, his hair brushed back and you could see how he ran his fingers through it. But nothing got me more than him holding that fucking fishbowl.

I tried to make it seem like I didn't care. I grab the tray of coffee and turn to walk down the corridor, not letting him see that my hands are shaking.

"I have a date in twenty minutes, so you have five min-utes," I tell him, putting the coffee on the counter and then crossing my arms.

He smiles at me and puts the fish down now, leaning back on the counter to face me. "You didn't text me back," he says, and I look at his hands, the hands that brought me more pleasure that I would ever acknowledge.

"There was nothing to say." I look into his eyes, and it's the wrong thing to do. The minute he sent me the text, my hands got so sweaty, I almost dropped the phone. I ignored it, but I would look at my phone every second to see if he texted me back. When he finally said he was coming over, I knew I had no choice but to answer him. I thought by answering him, he would go away, but he didn't.

"I think there are a couple of things to say," he says softly, and I just look at him. "Take for example us running in the same circle."

"We don't run in the same circle," I point out. "I go to hockey games, and you play hockey."

"Do we ignore each other when we are in the same room?" he asks me, and my stomach drops. I wasn't planning on ever being in a room with him. "Or do we just pretend that we haven't seen each other naked?"

"We are both responsible adults," I tell him. "I'm sure we can be in a room without being awkward."

"What about us being friends?" he asks.

"I don't think that's a good idea," I say. I'm sure I have reasons, but I just can't think of them right now with him in my space. I should have just called him and spoke to him on the phone.

"Why?" He tilts his head sideways. "We have a lot in common."

"Men and women can never be friends," I tell him. "It's impossible."

"You're friends with Matthew." He smirks, and now I'm so angry with him. I wish I could put my heel through his toe, but then Matthew would kill me if I injured his star goalie.

"He's like my brother," I counter. "We can't do that."

"Why not?" he says.

"Because we just can't," I say loudly, throwing up my hands. "It's not going to be fair to you. You want more than I have to offer."

"I want your friendship," he tells me, and I try to swallow, but my mouth is drier than a desert under a hot sun in the summer. "Surely, you can offer me a friendship after everything."

"It just isn't going to work," I say. "Men and women can not be just friends. It's scientifically impossible."

He rolls his eyes, and I want to go over to him and grab his face in my hands and then jump on him and wrap my legs around his waist. "I think I can be around you without wanting to sleep with you." He smirks and then adds, "And I'm assuming you can control yourself." He winks, and I glare now.

"Trust me, I can control myself. That isn't the issue. The issue is that we were very intimate with each other, and it's just weird after," I tell him. I honestly don't have an answer. I have no idea what to say. "I mean, just standing here, there is no attraction."

"Really?" he says and then looks down and looks up. "So if I were to come to you right now and put my hands down your pants, you wouldn't be ready for me?"

I point at him. "That is why we can't be friends."

"I was just pointing out as your friend that you were wrong about us not being attracted to each other." He smirks. "Anyway, I have to run," he says, pushing off from the counter. "And you have a date to get to." He walks over to me, and I swear I don't move, I don't blink my eyes, I don't even breathe. He comes into my space and leans down, and I can smell his musky aftershave that I know he puts on when he trims his beard. I know that he puts two drops in his hands and than slaps them together and rubs his face. And I know he does this while naked usually. He leans down, and I wait for his lips to touch mine, but they don't. Instead, he kisses my cheek. "Have fun, Vivienne," he whispers in my ear right before he steps away from me and walks out of the kitchen, leaving his kiss to linger on my cheek.

I wait for the door to close before I raise my hand to my cheek where he left his kiss. I walk out of the kitchen and toward my room in a daze. "What just happened?" I ask and sit on the bench in front of the bed. "What in the fuck just happened?" Rubbing my face, I then get up to get my phone beside my bed and walk back to my office.

I sit in my chair, moving the mouse on the pad and watching the computer come to life. Opening my blog page, I start writing.

Can a man and woman be friends, especially after being intimate? I have the answer for you, it's no. NO, NO, NO, NO. There is no way this can happen. I think it's scientifically impossible. You can't sit down and eat a meal with someone, knowing what he looks like naked. Wanting him to be naked, preferably with you sitting on his lap. I just don't see it.

How many of you have gone on to being friends after?

I press publish and then turn off the computer. Walking back to my bedroom, I strip out of my clothes, pin my hair on top of my head, and get into bed. The sheets are cool and crisp when I turn on the television, and it's still on the sports network from last night. I pretend that I was watching the game for Matthew. Ignorance is bliss, they tell me.

The night comes and goes, and my dreams are all of him, and when I get up in the morning, I do it on the wrong side of the bed. I drag my ass to the kitchen to make myself coffee, and when I turn to make my coffee, I see the tray from yesterday still sitting on the counter. Grabbing it, I walk over to the sink to pour it out, and I spot the fishbowl. "Motherfucker."

The coffee starts, and I run to grab my phone, but I don't bother texting him. Instead, I just call him, but I'm sent straight to voice mail. That irritates me more when I see it's ten, and I know he's up.

Me: **It's Vivienne, you left your fish here. Let me know when you're going to be home so I can have it delivered back to you.**

I toss the phone down on the counter, and when the phone rings, I assume it's him, so I don't even bother checking the caller ID.

"You better be on your way to get your fish," I say into the phone and then grab my cup for my coffee.

"What fish?" Karrie asks, laughing.

"I thought you were Mark," I tell her and close my eyes.

"Really? So Mark came over?" she asks, snickering, and it takes my pissed-off mood to the next level.

"Don't start," I hiss. "He wanted to go over a couple of things."

"I'm taking from the attitude that you didn't have the happy ending." She laughs, and then I hear her sip her drink.

"He wants to be friends," I tell her. "He came over with coffee to discuss us being friends."

"You can't be friends with him," she says right away.

"Merci," I say. "I told him that, but he disagrees."

"Of course, he does," she says. "But until you're over him, you can't be friends with him."

I stop making my coffee and snap at her. "I am over him." I'm hoping she doesn't call me on anything, but she's Karrie, and she knows me better than I know myself.

"Bullshit," she says to me. "You are not over him at all." I roll my eyes and take a sip of the hot coffee. "When you saw him, how did you feel?"

"Horny and wet," I tell her the truth.

"I mean you, not your vagina," she groans.

"I felt nothing," I lie to her, and she doesn't say anything. "Okay, fine. I felt happy to see him, but it's just because I haven't seen him in a while."

"You felt happy to see him," she repeats what I just said. "And the reason you felt like that is because you missed him."

"Karrie," I say her name. "You're not helping."

"I'm trying to help," she says softly. "But unless you admit that you liked him ..."

"Of course, I liked him," I say, sitting on the couch. The stinging of tears hits my eyes, but I blink them away fast. "That isn't the issue here."

"You never let anyone in the way you let him in," she points out. "You never let anyone close enough to like them before, so …?"

"How long before this feeling goes away?" I ask.

"Well, let's see. I've loved Matthew for what twelve years, so I'm thinking never." She laughs, and I groan. "But maybe being friends with him will help."

"Yes, because spending more time with someone I like is going to help the feelings go away." I exhale loudly.

"You never know," she says. "Maybe you need to put him in the friend zone to get him out of the like zone."

"I don't want him in any of my zones," I tell her. "I want it to be a no-Mark zone."

"You need to be in control of this," Karrie says, her voice going louder. "You need to be the one in charge of this, so if he wants to be friends, you be friends with him and make sure he stays in that zone."

"But what if I can't just be friends with him?" I ask softly.

"Then I think you guys need to talk about it," Karrie says. "You are the most honest person I know. You need to be honest with him also."

"I do," I tell her, knowing I have to.

"I mean, what is the worst thing that can happen?" she asks, and I stop myself before I answer her. The beeping noise lets me look at my phone, and I see that it's Mark.

"It's him," I tell her, and she laughs. "I'm breaking up with you," I tell her and then disconnect going to the other line. "Allo," I answer.

"Vivienne," he says like he doesn't have a care in the world. "How are you?" I want to punch him in his balls. Two can play this game.

"Mark," I say with my fake voice. "I'm fine, thank you. How are you?"

"Great actually," he says, and I want to ask him why. Is he great because he banged someone last night? Is he great because he has a date? My stomach feels like it's swishing around. "Just finished my workout and I got your message."

"Yes," I say sweetly. "You forgot the fish, so I would like to get that back to you."

"Um, let me check my calendar," he says, and I sit up. "I'm booked today."

"You know what? I was just thinking maybe we should have dinner," I tell him. "I was thinking about what you said last night."

"Really?" he says, surprised. "Um, okay. How is Friday?" he asks me.

"It's Tuesday," I tell him.

"Yeah, I know, but I don't have time," he says. "I mean, I guess we can do Thursday night, but I would have to get back to you."

"Mark, I have your fish," I tell him, raising my voice. "I am busy, too, but I can squeeze you in tonight at five thirty. It can be at Starbucks for all I care."

"Um, five thirty ..." he says, and I picture him tapping his chin. "I guess I can move my date to seven thirty instead." Asshole. I want to snap at him, but I don't.

"Great, why don't we meet in the middle?" I tell him, pretending he didn't just tell me he has a date with someone else.

"Sounds good, Vivienne," he says my name, and I suddenly hate it. "See you then," he says and then disconnects. I put the phone down, and I swear in French, English, and all the other languages that I know. I also run out and grab some fish food so Elsa doesn't starve to death.

I choose an outfit that doesn't look like I spent an hour trying on everything I own. I finally settle on tight dark blue jeans with a cashmere sweater with ruffled sleeves tucked in the front and falling off one shoulder. I grab my camel thigh-high suede boots and put them on, making my legs look even longer than they are, and grab my brown Gucci belt. I walk out the door right on time, my hands shaking and my stomach dipping. I really need to eat something, so I grab a cab there, and when I walk into the Starbucks that we decided on, I look around and see he isn't here yet. I look at my clock, and it's 5:35. I walk to the counter and order myself a chai latte and then go to sit in the corner, facing the door. I wait, checking the door the whole time, and I finally see him walking up to the door. It's a good thing I am watching the door to prepare myself. He pulls open the door and steps in, and all eyes turn to him. He runs his hands through his long hair. He is wearing a black suit with a white button-down shirt, opened at the collar.

His eyes roam the room to spot me, and when he finally does, he smiles at me and walks over. "Hey there, sorry I'm late," he says, leaning down, and again, I wait for his lips to hit mine, but he kisses my cheek again. His hands graze mine as he sits down, sending a tingle all up my arm, and by the time I look down, his hand is gone.

"No worries. I just got here," I tell him, and grab the menu. "I didn't get you anything. I wasn't sure."

"That's okay," he says, smiling. "I have to say I was surprised to get your phone call this morning," he says, and it's at that moment I gasp.

"I forgot the fucking fish."

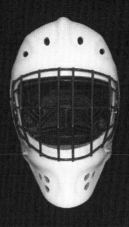

TwentySix

MARK

"*I* FORGOT THE fucking fish." She gasps, and I want to laugh at her. Was she as nervous as I was about this meeting that she forgot the whole reason we were supposed to meet?

After I left her place last night, I could still smell her on me. I knew I was leaving the fish, so I was just waiting for her to call me back. When she called me this morning, I purposely let it go to voice mail. It was a free day, so I didn't have to go into the arena and I didn't have to work out. I spent the day going over emails and planning things with Tracy about opening another location in LA.

"Are you trying to get me to meet you again?" I ask her, and she rolls her eyes. I lied about my schedule being full. The only thing it's full of is plans to win her back. "I must say, this is a change from last night."

"Don't flatter yourself," she says, taking a sip of her drink.

"I'll have it delivered to your house tomorrow."

I put my hands on the table and lean in. "What did you want to talk about?" I smile at her. "I mean, besides the fish."

"Well," she says, and I want to lean over and brush her hair back and kiss her bare neck. "I was thinking about how you said you wanted to be friends."

"I thought you said we couldn't be friends." I repeat what she told me yesterday.

"Yes, well, you were right. We are both mature adults," she starts, "and as you said, we will be seeing each other from time to time." I nod at her. "And we do have lots in common, and it wouldn't be that horrible if we kept in touch."

"I agree," I tell her, surprised she said that.

"And I mean, if one thing leads to another and we end up in bed …" she says with a smirk.

"Not going to happen," I tell her, shaking my head. Shock shows across her face, but then she covers it up as fast as she can. "I don't have sex without being in a relationship."

"And I don't have relationships, so we got that topic crossed off," she says.

"I think we can agree on that one. Sex is off the table," I tell her. Even though my hands want to grab her hair and grip it back while I pound into her, forcing her to admit that she misses me as much as I miss her. "I want to be your friend, Vivienne," I tell her. "Go out, have dinner, and catch up."

"I guess we can do that since we are on the same page for everything else," she says, and I look at my watch.

"I have to run," I lie, and she gets up at the same time, grabbing her drink. When I see her with her fuck-me boots on, my cock goes rock hard in under three seconds. We walk out side by side, and my hand grazes hers lightly. I'm expecting her to move her hand out of the way, but she doesn't. She keeps it there like it doesn't bother her, but I see her shiver. When we walk out of the shop, I turn to her and hug her. She lets out a gasp and then doesn't say anything else when I lean in and kiss her cheek again. "This was nice. We should do it again."

"Yes," she says, smiling and walking away from me to the edge of the sidewalk and putting up her hand to flag down a cab. "We should." A cab stops in front of her. "I'll send the fish over tomorrow, since you're out tonight."

"I'll text you when I get in tomorrow," I say to make her jealous, and she just nods as she gets into the car, and I watch her drive away. The red brake lights end up in a sea of brake lights. I walk back to my house and let myself in and shrug off my jacket, tossing it on the stool in the kitchen when I grab my prepared meal out of the fridge and zap it in the microwave. I eat standing in the kitchen and then pick up my jacket and go to my room.

My phone pings in my pocket, and I take it out and see that it's Vivienne.

Vivienne: *I forgot to mention that I bought food for the fish, but I'm not sure if it's the same food you use. Have fun on your date.*

I shake my head and look at my watch. It's right before seven thirty. I think about answering her, but I don't. I get into bed and turn on the game, and the whole night, I wonder if she's in bed or if she's watching one of her movies. When I finally fall asleep, I swear I could feel her next to me.

The next day, I walk into the rink with my shake in one hand, and then for five hours, I lose myself in work. When I finally walk back out, I look at my phone, and see it's almost four o'clock.

Me: ***Sorry I didn't call you this morning. I was late rushing into the rink. I'll be home in an hour if you want to send the fish over.***

I wait for her to answer, and when I walk into the apartment, it feels so empty. We have a home game tomorrow, then we leave for Florida.

She doesn't text me the whole night, and then the next day, I call her as soon as I leave for the rink. She answers right away, her voice sounding horrible.

"Hey," I say softly, and she coughs. "Are you okay?"

"No," she says. "I'm dying." I try not to laugh. "I was fine, and then I got home from our coffee, and my body started to ache, and then yesterday, I had a fever and then the cough came."

"Did you go to the doctor?" I ask her with worry and wonder if I can go check on her before I have to get to work. When I look at my watch, I see I can't.

"Yes, it's a cold," she says. "I want a second opinion since he looked like he could be in high school. He didn't even have facial hair," she says and then starts to cough again. "I'm sorry about not sending Elsa, but I checked Google and she can't catch my cold." I almost want to laugh when I think about her googling it. "Anyway, I have to go lie down."

"Take care and call me when you feel better," I tell her, and she groans as she disconnects. I get my Uber app out, and I order her a shit ton of soups to be delivered every hour. Then I call Amanda, who answers on the second ring. "Hey," I tell her. "I kind of need a special favor."

"Seriously, this woman has you doing all types of things you never did. I can't wait for you to just propose and get it over with," she says, laughing. "Then you can be normal and send her flowers."

I laugh. "Funny. But I was wondering if you can maybe put together a care package." She doesn't talk. "Get every single cough medicine that you can get and put it together with some flowers."

"Cough medicine," she repeats.

"And flowers." I mention that. "But nothing that says I like you or anything like that. What flowers would you send to a friend?" I ask her, and she laughs.

"No flowers," she answers. "Yellow rose is the friendship flower."

"Fine. Send her five dozen of those with the care package," I say, getting into my car.

"Five dozen?" she shrieks.

"Too much?" I ask her, and she laughs.

"A touch overboard, yes," she says. "Don't worry, I'll take care of it."

"I knew you would," I say and disconnect the phone. The game is a blur, but we win it in the last minute, thank God, and when I get back into the dressing room, I see that she sent me a text.

Vivienne: ***Thank you for the soup and the medicine and the flowers.***

I smile and answer her right away.

Me: ***And you said we couldn't be friends.***

She doesn't answer me, and for the rest of the night, I wonder if she's okay or if I should call and check on her. I've paced my apartment from top to bottom, and when it's finally a decent hour, I call her, and she answers on the fifth ring.

"You sound better," I tell her, and she hums.

"I feel so much better," she says. "I have to say the soup did wonders and so did all the medicine that you sent."

"Glad I could help a friend," I say, smiling. "I'm leaving today for Florida, so you'll have to keep the fish for a couple more days."

"That's fine," she says. "We'll talk more when you get back."

"That sounds good," I tell her, and I want to tell her that I miss her. I want to go to her and take care of her. But I don't.

"Have a safe flight," she says, and when she disconnects, I look at my phone in my hand. Am I the only one who feels like this? Maybe she really doesn't like me that way.

I walk to the plane, and on the way to Florida, I just zone out. The whole way there, I look out the window. I go over everything we have been through, and I know deep down she misses me.

Florida goes by slow, so fucking slow, and we end up losing bad. I smash my stick after the fourth goal, and when we get into the locker room, I don't even make eye contact with anyone. I shower and head to the bus. Matthew comes over once the plane takes off. "Is everything okay?"

"Yes," I say one word, knowing that my head wasn't in the game tonight.

"I mean 'cause if it isn't, we can see what we can do," he

274

tells me, and I look at him.

"I just had an off night," I tell him honestly. "Happens to the best of us."

"That it does," he says, and that is it. He doesn't say anything else, and when I finally get into my house, I dump my bag and make my way to my room.

I finally call her a week later—the longest week of my life—and she answers right away. "Hey there," she says, her voice upbeat.

"Hi." The smile that fills my face does it automatically. "I was wondering if you'd like to go to the library."

"The library?" she asks, shocked.

"Yeah, the library," I say. "Then we can get something to eat."

"Sure," she says. "What time do you want to meet?"

"Noon should be good," I say to her, looking at my watch and seeing it's a little past ten.

"Okay, I'll meet you at the entrance," she tells me and disconnects. I put on a track suit and a baseball hat and spot her right away as she walks up the stairs. She's wearing blue jeans again and a turtleneck with a brown suede jacket, her eyes so blue they look like crystals.

"Hey," I say, walking over to her, and it's her turn to come to me and lean up to kiss my cheek. My hand holds her arm for a second, and then I drop it.

"Were you waiting long?" she asks me, and I shake my head.

"Let's go inside," I say and put my hand on her lower back as she walks ahead of me. "I was expecting more people," she says, looking around. As we walk side by side, I make sure my fingers graze hers more than I should.

"It's Sunday; there's usually a ton of people on Saturday," I tell her. We walk up the stairs and into the library where most of the tables are vacant. "What's your favorite book?"

"*Kama Sutra*," she says, smiling, and I laugh out loud. Heads turn to me and someone shushes me.

"I mean with words in it."

"The *Kama Sutra* has words in it." She winks at me and laughs quietly, and I know at that moment with her looking at me like that, I'm not in this alone. I just have to show her. And I'm going to love every single moment of it.

TwentySeven

VIVIENNE

"*I*'VE NEVER BEEN friends with a man before," I say, taking a drink of my wine as we eat dinner. We spent the day walking through the library slowly, almost like snails. He would reach for the same book as me just so our hands could touch. Or he would touch me ever so gently that by the time I look at where I felt the touch, he was gone. It was driving me insane.

When he didn't call me for a week, it was almost like I knew he was moving on in a way. I would wonder if he was with his girlfriend, or if he had a date, and no matter how many times it made me sick to think about, I knew I didn't have a right to.

"Like ever?" he asks me, grabbing a French fry and eating it. "You are friends with Matthew and Max?"

"Well, yes, but ..." I try to gather up my words and not think about his mouth and the ways he used to make me scream with it. "Matthew is like my brother, and Max is a brother-in-law of sorts."

He nods, grabbing his glass of water and drinking some of it. "Apparently, there are a lot of people who stay friends with their exes," I tell him, and then he looks at me and laughs.

"How do you know that?" he asks, and I almost let it slip that I posted about it.

"I googled it," I tell him. "Although I have to say it did say no."

He laughs now, and I want to keep that smile on his face for the rest of the night if I can. "What? It's not funny. Look," I say, taking out my phone and typing it in. "Most men do not view friendships the same way as women do." I put the phone down and put up my hands. "I didn't say it. Google did."

"Well, I'm friends with many women," he says, and I try not to let it bother me because who cares. *You do*, my inner voice almost yells it. "So I know it can happen."

"Well, I'm glad we're friends," I tell him. "How is it being on the road?" I ask him, taking a bite of my chicken.

"It sucks, but it's part of the job. Luckily, we're here for Halloween," he says, taking a bite of his own fish.

"Are you going to the monster mash up or whatever it is?" I ask him and wonder if he'll bring a date.

"No," he says right away. "I don't do those things."

"But you have to show up," I tell him.

"No, I don't," he says. "I already declined the invitation, and it's not mandatory. The only thing I will do is the hospital visits with the kids."

"Yeah, that is one I never miss," I tell him.

"I know," he says, and I look at him. "Not going to lie, it was one of the reasons I went in the first place, and then it just was the right thing to do."

"You went for me?" I ask, shocked in a way.

"Vivienne, you know I've wanted you for a long time," he says, chewing. "This isn't surprising to you."

"I know," I say, looking down at my meal. "It's just, I didn't know."

He shrugs and laughs. "Not something I announced to the world."

I don't say anything because I can't. I want to tell him that I want to go home with him. I want to wake up with him tomorrow and then have dinner tomorrow night. "How is your chicken?" he asks, and I just nod at him.

"Great. Good," I say, and then for the rest of the meal, I'm quieter than normal, but I'm blaming the wine when I finally walk into my house and walk to the kitchen and see that the fish is still moving. He didn't even ask for the fish this time. It's like he's really over us. I should be happy, but I'm not. I walk over to the fish and give her a little treat of extra food and then turn off the light, but his bowl still lights up. I got bored one day and ordered a glow in the dark fish toy so he isn't in the dark the whole time.

I get into bed and text Karrie.

Me: **When are we getting together?**

Karrie: **I can come up tomorrow lunch?**

Me: **Yes.**

I put my phone down but text him one more time.

Me: **Thanks for today, it was a lot of fun.**

I put the phone next to me and turn off the lights. And I wait for his reply, but there isn't any, and the next day when I'm getting ready for lunch with Karrie, there is a knock on my door. I walk to it with my kimono flowing around my legs, and I find one of the bellboys holding a box for me.

"This came for you," he says and hands me the white box. Grabbing it, I walk to the kitchen. I pull on the white satin bow on top of it, and it falls to the side. Lifting the top, I see a white card sitting on top of silk.

Here is a little bit of some words to go with your Kama Sutra.

Mark

I laugh and put the card down and when I lift the silk, I come face-to-face with four books with brown covers on them. I pick them up and turn to see the gold writing on the spine of the book.

Pride and Prejudice. I gasp, opening the book and seeing the pages are yellow and old. The next book is *Sense and Sensibility*. I stand here wondering how he even got these, and I look down, thinking this has to be the most thoughtful gift anyone has ever gotten me. I don't move from my spot when I hear my door open and then hear clicking of heels.

"Vivi!" Karrie yells. "I'm here," she says and then stops walking when she sees me. "Hey." She smiles and comes into the kitchen. "What do you have there?"

"Jane Austen books," I say softly.

"Aww, your favorite," she says. "Didn't you read this one every single week for five years?"

"It's a classic," I say, looking at her and taking the book out of her hand.

"Holy shit, did Mark send those to you?" she shrieks when she picks up the card.

"Yeah," I say and then turn to her. "We went to the library yesterday, and he asked me what my favorite book was."

"That is so sweet," she says with hearts in her eyes, and I shake my head.

"I told him *Kama Sutra*," I tell her and rub my face with my hands while she laughs.

"Matthew and I bought that for me one year, and he wanted to do a position a day." I look at her, and my mouth hangs open. "I was all for it until he wanted to do a handstand against the wall so I could suck his dick." I laugh now, putting my hand over my mouth. "It's all fun and games until you get hit in the eye with his knee cap." She shakes her head. "It was not pretty."

"Oh my God," I say, and then I look at her. "I think I like him."

"No shit," she says and then walks over to the cabinet and comes back with tequila. After pouring two shots, she tells me to drink.

"I like him, Karrie," I whisper to her and take a shot, the liquid burning all the way down. "Like, like him."

"There is nothing wrong with that," she tells me, and I look at her.

"Everything is wrong with that!" I shout. "I don't want to like him. I don't want to have that feeling and then be let down when he leaves."

"What if he doesn't leave?" she asks me, and I take the second shot she poured. I take it and don't answer the question.

"I can't be friends with him," I tell her. "I thought I could, but I can't."

"You kept the fish." She gasps. "Oh my God."

"I don't think he wants it," I tell her and then pour myself another shot. "He hasn't asked about Elsa once."

"You named the fish Elsa?" She holds her stomach while she laughs.

"I'm going to put an ad in the paper looking for a new friend," I tell her, and she laughs even harder, but I just shake my head. Instead of going out, I have food delivered. She doesn't bring up Mark again, and when she leaves with kisses and hugs, I send him a thank-you text.

Me: ***Thank you for the books. I didn't know books came without pictures! Mind blown.***

He doesn't answer me, and I put the phone down. I think about that last time we were together, in the shower at my house, and I walk to my bedroom and take out my treasure chest that I keep. A woman can never have enough toys. I put the box on the bed and take out my purple trusted friend. I have been around the block a time or two with this one. I lie on the bed and close my eyes, seeing Mark in my head. His body, his arms, his fingers, his cock. I'm so turned on my nipples ache. I play with myself over and over again, but I never, ever get my happy ending. *Maybe I need to relax*, I think to myself, so I start a bath and bring my waterproof toy with me. The warm water makes me relax, but I just can't get myself there. I grab my iPad and put on porn and nothing. I spend the whole night playing with myself to the point of exhaustion, and the next day, I call Karrie crying.

"He broke it," I say into the phone.

"Oh my God, what did he say to you? Are you okay?" she asks in a panic. "I am leaving right now," she says, and she hangs up the phone, and I cry into the pillow. I don't know where she was, but she's here in twenty minutes. She comes running down the hall, and she gasps when she steps into my room. I'm lying in the middle of the bed, naked, with my toys surrounding me. The treasure chest was knocked over at some point, and her mouth hangs open when she spots porn on the television. "What in the fuck is happening right now?"

"He broke it," I say, sobbing so hard that snot is running out of my nose.

"Who broke what?" she asks, afraid to even come into the room.

"My vagina," I say, pointing at it. "My vagina is broken." She looks at me shocked. "I can't orgasm," I say, putting my head back. "I've tried for the past twelve hours and nothing. Nothing, not this one," I say, holding up my rabbit. "Not the dolphin," I say, lifting that one and tossing it to the side. "Not even the dual pleasure can get me there."

"Oh my God," she says, and she still doesn't move from the doorway.

"Karrie, you need to check," I tell her frantic now. "You need to check and see if anything is broken inside." I open my legs.

"I am not checking your vagina!" she shrieks, holding her hands up to block her eyesight. "Jesus, can you cover it?"

"I would do it for you," I tell her, and then she shakes her head. Finally entering, she goes straight for the television and turns it off right before the woman has a squirting or-gasm.

"This room smells of rubber," she says, and she tosses me my kimono. "You need to take a shower," she says, grab-bing one of my shirts and then picking up all the sex toys scattered around the room. "Are those anal beads?" she asks me. "How many butt plugs does one person need?"

"You can take all those home. I don't need them," I say, getting off the bed. "I'm broken."

"One, I'm not taking your sex toys home, and two, you ar-en't broken. Maybe you just weren't in the mood," she says, and she tosses the T-shirt down and looks around. "I can't even sit down." She throws her hands up. "Go shower and don't use the showerhead." She points at me and walks out of the room. I take a shower, my whole body hurting me, and I find her in the kitchen heating up some food.

"I'm exhausted," I tell her, sitting down. "My arms feel like hundred-pound weights."

"You need to drink. You might be dehydrated," she tells me.

"I think he broke me for all other men," I tell her, grabbing the plate of pasta she put in front of me.

"You are not broken," she says. "But I need you to prom-ise me right here and now that you will never again call me crying about your vagina being broken."

"It is," I tell her, and the tears almost come again. I look down at myself. "And I've been told I have a nice vagina on top of that."

"By who?" Karrie says. "It looks normal."

"One year, I spray painted it the color of the French flag," I say, and she just looks at me. "Then when we went into the hot tub, the paint floated to the top."

"Oh my God." She laughs now.

"His parents were less than thrilled," I tell her. "I was so carefree and so was my vagina." I take another bite. "You know what I can do? Lure him into having sex with me."

"Well, if you take a picture of your dungeon back there, I can guarantee he'll run over here," Karrie says while she eats her pasta.

"You think so?" I ask her. "Maybe I could send a picture of me pleasuring myself," I say, and her eyes go big. "Well, without the pleasure part."

"Promise me that you will never do that," she says. "One of the guys went to send a dick pic to a girl on Snapchat, and he put it on his story instead."

"Oh my God, was he big?" I ask her, and she just shrugs.

"I don't have Snapchat. Matthew told me," she says. "Speaking of, I should call and tell him I'm still in the city."

"What were you even doing here?"

"Going over the Halloween party with Zara. It's a good thing she didn't come with me. There is no way we could explain all that."

"Oh, please, she has enough sex. How do you think she got pregnant?" I tell her. The rest of the afternoon flies by, and when she leaves, I walk back into the room and put all my toys back into the box and set it aside. *Maybe Karrie is right*, I think to myself and then walk to my computer and type up a blog post. When I finish it, I turn it off and make plans to go straight to sleep. It doesn't take me long before I find him in my dreams.

TwentyEight

MARK

*I*T'S BEEN THREE weeks since we had the library outing. Between being on the road and having home games, I've had one day off, and I wanted nothing but to sit at home with her. I text her every two days like clockwork. I live for the day I know I'm going to text her, knowing that she will text me back.

This time, though, I need to hear her voice. It's just been too long. She picks up on the third ring. "Allo." My heart speeds up just a touch when she answers, and then the smile just appears. I could be having the shittiest day, and hearing her voice makes everything better.

"Hey," I say, taking a sip of my coffee. "Long time."

"I know," she says, and then I hear her moan as she stretches. "What's up?"

"Were you sleeping?" I ask, looking over and seeing that it's almost ten.

"No, just lounging in bed. It looks dark outside," she says, and I picture her in bed and wonder if she still sleeps naked or if she wears something in the winter.

"It is. It was softly snowing before but melting the minute it touched the ground," I say, looking out of the window at the gray sky. "Are you coming to the game tonight?"

"That is the plan," she says. "Although I'm obsessed with Netflix these days, it's time to get out," she says, and I want to know everything.

"How about dinner after the game?" I ask her, and she doesn't say anything. "I know that the guys usually get together and have dinner, but …"

"Oh, I wasn't going anywhere after the game," she says.

"I know of a small little place that closes at ten but will stay open if I call them," I tell her, and if I can't find a place, I'll call in a couple of favors.

"Just the two of us?" she asks softly.

"I mean, if you aren't comfortable with that …" I say. My stomach drops, and I put the cup of coffee down on the counter and close my eyes.

"No," she says right away. "It's fine. It'll be good. We can catch up."

I try not to make it a big deal.

"Yeah, that would be nice," she says. "I've been cooking lately, so having someone else cook for me sounds like heaven."

"Perfect. I'll send you the address, and you can meet me there," I say, and then I close my eyes. "Or you can wait for me, but …"

"But people will see," she says, laughing. "I get it. I can

290

meet you there."

"Great," I say, hating that I can't go with her but knowing that it will raise too many questions. I don't want to freak her out and push her further away with the pressure.

"See you then, Mark," she says, and I can picture her saying it with a smile, but I'm hating that she hasn't called me Markos. "And break a leg."

"Let's not put that thought into the universe." I laugh at her, and now she laughs.

"See you later," I say and disconnect and text my guy over at the Italian restaurant I want to take her to.

I relax most of the day, doing stretches and ignoring the butterflies in my stomach. And when I'm slipping my suit jacket on, my phone pings to let me know everything is set for tonight.

I grab my cashmere jacket and beanie for later and make my way to the rink. The camera crews are set up since it's a Saturday game. Walking into the room, I see I'm one of the first ones here, and I take off my jacket and grab my phone with my AirPods so I can ignore the noise from everyone else. After undressing and putting on my track suit, I go into the kitchen and grab my pre-game shake and then go walk on the treadmill while the music plays in my ears. After I walk on the treadmill for thirty minutes, I go back to the kitchen and make myself a peanut butter sandwich, the same thing I do for every single game, then walk back into the now crowded locker room. Grabbing my glove and a tennis ball, I walk to my quiet wall in the garage that no one really knows about.

It's off to the side on the second floor, and no one parks

there, so I walk out the door and see some of the wives arriving. Then I spot Vivienne getting out of the car, and I watch her smile to one of the girls walking in. She must feel me watching her because she turns, and when she sees me, it's a different smile altogether. Her eyes light up, and her smile fills her face so her eyes crinkle at the sides. She stops walking, and she doesn't know if she should come to me or not. I know I shouldn't, but I motion with my head for her to follow me. She turns around and says something, and I watch her walk to me. She is wearing black pants with white lines that look like squares and a black cashmere jacket with the collar closed so it looks like a turtleneck, and she has it tied at the waist. Her black heels click on the concrete, and she finally reaches my side. "Hello there," she says and doesn't try to kiss me, so I lean in, putting one hand on her waist, and I put my cheek against hers, kissing her softly.

"Hey," I say to her and then turn to walk to my secret place.

"Where are you going?" she asks. She looks around as we get farther away from the noise, and I lead her to the iron stairs that lead upstairs. "This feels like those movies when the killer is waiting in the empty parking lot, and just when you think you're imagining it ..." She laughs. "Boom, you're dead."

"Don't worry, I'll protect you," I say when I finally get to the second floor and wait for her. "I come up here to practice," I tell her and walk toward the corner part.

"I'm no expert, but shouldn't you practice with people?" she says, standing there holding her purse in front of her with both hands.

"Watch," I tell her, and I throw the ball against the wall, and it bounces back at me, and I do it over and over again. My eyes never leave the ball as I try to catch it. "The game is to never have the ball in your hand more than two seconds," I say to her. "And to go right to left each time."

"Do you ever miss?" she asks me, and I nod. "What happens when you miss?"

I catch the ball and turn around to look at her. "Then I start again." I smile at her.

"Do you ever just give up?" she asks, and I turn and face the wall again. "And say fuck it."

"The endgame is that much better if you fight for it," I tell her, and then I catch the ball and turn around and walk to her. Standing right in front of her, I make her look up at me. "If the game is easy, it gets boring," I tell her, and then I lift my hand to push her hair away from her eyes. "The chase is what makes the game exciting." I lean in just a touch more, and I only hear her small gasp because it's so quiet up here. "Getting that prize and claiming it," I say, leaning in to whisper in her ear. "Holding the prize in your hands, there isn't another feeling out there."

My cheek grazes hers, and when I stand, I see that her eyes have shaded over, and I bet if I kiss her neck, I would be able to feel the beating of her heart. "I should get back," I tell her and walk away from her. I turn over my shoulder and see her back to me. "You coming?"

She turns around, and I see that she put her game face on because she gives me the same fake smile she gave the girls when she got here. "Yes, I need to get in there."

We walk to the door together, and I open it and wait for her to walk in. She goes one way while I go the other. Neither of us saying anything to each other, and when I walk into the room, the guys are already suiting up. I put my glove away and then start getting ready. The camera crew comes in when we are all dressed, and he goes around the room to catch everyone. I'm the first one on the ice as always, and then I see the kids by the glass. I skate to side and start my stretching by getting on my knees and going side to side. I get on one knee and kick off with the other foot, going in circles and stopping at all four points back and forth on each leg. Evan comes over and starts his stretching beside me. Getting on his knees, he kicks out his legs while I stretch my legs out from one side to the other.

"I really want to win tonight," he says. Looking at all the kids lined up, I spot Vivienne with Chase on her hip. Her jacket is off and now I see her wearing a bright white button-down silk top, and you can see the lace details of her bra underneath. A bra I know that snaps off with just a flick of the wrist. She points out the players to the little boy. He looks at her and laughs while she leans in and kisses his neck, making him squirm and try to get away from her. I get up and skate around in a circle to the goal now, taking my position.

When we get off the ice and then go back on, I skate back and forth in the crease, making some powder, and then I move from one post to the next. I take off my mask when they sing the national anthem, and then it's game time.

Six seconds into the game, I've already stopped the first

puck. I wait for the referee to come over and grab the puck from my glove and the face-off takes place to the right of me. The guys win the face-off, clearing the puck and going toward the other goal, but a stupid pass in the neutral zone has the team coming back at me with a two on one. I advance and then slowly start moving back, and because I'm big, I cover a good part of the net. I see the puck go from side to side, and I also see the other guy passing our defenseman, but I know he's too deep in the zone to make a pass, so I know the guy is going to take the shot. He does, but it's right on me, so I have no trouble saving it.

The rest of the game is crazy with the shots on the net being sixty shots on me and twenty-seven on the other goalie, but we end up winning two to nothing, with me having my second shutout of the month.

I am named first star and do the turn on the ice, tossing the puck, and I'm almost dreading the room now knowing the reporters will be all up in my face. "Good game, Mark," Matthew says to me when I finally get off the ice. "Heads up, the reporters are already in there."

"Don't we have a grace period?" I ask, annoyed that I won't even have a chance to take off some of my equipment.

"When you steal the show by blocking sixty shots on the net, you don't get a break," he says, slapping my shoulder, and I wonder if this is going to go longer than I thought. When I walk into the room, I make my way to my seat, grabbing the Gatorade waiting for me with my post-workout mix. I put my mask on the top shelf and hand the glove and blocker to the equipment guy waiting for me, and I sit to take off the pads. The minute the pads are off, the press come over.

"Mark, you were on point tonight," one of them says. "How did you feel about all the turnovers in the neutral zone?"

It's a shitty question, and if I was a rookie, I would throw my team under the bus with my answer because they sucked tonight, and the turnovers were sloppy. "I mean, in the end, I did the job they pay me to do. Kept the pucks out of the net."

"There were half the shots on net to the other team. Is it safe to say you were the best one on the ice tonight?"

"I didn't put the two goals in the net, so I guess it's a group effort, wouldn't you think?" I tell him and take a gulp of my drink.

The questions last ten minutes more until I nod at them and walk away to go to the shower. I rest my head under the hot water for a minute and then rush to get to the restaurant.

I pull open the door, and the bell over the door makes noise. I look around, and I spot her sitting in the middle of the restaurant at the lone table with no one else there. Her eyes fly up from her phone when she hears the bell, and she smiles. "Well, there he is, the first star of the game," she says, and I smile at her and walk over to her. She stands up to greet me, and this time, I kiss her just near her lips, closer than ever before.

"Sorry I'm late; the press was all over me," I tell her and shrug off my jacket and also my suit jacket. I roll up the cuffs of my shirt to my elbows and take the beanie off, brushing my hands through my hair.

"Your hair is still wet," she says, and I nod. "You should have taken your time so you don't catch a cold."

I smirk at her. "If you start that, I'm going to think you like me." I wink at her, and right before she says something, the waiter comes over.

I watch Vivienne watching the waiter as he tells us the specials of the night, and I think of the chef who is staying late for us. "It all sounds so good," Vivienne says when the waiter walks off to give us time. "Are you hungry?" she asks me.

"Famished," I tell her, and I don't smile. I just look at her. "I feel like I haven't eaten in months."

TWENTYNINE

VIVIENNE

"*FAMISHED*," HE SAYS, and I just look at him while he stares at me. "I feel like I haven't eaten in months." My body shivers internally, and my body goes tense. "What about you? Are you hungry?"

Oh, if only he knew how fucking hungry I was. "No," I say, shaking my head. "I ate during the game," I tell him, and he just nods. My whole body is on edge. I've been jumpy since I saw him in the garage, and he took me upstairs. I swear to God I thought he was going to push me against the wall and finally kiss me. At least that is what I was hoping; this dancing around is almost like a mating dance, and I, for one, am ready to get in the ring and oil wrestle with him. Naked. After the game, I quickly kissed everyone and said I was heading home to bed with a headache, but Karrie knew exactly where I was going. How could I not tell her after the garage part? When I walked into the lodge after that,

I downed two glasses of wine, one after another, not even giving myself time to think about it.

The waiter comes out with three plates. "The chef sent this out for you to snack on." He puts down a plate of calamari, meatballs, and rice balls. He then takes our order, and I grab a meatball and put it on the plate in front of me.

"That was a great game tonight," I tell him, and he smiles at me while he picks up a piece of calamari and dips it in the sauce and puts it in his mouth. His tongue darts out, licking the sauce from the corner of his mouth. I want to lean over the table and pounce on him like a cat in heat.

"What part was your favorite?" he asks me, and I'm in a daze of him throwing me on the table and having me as his meal. "Vivienne," he says, and I snap out of my head.

"Yeah?" I say, confused.

"What part was your favorite?" he asks me again.

"Um, the part where you guys won," I say to him, and he laughs. "I mean, I was drinking and eating, but I heard the crowd really, really into it." I smile at him while I pop a piece of my meatball in my mouth. "So I'm assuming by the gasps of the crowd and the fact you guys had zero goals scored on you that it was a great game."

He laughs now, then takes a sip of water. "I guess I can live with that," he says, and the waiter comes back out with two plates of different salads courtesy of the chef.

"I don't know how I'm going to eat my plate at this rate," I tell him, grabbing some arugula salad and adding it to my plate.

"You can always box it up," he tells me. "So how have you been?" he asks, grabbing a meatball.

"Well, since yesterday when we texted, I'm still okay," I tell him. "Oh, and not that you care anymore, but Elsa is doing well." He laughs. "Why are you laughing?" I ask almost angrily. "You haven't asked for her once. Not one time. You don't even know if I'm feeding her."

"Oh, I know you're feeding her," he says, not looking at me, and I grab my glass of white wine and finish it off. "You won't let Elsa starve."

I watch him and get a little bit irritated that he isn't taking this seriously. "How do you know? I don't know the first thing about raising a fish," I tell him and take a sip of my wine and then another. "How do you know she doesn't wonder where you are?"

He puts down his fork and leans back in the chair, and it's the worst thing right now because him leaning back makes his shirt pull across his chest that is sculpted like the fucking *David* or whatever is better than the *David*. I want to lick him like a lollipop. "Are we still talking about the fish here?"

I tilt my head to the side. "What else could we be talking about?"

"Well, is that your way of asking me if I'm dating anyone?" he asks, and I want to slap my hand on the table and say yes, yes it is, and are you?

But instead, I throw my head back and laugh a forceful laugh. "Are you crazy? Why would I care?" I ask, the words tasting like acid coming up. "I mean, I'm sure you're not over there thinking about me dating, right?" He doesn't answer, but I see a tic in his forehead. Maybe it does bother him to think about me dating. I'm not going to tell him that he's ruined my vagina or that when I went to the doctor, I asked

301

him if my vagina could, in fact, be ruined from ever orgasming again. I don't tell him that the look on the doctor's face was utter disbelief or that the nurse whispered, "Oh my."

"Are you busy next Saturday?" he asks me.

"Are you asking me out on a date?" I ask, surprised.

"No." He shakes his head. "I have this gala with the SPCA, and I was wondering if you wanted to join me." His eyes never leave mine. "It's for a good cause."

"What type of event is this?" I ask him, knowing full well I'll go with him.

"Black tie," he says. "The richest of the rich." He laughs. "Just your average Saturday night soiree."

"I'll have to check my calendar when I get home," I tell him, and he just nods. Before he can even say another word, the waiter comes out with our meals. We dance around the subject of next Saturday, and when it's time to leave, I've finished a bottle of wine all by myself, and my laughter is coming out more. I get up, and well, I sit back down just as fast. He watches me when he rolls down his sleeves. "Okay, let's try that again," I say and get up, but now he's standing beside me. His hand comes out to hold my waist and pulls me toward him. I look up at him, and he's honestly the most beautiful man I've ever met. And I know that some men would cringe at being called beautiful, but that's what he is. "Thank you," I say, pushing out my chest a little like the hussy I am.

"You sure?" he asks me, and I could swear he's bringing me in closer and closer, or maybe I'm falling into him. Either way, no one moves, and we stay like this for what seems an eternity but is probably just three seconds before his hand moves from around my waist. He takes my jacket and helps me with it. I just smile at him and look down, my hair falling in front of my face, so I push it back around my ear. I watch him walk to his own jacket, and he puts on his suit jacket first and then the cashmere blue one, and like the suit, it molds to him. He places the beanie inside his pocket. "After you," he says, and I smile, walking out in front of him. The cold air pushes the door back closed on me, and he grabs my hips to steady me. "You okay?"

"Yeah," I say, looking over my shoulder at him and having him so close that I smell him all over me. It would take nothing for me to turn into his arms and pull him down to me and finally give in to everything. But I don't. Instead, I push the door harder this time, and he holds it open so it doesn't come back and smash me in the face.

I walk to the sidewalk and hold up my hand, and I feel him pull me back to him by my arm. "I'll take you home," he says as his truck shows up at the curb. The waiter comes out and nods to us, then goes back inside the restaurant. He walks to the passenger side and opens the door for me, taking my hand in his as he helps me into the truck. "Thank you," I say to him, and he closes the door, and I put my head back on the headrest and close my eyes. The pull to him is stronger than I've ever felt in my life. He gets in, and I want to just lean over and kiss him—just a little kiss on the lips— but I don't. Instead, I tell myself that this is for the best. He takes me home and gets out of the truck when he parks in front of my apartment, and the bellboy opens the door for me. "Do you need help upstairs?" he asks softly, and even through my coat, I can feel his hand on my back.

"I'm good." I smile up at him. "Thank you for dinner."

He smiles at me, and his hand goes to my hip now, and he leans in. "Anytime, Vivienne," he says softly, and I'm waiting for his kiss on my cheek, but it never comes. Just the tingle from his beard. "Let me know about Saturday," he says, and then I nod and walk into my lobby, never once turning back. Even when I get in the elevator, I wait for the door to close before I turn around and hold the railing in the elevator while my breathing returns to normal. I walk into my house, kicking off my wet shoes at the door and then walking to my bedroom where I hang up my jacket and undress. Walking to the closet in the spare room where I keep all my formal gowns, I knew the minute he said anything to me exactly what I wanted to wear. The gown is ready to be worn. I close the door and walk back to my bedroom, my phone buzzing from my purse. Taking it out, I see it's from Mark, and my heartbeat speeds up just a touch. I wonder when it's going to stop acting like this. It's been over two months, and still, it speeds up every single time I see his name.

Markos: *Just made it home. I wanted to come up and say good night to Elsa, but it was late, and she was probably sleeping. Let me know about Saturday.*

I contemplate dragging it out, but my head doesn't connect to my fingers that are typing faster than I can read.

Me: *I'm free. Send me details.*

The blue text shows up as delivered right away, then I put my phone on the side table and close my eyes. The room spinning just a touch or a lot. I don't bother undressing, I just lie on top of the bed and then curl up, and when I hear ringing the next day, my eye opens ever so slowly, and

I see the sun blaring into the room. I don't move, and the ringing stops and then starts up again right away. I slowly get up and my head pounds, so I close one eye and see that my phone is showing me Karrie's picture.

"Are you dead?" I slowly get off my bed and walk to the bathroom.

"Are you dead?" she asks me. "I've been calling you since eight."

"A.m.?" I ask her, sitting on the toilet and kicking off my pants. "When did you become a farmer?"

She laughs, and I hear water running in the background. "Please, I've already made breakfast and put lunch in the oven."

"What time is it?" I ask, confused and then put her on speakerphone while I wash my hands and face and then brush the cotton balls from my mouth.

"Almost noon," she says. "So how was last night?"

"It was okay," I say, trying not to say anything more, but she's Karrie. "He asked me to go with him to the SPCA gala next weekend."

"Are you going to go?" she asks me, and then the water shuts off.

"Yes," I say to her and then take off my blouse from last night and then pick up my phone and walk to the kitchen to start my coffee. She doesn't say anything. "I'm going to stop doing this after the gala."

"What do you mean?"

"I have to stop being friends with him," I tell her, closing my eyes, and my heart breaks just knowing that it's coming. "It's just I thought I could handle it, but I can't. I want him."

"You know you could have him," she says softly.

"It's not fair to him. He is going to want marriage and kids and all that traditional stuff. How does this happen?"

"How does what happen?" she asks, laughing.

"How does the one person who hates commitment sleep with a man who only wants a commitment?"

"Opposites attract," she says. "What are you going to wear?"

"My champagne silk gown," I tell her and wait for her to gasp.

"The one that you bought 'for the next biggest milestone of your life.'" She imitates me. When I saw it hanging on the hanger in the store, I knew I was going to buy it, but I didn't have a reason for it. So I said the next biggest milestone in my life I was going to wear this dress. But it's been two years, and there hasn't been anything big in my life.

"I don't need to hear it right now," I tell her, grabbing my coffee and phone and going back to my bedroom. "What I need is for you to not make a big deal about it, and," I say softly, "for you to come over on Sunday and hold my hand."

"Done," she says, "And done. I'll bring all the cheesecake and croissants for us. With all the wine and tequila in the world."

"Perfect, and then from then on, no more Mark. I won't answer his texts," I tell her, and then I say, "What if he wants to ask about Elsa?"

"Give him Elsa back," she says, and I gasp.

"I can't just give her back!" I shriek. "I just got her pink glow in the dark rocks." She laughs so hard. "I have to go now. I forgot to feed her," I say, disconnecting.

The rest of the week goes by slowly. Mark texts me on Thursday to tell me he's going to pick me up at seven. I know that he's on the road, and they lost both games.

Saturday comes, and for the whole day, I have stomach pains. My stomach goes up and down and flip flops all around, and I know I'm just nervous. But I don't know if I'm nervous about seeing him, or the fact that I know after tonight, I won't be talking to him anymore. I can't be friends with him. I spent Thursday on Pinterest finding pictures of him on fan pages. I can't go on like this. I also check Page Six and all the hockey gossip pages I know to see if anyone had "spotted" him with someone, and I've come up empty, which isn't a surprise since he's never been on those sites before.

I slip into the gown and pull it over my shoulder and zip the side and look at myself. The gown is sleeveless, and the champagne satin comes up to my neck. The side looks like it's folded over, pushing in my waist and having the extra material fall on the sides to the floor like a cascading waterfall of sorts. I slip on my gold shoes and then put on my pearl and diamond earrings with the matching ring. I look at myself and put my hand on my stomach and then finally put on the bracelet that I never thought I would wear again, the pink quartz one. As I grab the matching purse and stick my lipstick and ID inside, the sound of knocking makes me look up. I grab my purse and my shawl and make my way to the door. I don't know what I was expecting, but it wasn't this.

He stands there in a black tuxedo looking like he stepped out of a magazine ad. His hair perfectly pushed back, and his beard trimmed. His eyes light up when he sees me, and it takes him a second to say anything. "You just …" he says, and I smile and do a turn, showing him that there is no back to the dress, the skirt twirling between my legs. "I can lend you my coat," he says, and I laugh at him.

"I have a shawl, thank you very much," I tell him. Walking out, I close the door behind me and put my keys in my purse. He puts his hand on my back, and my whole body wakes up. "You look very dapper," I tell him when we wait for the elevator, and my hands come up to touch his jacket.

"You didn't drive?" I ask him when I see the town car waiting for us at the curb.

"No, figured I could maybe have a drink," he says, and I laugh now. "Or not. We'll see."

The chauffeur opens the door for us, and I grab the bottom of my dress, stepping into the car, and he gets in after me. When we walk into the ballroom, I see all the glitz and glamour that you see in the movies. Men wearing tuxes as the women hold on to their purses and air kiss the other people. The diamonds dripping off them, a man with a camera walking around taking pictures. The tables around the dance floor are filled with lavish high vases so you smell the flowers everywhere. Candles are lit up around the room, giving the room a certain glow along with the crystal center chandelier that hangs in the middle of the room over the grand dance floor. Dim lights around the room keep it from being too dark. Mark grabs a glass of champagne from the passing waiter and hands it to me.

"Thank you." I smile at him and take a sip. He has people come up to him, shaking his hand and thanking him for coming. He introduces me to a couple of people who are with the SPCA, resting his hand on the lower part of my back the whole time.

"Well, well." I hear a voice that sends shivers down my spine, and I'm hoping that it's just my ears playing tricks on me. "If it isn't my favorite dog walker in the world."

Mark and I turn at the same time, and my eyes meet his for the first time in ten years. His face goes from a smile to shock, and then he catches it and smiles, coming over and shaking Mark's hand. "I was wondering if I would see you here," he says and I look at him. I want to say that the years have not been good to him, but he looks the same.

"Scott," Mark says smiling. "So great to see you. Where is Juliette?" he asks him, and Scott turns to look behind him, and the woman wearing a black dress comes over with a smile on her face. I've never seen her close up; I only saw her that one time from a distance. She has her blond hair tied up in an updo. I try to control my breathing, try to ignore the bile rising. I want to run away and hide.

"The most handsome man I've ever seen," Juliette says, coming to Mark and kissing his cheeks. My eyes fly from hers to Scott's, and I see him just looking at me. Juliette takes her place right beside Scott.

"Vivienne, this is Scott and Juliette, one of the very first clients I've ever had," Mark says, and I smile and put my hand out to shake Juliette's hand and then Scott's. "Their kids," he continues, saying, "how old are they now?"

"Sebastian is going to be ten, and Stella is turning eight," Juliette says, her eyes beaming with pride.

"They still in love with Lucky?" he asks, and I know that I

have to get away from this. But my feet stop me from moving.

"Yes, they talked Scott and me into another one, so we have two dogs," Juliette says, and I stand here and just smile.

"If you guys will excuse me." I finally get my voice. "I'm going to find another glass of champagne." I look at Mark, and my heart speeds up. "Stay here." I pretend everything is okay.

"I'll be right here," he says, assuring me, and I turn to walk away, hoping that the crowd swallows me up. I walk out of the ballroom, and I turn to go to the side and find a hallway with another room that looks like a sitting room with couches all around the room, but it's empty. I walk to the roaring fireplace and put my hand on my stomach, trying to blink away the tears that are stinging to come out.

I breathe in and out and close my eyes. I don't hear anyone else walk into the room until I hear the two words I erased from my memory ten years ago. "Mon amour."

THIRTY

MARK

$\mathcal{I}$ watch her walk away, but instead of going to the bar, she turns and walks out of the ballroom.

"I think I'm going to grab a drink myself," Scott says and then turns to Juliette. "Do you want anything?"

"A white wine would be lovely," she says, smiling, and then I look at Juliette as she continues to talk about their kids, and when I look back, I see that Scott has also walked out of the ballroom. I don't know what it is, but the minute she turned around, I felt her whole body go tense, and I saw her hands shake just a touch. I don't even think she knew she was shaking.

"Excuse me," I tell Juliette. "I'm going to go find Vivienne."

She just smiles at me, and I walk out of the ballroom, seeing guests lingering everywhere. I walk to the side and see a small hallway, and I'm not sure what I expect to find, but my heart races so fast it sounds like roaring in my ears. I get close enough to hear her voice. "Don't call me that ever again, and don't fucking touch me."

I get to the doorway, and she is standing there with her back to the fire. Scott is in front of her, and he has his hands on her arms, on her bare arms. "Mon amour, please."

The minute he calls her that, I see black. "I'm going to give you less than a second to get your fucking hands off her before I put you through a wall," I say, my voice staying low. Vivienne's eyes come to mine, and I see her with tears in her eyes. Scott turns around and sees me, his hands slipping off her arms.

"Mark, it isn't what it seems," he says, and I put my hands in my pockets instead of going to him and grabbing him by his jacket and putting him through a wall.

"I know one thing," I tell him, walking into the room. "She told you not to touch her."

"It's a private conversation," he says, and I laugh.

"How is this for private? If I see you touching her again, after I finish putting you through that wall, I'll make sure I break every fucking bone in your body?" I tell him when we stand toe-to-toe. Except he's smaller than I am, so I look down. "Now it's safe to say our business relationship is also terminated." He nods at me, then turns to look at Vivienne one last time before he walks away. "Oh, and Scott, don't cross me. I would love nothing more than to bury you, and we both know I have the means to do it."

I watch him walk out of the room and turn back to look at Vivienne, my beautiful Vivienne. "Mark," she says my name softly, and I look down. I knew today we would either continue or it would have to end. I couldn't do this anymore. I couldn't stand not going home with her. I couldn't stand not waking with her, it was just too much, and I was over it. She either was with me or she wasn't. I just never thought that it would come to this right here. She steps forward and puts her hand on my arm, and I just look down at it, the hand that I want to hold for the rest of my life.

"Um ..." I start, then I stop talking because there is so much that I need to say, there is so much that I want to say, but my heart is beating so fast, and my hands are trembling. "I think we should go."

Her hand falls off mine, and I look at her. She puts her shoulders back. "Perhaps I'm the one who should go."

"Vivienne," I say. "I don't want to do this here."

She nods at me and walks ahead of me down the stairs, and I follow her. She walks over to grab her shawl and then comes to me. "I think it's easier if I just grab a cab."

"You can do that," I tell her, and she nods and tries to walk away. "Either way, I'll show up at your house." She stops walking and turns around. "I'm not doing this here in front of everyone." I look around to make sure that no one is paying attention to us. "Now the car should be out front."

She nods and walks out, and our car is there waiting like I told him to. The driver gets out of the car and opens the back door, and she steps in, and I walk around. I sit next to her, but she glues herself to the side of the car, and when we pull up, I get out and walk in with her. Neither of us saying anything.

The whole ride up in the elevator, I hold my tongue to wait for when it's just the two of us. She unlocks the door and walks down the hallway to the living room. She puts her shawl and her purse on the table and takes out the tequila, drinking a shot and then another. "It was in this room ten years ago that I broke up with him," she says the words without looking at me, and then she takes another shot.

"It was my birthday." She puts the glass down softly and then turns to me, and I see the tears running down her face. "He was going to meet me at four, so I went out with Karrie to celebrate." She puts her head back and looks up at the ceiling, and then looks back at me. "I saw them on my way home." I don't say anything, and again, for the second time tonight, I put my hands in my pockets instead of going to her. "I knew he was married. I found out after four months," she says, and two more tears roll down her face. She turns around and takes another shot, this time hissing and then wiping her mouth with the back of her hand. "I know I disgust you with all this." She starts to talk, and I feel like with those words, she just shattered me. "I had an affair with a married man.

"But he told me he was leaving her," she says loudly. "And I believed him until I saw them that day. She was getting out of the car with him and she turned around to say something to him, and I saw her stomach." She swallows now and puts her hands to her mouth. "That night, he came over, and I kicked him out."

"Do you love him?" I ask the only question I really care, the only question that really matters.

She shakes her head. "No." She folds her hands together and wrings them. "At the time, I thought I did," she answers softly. "I was ending this tonight," she says, and I look at her, not getting it. "This whole being friends with you. I was ending it because I couldn't do it anymore."

"Why?" I ask her, my mind begging her to say it.

She walks away from me and goes to the window and looks out, and I wait with bated breath for her to say anything at this point. She turns around. "When Scott left, it took me three days not to think about him," she says. "Three days and then it took me seven days to think back when was the last time I thought of him." She turns back to look outside, and I hear her. "It's been two months since I've felt your kiss, and I haven't gone ten minutes without thinking about you." My heart beats so fast and so hard, but I don't know how to react. She turns back and now the tears are just pouring out of her, and she looks at me. "I love you," she says. "Like love, love you. Like my world would shatter without you." Her breath hitches while she tries to keep her composure. "I knew I liked you. I knew, but tonight, seeing Scott …" She takes her hand and wipes away the tears. "The only thing that I could think about was you not finding out what a horrible person I was. Hoping that even with all this, you could somehow …" She puts her hands on her stomach.

"Are you done?" I ask her, not wanting to cut her off but not wanting another minute to go on where she thinks I'm judging her. "I want you to know before anything and above everything, I will never judge you." Her eyes open a bit more. "I love you."

"What?" she whispers almost as if she doesn't believe it. "Even after …?"

"When you left me, I told my father about you," I say, and she gasps. "Told him I lost the girl I loved, and he said if I loved you, I wouldn't just let you get away." I take a step closer to her. "I sat there outside on my patio with my heart broken, and my father told me that if I let you just walk away, then I didn't really love you." I take another step to her. "So I made a plan." Another step. "To make you see that you loved me." I finally stand in front of her and now my hand comes out and stops the tear from rolling down her cheek. "I knew you loved me. You were just scared." She nods her head. "You can't just walk away from me, Vivienne, because I'd follow you," I tell her. "I'd follow you wherever you go. As long as I'm with you, everything is okay." I smile. "I was ending it tonight, too." Her mouth opens. "I was done giving you space. I was done with the games and showing you I loved you. I was done not waking up with you or going to bed with you. I was done with not telling you."

"I'm done running," she finally says. "I'm done with it all."

"Can I kiss you now?" I ask, my voice almost a whisper.

"Please," she says just as softly, and finally, after two long months, my other hand comes up and takes her face—her beautiful, beautiful face—and I lean in and kiss her lips. Her hands rest on my chest right over my heart as my tongue slips into her mouth. The kiss goes from soft to urgent to frantic in seconds. I bend and pick her up, carrying her in my arms, her legs falling over my arms. Our mouths never letting the other one go. When I get to her bed, I stand her up and slowly undress her, the satin dress falling to her feet, leaving her in front of me in just a pair of see-through panties that shred in my hands the minute I try to take them off.

"Make love to me," she asks, pushing the jacket from my shoulders. Her fingers unbutton my shirt, and then finally when it opens, she pushes it off my shoulders, and I look at her.

"You haven't been paying attention," I tell her, and she looks at me. "I've been making love to you this whole time. Every single time I slid into you, I was making love to you."

I pick her up and place her in the middle of the bed. After I finish undressing, I get on the bed with her, then turn around to get a condom, but her hand comes out and stops me. "Nothing," she says softly. "Nothing between us."

"Are you sure?" I ask her, and she just nods and opens her legs for me. "I want to do all those things, but I need to get into you," I tell her, grabbing my cock and rubbing it up and down her slit with one hand on my cock, and with one hand by her head, I sink into her. My other arm goes to the other side of her head, and her mouth finds mine, and for the first time, she knows I made love to her.

THIRTYONE

VIVIENNE

I FEEL LITTLE kisses on my shoulder, and it takes me a second to realize it's not fake and I'm not dreaming. Last night wearing the dress I knew I would wear for a big milestone; I finally gave in to the fact I was in love with Mark.

When I turned around at the gala and saw Scott, my whole world felt like it was tilting on its axis. Hearing him call me amour just made my stomach sick. Looking at him, I wondered what I ever loved about him in the first place. His hands on my arms repulsed me so much, I was about to tell him to fuck off when I heard Mark and my heart sank. I don't know what was worse about him catching me with Scott—the fact that I just realized what a douchebag Scott was or the fact that I was head over heels in love with Mark.

It happened so fast; everything felt as if it was all crumbling down, and then when I looked at Mark, he wouldn't even look my way. During the whole car ride, I kept telling myself I would be okay.

It would be hard, and I would never be the same, but this feeling was so much worse than before. I could hardly breathe, I could hardly think, so I told him everything. If he was going to walk out on me, he was going to do it knowing the truth, the whole truth.

I have never been more afraid of anything in my life, but if he walked out on me, I wanted him to know that, in the end, what I felt for him was so much more than even I knew.

The little kisses sting just a bit, and I know that he just nipped me. "I know you're faking," he says. When he picks up my hips, I brace myself for him to bury himself inside me. The whole night, I couldn't let him go for longer than an hour. I would fall asleep and then wake up, reaching for him. "Missed you," he says just like he has said for the past fourteen hours.

"God, yes." I close my eyes and just feel his hands on my hips as he thrusts into me over and over again. He collapses on me and brings us to the side. "I need a shower."

"Hmm." He agrees as he catches his breath. "Me, too." He slowly slips out of me, and I get up and walk to the shower. Turning it on, I look at myself in the mirror. I have hickeys just about everywhere. Little red dots from his beard all around my mouth and neck. He comes in, and I just look at him. He stops beside me. "I love you," he says and kisses my neck. Walking to the shower, he opens the door that has now filled with steam from the hot water. I follow him in, and he just sits on the bench and puts his head back. "I think we should take a bath," he says.

"We can take one at your house tonight," I tell him, and

he just nods. I wet my hair and throw my head back, letting the water wash over me. His hand comes up to play with my nipple. "Maybe we shouldn't shower together." I laugh and see his cock already getting ready for another round.

"It's been over two months. I'm not letting you out of my sight," he says, and I lean down to kiss his lips.

"Why don't I make sure you're clean?" I tell him, my hand going to his cock as the water pours down over my arms and onto him. I get on my knees, taking the tip in my mouth. "Make sure you are all clean," I say, and just when I'm about to take him deep in my mouth, I hear Karrie's voice.

"God, I hope you're not drowning yourself." She laughs, and then she must spot Mark sitting or me on my knees; either way, she shrieks and yells. "Oh my fucking God," she says and runs out of the bathroom. Mark covers my head, assuming to protect me, and I have to laugh.

"Was that Karrie?" he asks me, and I get up and kiss his lips.

"I forgot she was coming," I tell him and walk out of the shower, grabbing the robe. "I'll go make sure she's okay."

"I think she saw my dick," he hisses, peeking his head out of the shower to make sure Karrie isn't there, and I hand him a white towel.

"She's seen a dick before, Markos," I tell him, and he wraps his towel around his waist. "I don't know if she's seen one so big before, but she's never complained about Matthew, so I'm assuming that he's well endowed."

"Can we not talk about Matthew or his dick right now?" Mark says and then looks at me. "What if he's here?"

"He isn't here," I tell him. "Karrie was coming by herself."

"Why?" he asks me, and I look at him.

"Get dressed," I tell him. Walking out to the kitchen, I find Karrie at the liquor cabinet, and I laugh.

"How long would it burn if I poured tequila in my eyes to disinfect them and erase what I just saw from my mind?" she asks, and I see her all flushed.

"Not worth the pain," I say with a huge smile on my face. "Sorry about that. I forgot you were coming."

"How could you forget I was coming?" she shrieks and then stops talking when Mark comes out of my room wearing his black pants from last night and one of his shirts he forgot here.

"Karrie." He nods to her, and she avoids his eyes.

"I didn't see anything," she says fast. "I mean, I saw this one"—she points at me—"on her knees, and I saw your chest." She takes another shot. "But apart from that, I can say I didn't see anything else."

I laugh at how uneasy she is. "Karrie, he's a meal only the fine can appreciate," I say, walking to the kitchen to get a coffee. "Oh, she brought food."

"This is …" Mark starts.

"The most uncomfortable moment of my life." She finishes for him. "More uncomfortable than when I came over, and she asked me to inspect her vagina."

"Oh." I peek my head out of the kitchen. "Good news, it's not broken." I smile at Karrie who glares.

"Do I want to know?" Mark asks, and I start the coffee.

"No," Karrie says, and I laugh.

"I thought you broke my vagina. I couldn't orgasm for two months!" I yell from the kitchen while I pick up the boxes and set them in the middle of the table. "Are we doing mimosas?"

"Yes to the mimosa," Karrie says. "And how are you just walking around in a kimono with not even a care in the world that I just walked in on you on your knees?" she asks. Going into the kitchen, she comes back with the champagne bottle and pops it. Then she takes a drink straight from the bottle.

"Sit down," I tell him, and he walks over to the table and sits. I walk to him, and he puts his hands around my legs. "I'll get you coffee." Then I look at Karrie. "You need to relax. It's human nature."

I lean down and kiss his lips, and Karrie comes out with the orange juice and gets the champagne, and ten minutes later, I'm sitting down. "Well, I guess you're wondering." I look at Karrie, and Mark just leans back in his chair.

I open the boxes that Karrie brought, and she did not go wrong. "I am wondering all sorts of things," she says, grabbing a piece of cheesecake and a fork. "But I'm also very afraid."

"Markos, do you want me to order some eggs and meat? You need your protein." I wink at him, and for the first time, he blushes.

"I'm still here," Karrie says. "Right here."

"So the gala," I tell her. "Scott was there." I say his name, and I'm not angry, I'm not bitter, I'm nothing. Her eyes fly up and look at mine and then at Mark. "He knows. I told him."

"You told him?" She slaps the table. "It took you ten years to tell me."

"Don't be jealous, Karrie. I love you both equally," I tell

her and then look at Mark. "Sorry. Anyway, I saw Scott and his wife, and well, then Mark caught me telling him to fuck off."

"High-five," Karrie says, lifting her glass at him.

"So minus all the crying and me feeling like scum for sleeping with a married man—"

"That's enough," Mark snaps, and Karrie looks up at him. "I'm not going to let put yourself down." I look at him and smile and then look at Karrie.

"He's so going to get laid for that." I wink at her, and she drinks again.

"Like you wouldn't bang him regardless," she says, and I shrug.

"I professed my love to Mark," I tell her, feeling so free. "And then we made up for lost time."

"There will be no details of that," Mark says, chewing. "We are not discussing that."

"I second that," Karrie says.

"Please, do you know the number of times I heard you and Matthew going at it?" I say, laughing.

"You did not," Karrie says, shocked.

"You aren't as quiet as you think you are," I tell her. "And besides, once you left the baby monitor on, and well"—I put my hand up—"high-five for banging in the middle of the day." But she just glares at me.

"Mark and I are together," I say with a smile on my face. "I have a boyfriend."

"I saw," Karrie says.

"We haven't figured out how or if we are going to tell people just yet, and I would like Vivienne to meet my family before we announce it," Mark says, and I look at him. "I told you I don't share my personal life with anyone really."

"Buddy, you have chosen the wrong person," Karrie says and drinks the rest of the champagne.

"Hey, no one even knew we dated before," I tell her. "I think that it would be good to keep it to us."

"So are you going to go to the games and whatnot to cheer for him?" Karrie asks.

"I cheered for him this whole time, and no one knew." I fold my hands over my chest. "On the down low."

The rest of the lunch goes smooth, and Karrie calls herself a car service to take her back to Long Island. I hug her at the door, and she waves to Mark who just nods at her.

"Go get dressed so we can go to my place," he tells me, and I nod at him.

"We have to bring Elsa," I tell him from the bedroom while I pack a bag, slipping into my yoga pants. "When is your next game?"

"We leave tomorrow and come back Thursday," he tells me, coming into the room. "You can come back here or stay at my place, but," he says, sitting on the bed, "I don't want to sleep without you." He looks at me. "If I'm home, I want to be with you. Whether we sleep here, or we sleep at my place."

"Okay," I say and watch him exhale heavily. "What is with the big exhale?"

"I thought you would give me a hard time," he tells me, and I laugh. "Can we go now?"

"Go pack Elsa and I'll grab my stuff." I wink at him.

"You know, she can stay here alone for two days, right?" he says, and I walk out of the closet.

"Don't even joke like that," I say, and he laughs.

"How the tables have turned from you dropping her off at the fire station," he says, grabbing my hand while he holds Elsa in the other. We get into the car, and I hold Elsa on my lap as he makes his way to his house. When I walk into his house, I get this feeling like I'm home, which is just a touch weird, considering I have my own home. I put my bag down in the closet while he puts Elsa in the kitchen. "Did you buy light up rocks?" he asks, coming into his room.

"You kept my robe?" I ask him, looking at the robe hanging next to his.

"Yeah," he says, pulling off his shirt and pants and kissing my neck. "I'm going to take a shower."

"Want me to join you?" I ask him, and he looks at me with a twinkle in his eye.

"Is that even a question?" he asks, and I follow him into the shower.

"Is it okay that I left my stuff by the sink?" I ask him, walking out and seeing him already in bed. "I have my face creams and all that. I can pack it back in the bag if you want."

"I like it there," he says. "Leave it."

I get into bed with him, and he pulls me over to him. "I love you," he says, and I look up at him. This man has held my hand and helped me love without even knowing.

"I love you, too." I smile at him, and for the second time in my life, I sleep more peacefully than ever.

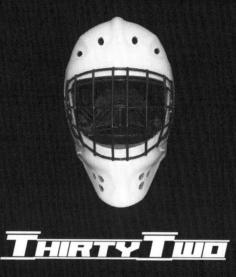

THIRTY TWO

MARK

I WALK INTO the rink two days later with my bag in my hand. I just dropped Vivienne and Elsa off at her house, and I already miss her. Yesterday when I came to practice, she stayed at my place, and when I got home, she was there on the couch with her laptop, and it just felt good.

I walk into the room and see that most of the guys are there. "Hey," I say to them, and Evan looks up at me while he's reading something on his phone.

"I can't fucking believe this," Evan says, slapping his leg. "She finally fell in love."

"Who did?" I ask him, and he looks up.

"Life of a Serial Dater," Evan says, and I look at him confused. "It's a blog about this woman who lives in New York or at least that is what she says. Candace came across her blog a couple of years ago, and from time to time, she sends me some of her posts. This chick," he says while I sit down. "She's out of her mind. Dude bought her a fish, and she about lost her shit."

My head snaps up when he says that. "What?" I ask him, and he laughs.

"She started dating this guy or banging him," he says. "She never really stays with anyone longer than one night, but this guy, he takes her out to this romantic date and then sent her a fish."

I swallow, and I try not to look shocked. "She lost it."

"What is this blog called?" I ask him, taking out my phone.

"Life of a Serial Dater," he tells me, and I google it. But I don't have a chance to read anything else because Oliver comes in, and we get on the bus. I don't have a chance to read it until I finally get into my room. I pull up her latest post.

Stick a fork in this turkey, the goose is cooked.

I never thought this would happen, never thought I would find someone who I wanted to wake up to every single day, but people, I did.

I smile and then scroll down to the one under it.

My vagina is officially broken or cursed.

I laugh but continue reading.

I just spent the last ten hours trying to make myself have the happy ending, and you know what I got? Carpal tunnel.

I swipe up.

I don't care what anyone says, size does really matter.

I scroll and find another one.

Can you really miss someone if you haven't been to-gether long? I knew him less than a month, yet I look for him wherever I go. I actually go out of my way to walk by his house with a chance to see him. Is this what women actually do? The answer apparently is yes.

I smile and then go to the next one.

He sent me a gift. I know what it sounds like—woohoo he sent me a gift. But it is more than that. He sent me Jane Austen books. The same books I spent five years reading weekly. It's the most thoughtful gift I've ever gotten, but how did he know?

It's been seven days since I last saw him, and it feels like just yesterday. I don't understand what this is or how to make it stop. How long can this go on?

I don't know why I'm so happy, but the next one kills me.

How can he think I would be in a relationship? How did he not know that I don't do relationships, and in this day and age, how can one refuse to have sex with a woman who is willing and able? I'm a serial dater, for fuck's sake.

I'm about to read the next one when my phone rings with FaceTime, and I see it's Vivienne.

"Hello," I say when it finally connects, and her face comes into view. She has her hair piled on her head, and she's wearing the same shirt she wore home, which is mine.

"Hey," she says, smiling. "What are you doing?"

"Nothing," I tell her. "Just reading something I found online. What are you doing?"

"I am just going to order myself something to eat, and I thought I would check in," she says softly. "When are you coming back?"

"We leave here tomorrow night after the game, so probably around two or three in the morning," I tell her. "Where are you going to be?"

"Probably here." She looks at the camera. "Do you want to come here?"

"I can," I tell her, and we talk for an hour, even after she gets her food, and the next night when I get to her apartment, I'm shocked to find her waiting for me at the door. "Hey," I say, grabbing her around her waist and carrying her to her bedroom. After dumping my bag on the floor, it takes her five seconds to get naked and a second more for me to plant myself inside her. She is fast asleep when I come back from my shower, and I collect her in my arms and pull her close to me.

"Good morning," she tells me the next morning when I walk into the kitchen while she is making eggs. I walk to her and wrap my arms around her waist and kiss her neck.

"Is that my shirt?" I ask of the dress shirt she's wearing.

"It smells like you," she says, smiling, looking at me from the side. "Go make coffee. It's almost done."

I make myself coffee and then bring it to the table, and she walks out two minutes later with two plates. "I made spinach and feta omelets," she says, putting the plates down and then coming back to the kitchen. "And bacon and some sausage." She puts down two more plates and kisses my lips before she sits down in front of me.

"What time did you get up?" I ask her, looking at the spread.

"I think it was about an hour ago. I had some things to do," she says and takes a piece of bacon and bites off a piece.

"Strange thing happened to me this week," I say. "I came across this blog." I look up at her and see that she's stopped eating her bacon. "Really, really good blog. The Serial Dater."

"Mark," she says, and I shake my head.

"My question is are you going to change your name?" I ask her. "Because you aren't a serial dater anymore."

"How did you find me?" she asks me.

"Evan," I answer her, and her mouth drops open. "He doesn't know it's you, though," I tell her, and she releases a big sigh. "I take it no one knows?"

"Karrie," she tells me. "She's the only one who knows about it."

"What about Matthew?" I ask her, and she shakes her head.

"God, no. It started as a joke, and then it just exploded, and I, well ..." She puts her hands up.

"I never mentioned you by name."

"I know. I read it," I tell her, and she looks at me shocked. "Not everything. I stopped when it started talking about other men or, as you called them, conquests."

"That was before," she says, and I nod my head. "It's not now."

"I am going home for Christmas," I tell her. "And I want you to come with me." I watch her, and I don't know what I'm expecting or, if I'm honest, I'm expecting her to come up with excuses.

"Mark," she says, "what if your parents don't like me?"

"What do you mean?" I ask her.

"Mark, I have no filter," she tells me. "My best friend walked in and saw me on my knees, and I didn't even care." She laughs nervously. "What if I say something, and then they don't like me?"

"One, I don't think that my family will ever catch you on

your knees, and ..." I push away from the table and then hold out my hand. She gets up from her side of the table and walks over, sitting on my lap. "My family is going to love you." I push her hair away from her face. "You know why?" She shakes her head. "Because I love you, so my parents will do what they need to do in order to love you, too." I smile at her. "It's the way it is."

"I've never met parents before," she says while her finger plays with my collarbone. "But I swear I'll be on my best behavior," she says. "I mean, I'm going to talk to Karrie, and maybe I can take a course or something of what to do and what not to do." I laugh now and kiss her lips. "I think we should see what the omelets taste like cold." She moves in my lap and straddles me now. Moving my shorts down, she slowly lowers herself down on me. My hands rip open the shirt she's wearing, and I cup her tits while she rides me; the only sounds in the room are the pants coming from both of us. When she finally comes, I let go, wrapping my arms around her waist, and she buries her face in my neck. I get up and carry us both to the shower.

"I want to show you something," she says to me while she stands next to the sink putting on cream. I'm running my hands through my hair, and a towel is wrapped around my waist. I nod at her, then slip on my boxers. She holds her hand out to me and walks me toward a door that is always closed when I am over, but I never thought anything of it. She turns the handle, and we walk into her office. It's clean and bright and cheery, but that isn't what I'm looking at. Instead, I'm looking at where she has her articles. "This article was the first one I published with the magazine." She points at it and smiles. "This is the first blog post ever." She points at it, and I look around, and I'm so proud of everything she has done.

"This is incredible," I tell her, smiling. "But why not own it?"

"Because it's just easier." She shrugs. "Plus, it's almost like a diary. And you don't want people to actually read your diary." She sits in the chair. "I'm sorry I never told you."

"It was interesting to find out all that you did after we ..." I tell her. "We parted ways."

"Also, I would like to add that you can't use anything that I say in my articles." She points at me. "Nothing."

"So ..." I look at her. "Size doesn't matter?"

She slaps her desk and laughs. "No, that is all true."

"Did you really play with yourself for over ten hours?"

She nods her head. "I thought my vagina was broken. I even went to my doctor."

I put my hand in front of my mouth, and before I say anything, my phone rings. I turn and follow my ringing to the bedroom, picking it up and seeing it's my father. "Hey, Dad," I say, smiling, and then look up at the doorway and see her there smiling at me. I make a decision I know she is going to kill me for, but I don't care. "I'm going to FaceTime you because I want you to meet someone," I say, pressing the button and then looking at the shocked face she gives me. He comes on the screen, and I see my mother is there with him. "Hey, guys," I say and then look at her and put my hand out. "I'd like you to meet someone."

"Oh my God, it's a woman," my mother says, and then she claps her hands. "I knew it."

"Vivienne." I say her name, and she comes over to me, taking my hand in hers and sitting next to me. I put my arm around her and bring her close to me, kissing her forehead, and see the both of us in the square in the corner. My mother puts her hand to her mouth.

"Oh my gosh, she's so beautiful. Look." She grabs my father.

"I can see, woman. I'm holding the phone," he tells her, and it's just the thing that Vivienne needs because she throws her head back, and just like that, I check one more thing off my list to make her mine forever.

THIRTY THREE

VIVIENNE

"SO YOU ARE really leaving for Christmas?" Karrie says from the couch in front of me. It's another Saturday night, and I'm at the game. I've come to every single game, but I leave as soon as the game is over and go to Mark's place where we have dinner together and then get lost in each other. There are times we go out after the game, but it's easier for us to just meet at his house.

"I have to," I hiss at her and look around. "Do you think I should take something?"

"What do you mean?" She looks over at me.

"Should I take something to not be myself?" I ask her, looking down and then looking up at her again. "I mean, I'm me, and he's, well, he's him."

"Vivienne," Karrie says, coming close to me. "He loves you for you. All the crazy that comes with you. The walking around naked even if I'm there."

"It was one time." I roll my eyes at her. "And it's not like you don't suck dick." Then I look at Matthew, who is leaning on the bar watching the game. "You probably sucked his dick before you got here."

She doesn't say anything; she just drinks her wine. "Don't start. It's tradition."

"Nice." I nod at her, and then Zara comes over, and her little belly is starting to get bigger.

"I think I ate the whole cake," she says, sitting down in the single couch. "I might have even licked the plate." Both Karrie and I laugh out loud.

I look around, asking, "Where is Zoe?"

"She's not feeling well," Zara says, and I have a feeling she's lying about it. "I can't wait to be off for five days."

"Me either," Karrie says.

"When are you leaving?" Zara asks, looking at me, and I stutter, wondering what she is talking about.

"She's so excited to go to Paris," Karrie says, and I just nod.

"I leave tomorrow night, and I'll be back on Thursday," I say, drinking the rest of the wine. We are leaving tomorrow but at six a.m. and taking a private plane there. It's a one-hour flight. "The presents will be delivered on Monday."

I leave the game with hugs and kisses to everyone, and I'm just a touch sad that I'm not going to be with them on Christmas. Matthew kisses me on the head. "Going to miss waking up on Christmas morning and not having you sitting there in the corner wearing sunglasses."

I laugh at him and hug him. "One time," I tell him, and now he laughs. "Okay, fine, every time, but it's not my fault.

Your wife is a bad influence on me."

"Yeah, sure," he says, and he walks me out with one last hug and kiss, and I make my way over to Mark's place.

I'm taking out the food from the oven when I hear his key in the door. "In the kitchen!" I shout, and he comes in, tossing his keys on the counter and coming to kiss me. "Hello."

"Hey," he says quietly and grabs a piece of bread and tosses it in his mouth.

"I want to spend next Christmas with Karrie," I tell him, and he looks at me. "I know I said I wanted to keep things under wraps for now, but next year, I want to spend it here, and maybe your parents can come over."

"Okay," he says. It's all he ever says. I could ask him to go to Alaska and sleep in igloos, and all he will say is okay. He will never really say no to me.

"That's it? Okay?" I tell him, grabbing my wine glass. "Just like that?"

He leans against the counter in front of me and looks at me. "Will you be there?" he asks, and I nod. "Then okay." He grabs another piece of bread. "And for the record, I don't like that you're trying to start a fight because you're nervous about meeting my parents."

"I'm not trying to start a fight, Markos," I tell him, though, I have to admit, he's right. I am picking on every little thing the past couple of days to see if he will argue with me, but instead of giving in to my craziness, he just agrees and kisses me, and just like that, I'm okay. My nerves calm, and the next morning, I wake up way before the alarm and then look at him. "Do you think that the lady is going to come every day and feed Elsa?" I ask him, and he opens his eye at me. Instead of answering me, he plants himself inside me, and by the time he's done, I don't even know what I was complaining about.

We pull up to the house, and I look over at him. "If your parents don't like me, we can't date,"

I finally tell him, and he smiles at me and leans over to kiss me. "I'm not kidding, Markos. I will not be that woman."

"And what woman is that?" he asks me, holding my cheek in his hand.

"The woman whose in-laws hate her but just smile to keep the peace," I tell him. "The ones who they dread to be with."

"Vivienne, I promise you that my parents are going to love you," he says and kisses my lips, and when I look over at the house again, I see that his parents are standing in the doorway waiting for us.

"Oh my God." I duck and hide in the seat. "They just watched us make out." I try to hide my face.

"Hey," he says, taking my hands away from my face. "We basically live together." He laughs, and it makes me gasp.

"Oh my God." I put my hands in front of my mouth. "You think they know we have sex?" He just smiles and shakes his head, getting out of the car. He walks around to my side and opens my door, putting out his hand. "Do you think they'll know I sucked your dick this morning?" I ask him quietly as I get out of the car. I stop, and he turns around to look at me. "Does my face glow?"

"What?" he asks and just shakes his head and proceeds

344

to walk, but I pull him back.

"Does my face glow?" I ask him again. "If it glows, they will know we had sex." But he doesn't answer me; he just walks ahead, and I follow him not because I want to but because if I don't, I'm going to slip on my fucking ass. High heels and ice are not a winning combination.

"Mom, Dad," Mark says as he helps me up the five steps to their house.

"Markos," his mother says and grabs his face and brings it down to her lips, kissing his cheeks.

"Angela," his father says, pulling her back. "Give the man some space." They move away from the door, and we step in. Mark closes the door behind us.

"Hello," I say to them and lean in to kiss his mother's cheek and then to his father. "Thank you so much for having me."

"Mom, Dad," Mark says, putting his arm around my waist. "I know you've met through FaceTime, but this is Vivienne." He smiles like I've never seen him smile before, and he even puffs out his chest. "Vivienne, this is my dad, Angela, and Yanni."

"It's nice to finally meet you," I say to them.

"Look at how pretty she is," Angela says to Yanni. "She glows." She smiles, and I want to crawl into a hole, but I'm saved by the doorbell. I move to the side, and just like that, more people arrive.

"Here we go," Mark says from beside me, and he was not kidding. I thought Matthew's family was nuts. Well, Mark's trumps Matthew's. His aunts come in with enough food to feed a hundred people. His cousins all come in to say hello.

By the time everyone left, I was helping Mark clean up. His mother came out of the kitchen wiping her hands. "No, stop doing that. Come sit down and have a coffee," she says softly, and I'm about to answer her when the front door opens.

"Is there anyone left in this town who didn't come over today?" I ask Mark while I throw away another plate with food on it.

"I'm home," a man says, and then Angela's eyes light up.

"Christo," she says, walking toward the door.

"My brother is here," he says, and a second later, his brother walks into the room. If I didn't know Mark like I do, I would say they are twins, but Mark's eyes light up just a touch browner than his brother.

"Well, well, well," Chris says, coming into the room. "He finally brought you out in the open," he says, kissing my cheeks, but not for too long because Mark comes over and pushes him away, making us both laugh.

"I saved you a plate," Angela says, and Yanni comes into the room, and he slaps his hands together.

"Aha, now the family is all here," he says, walking over to his son and grabbing him by the cheek. "You good?"

"He's fine," Mark says from behind me; his hand on my hip. "Go eat, little baby," he says. Chris looks at him and waits for his parents to turn around before giving him the finger.

"Why don't you go sit down with them, and I'm going to get these dishes in the dishwasher, and then we can go so I can give you my early Christmas gift?" I tell him, and he just smiles at me.

"Pretty sure I got everything you can give me." He leans

down and kisses me, and then I hear Chris.

"Stop playing tonsil hockey with Vivienne and come sit with us." I look at him and roll my lips.

He grabs my hands and brings me to the table, but I walk to the kitchen instead and find Angela putting things in the dishwasher.

"I can do this," I tell her. "Why don't you go sit with the boys?" I look at her, and she looks down and then looks up at me.

"Nah, I'll give them their alone time. Yanni lives for these moments," she says as I help her fill the dishwasher.

"I always wanted a girl," she says. "I mean, your sons are your sons. But your daughter, she usually stays with you."

I nod at her. "My mother says that all the time."

"I always worried about Mark all alone in the city," she says, and I look over at her while I rinse out a glass and put it in the dishwasher as she puts the food away. "I would sit and wonder what kind of woman would he pick." I don't say anything. I just look down.

"I know that you wanted better for him," I tell her. "I'm not the innocent little girl who mothers want for their sons. I am my own person. Independent," I tell her. "I have my own money, so I don't need a man for that. I have a career that I'm proud of, and—"

"Do you love him?" she asks me, coming to stand next to me.

"Yes." I look down and then look up at him. "I told him that I would leave him if you don't approve of me, and I will."

"What? Why?" she asks, shocked.

"Because you're his family, and he loves you guys more

than anything," I tell her. "And I'm never going to get in the middle of that. I won't have him choose."

"You would do that, wouldn't you?" she asks me softly. "Just leave him."

"It would kill me but ..." I look over at the guys through the doorway into the dining room and see Mark throwing his head back and laughing while his father laughs and looks at his sons. "I would do it." I look back at her and try to blink the tears away.

"Good news," his mother says, coming over to me and putting her hand on mine. "We approve,"

she says, and I smile, but the tear comes out anyway. "How could we not? Look at my boy," she says, pointing at Mark. "You helped make him happy like that."

I look over, and he catches my eye and sees that I have tears. He gets up right away and comes in almost like he's ready for war. "What happened?"

I look over at him, and I don't mean to sob out. "She likes me." He walks over to me, and I bury myself in his chest. This man who didn't let me run away from him; this man who holds me in his arms every night when he can and loves all my crazy.

"Of course, she likes you," he whispers, and now Yanni comes in.

"What happened to her?" he asks with worry. "Angela, what did you do to her? Did you give her the talk?"

"Oh, would you hush," Angela says hisses to her husband. "They live together. You think I need to give her the talk?"

I try to stop the laugh from coming out, but I can't, and my arms wrap around Mark's waist and then I look up at him as he looks down at me. "Love you," I tell him, and he leans down and kisses me.

"Mom, that lasagna was amazing," Chris says, coming in and rinsing off his dish right next to me.

"What is wrong with you?" Angela asks Chris. "Vivienne is crying, and all you can think about is lasagna." She puts her hands on her hips.

He wipes his hands and is coming toward me, holding out his hand, and Mark holds out a hand. "Don't even try."

"See that, Mom?" Chris says. "He threatened me."

And just like that, everyone laughs, and I feel just like one of them.

THIRTYFOUR

MARK

I WALK UP the stairs to the little corner of the garage with my ear pods in and the tennis ball in my hand, and when I finally get to the last step, I see her leaning against the wall.

"Hey there," she says, putting her phone away. "How're you feeling?"

"Good," I tell her and go to kiss her. Tonight, we play for the Cup, and she's been a nervous wreck for me. We still haven't come out as a couple. Neither of us really cares, but at night, we go to bed together. Half of her stuff is at my house, and now she spends more time there than at her apartment. As much as I want her to just move in completely, I also don't want to push her.

"Are you nervous?" she asks me, and I just shrug.

"My parents just got here," I tell her, and she smiles. After Christmas with my parents, she and my mom have become five to check in, my mother does the same with Vivienne. At first, I thought it was too much, but then one night, Vivienne called her before she had a chance to check in. Plus, on Mother's Day she flew her in and took her to the spa all day and had her glammed up.

"I'm going to go and see them as soon as I go in," she says, coming to me. "Whatever happens tonight, I want you to know how proud I am of you."

"I know." I smile and kiss her. "Now get out of here so I can get in the zone."

"Fine," she says, and she kisses me on the lips and then wipes off her glitter.

I get in the zone, and when I go back into the room, the energy is just crazy. Half the team isn't talking while the other half is overtalking. "This whole year," Viktor says from beside me as he drinks his energy drink. "It's all led to this."

"I'm retiring," I tell him. Something I haven't really told anyone yet, but my contract is up, and it's time to hang up my skates. He looks over at me with shock. "I mean, I say that every single year."

"I celebrate one-year sober tomorrow," he says, tapping his finger on his bottle. "One year ago, it was a totally different story."

I look at him. "You did it, man." He really did. For the past year, he busted his ass to be where he's at. "You should be proud."

He just shakes his head. "Win or lose this game, I still win the year."

"Yeah." I smirk at him. "But how much better would it be

holding the Cup over your head?"

"Good point," he says, and we get up to walk out and get on the ice. The fans have already started coming in, and I look at the seats and find Vivienne sitting with my mother and laughing about something while my father and brother sit next to each other talking.

I look toward the box and see Matthew not even there. He's in the press box tonight, where he's been the whole series. We lost the first game at home and then won the next one and then went to St. Louis and took the two games. I start my stretches, and by that time, the national anthem has been sung by one of the top Broadway girls. I look ahead, and when the lights come back on, I take my spot between the pipes. I skate back and forth in front like I always do and then skate side to side.

The puck drops, and I get ready in the crease, head down for just a second, and it was at that second, I didn't see the puck passed from one side to the next, and it flies over my shoulder and into the net. Seven seconds in. "Fuck," I hiss, putting my mask on top of my head and squeezing the water into my mouth while I watch the replay.

"We'll get it back," Evan says, coming to me, and I just nod. I watch the face-off again, and this time, when they lose it and come back, they shoot, and I make a glove save. When the first period ends, the shots on net are eighteen to four. I put my stick next to everyone else's and have my skates sharpened.

"We need more shots in the fucking net!" the coach screams when he comes in. "We need to go out there and play our fucking game. We need to stop doing turnovers in the neutral zone, and for the love of fuck, can we stop giving them opportunities to shoot on Mark," he says and then storms out. I look down at the floor, not saying anything, and then I look up at Evan.

"I can't do it all on my own," I start, talking low. "I need you guys to put a couple of pucks in the net."

"Let's go out there, boys, and show them that they can't come into our house and sit at our table," Evan says, standing up. "Time to show them who we are," he says, and everyone gets up and gets ready. We start the second period on fire, and with one minute to go in the second period, Evan ties up the game in a tap in redirect. Just like that, the game is tied, and then right off the face-off, we hustle into the zone, and they pass it from one to the other. Viktor takes a shot, and Evan picks up the rebound, making it two to one.

At the start of the third period, I try not to let my nerves get to me. I am on point, but with four minutes to go, they pull the goalie, leaving it with six against five. They come into the zone, and our team makes good, blocking and not giving them a chance to shoot the puck. But one gets past, and after I block it, they scramble in the front for the rebound. I put my blocker down on the puck, and then one of the other team members slashes my hand twice. The referee blows the whistle while Viktor goes after the guy who hit my hand. Evan pushes him away from the guy while the referee picks up the puck. He skates to the side where they have a face-off. The hits are harder, the puck is all over the place, and I try to control my breathing while looking at everyone on the ice as they scramble for the puck. St. Louis does what they need to do to keep it in the zone, and luckily, the defenseman misses the pass, and it goes out of bounds, giving everyone a chance to change. Lucky for us, they have one player causing an offside so the face-off is taken in the neutral zone. I get down and ready for whatever is going to come, but we win the face-off. Evan just shoots at the net, and it slides into the open net. I put my stick up and look at the clock, seeing that there is twenty-five seconds left. I skate to the blue line and wait for the guys to come over and smack my glove and get ready for the face-off. With five seconds to go, the guys are already climbing over the bench. My mask is thrown off my face, I drop my stick and my blocker, and when the guys finally get to me, I'm pushed against the glass, and the guys just jump all over each other. I don't know what is said, and I don't know who I hugged and who I didn't. "We fucking did it," one person says.

"Holy fucking shit, we fucking did it," another one says, and then we skate to the middle of the ice and get in line to shake the other team's hands. The volume in the arena is almost deafening, and I can't wipe the smile off my face. When I get to the bench, Matthew is there standing next to Max, and he's already wearing the New York Stinger Champion hat.

He comes up to me and pulls me into a hug. "We couldn't do this without you," he says, and I just smile at him.

"You made this happen more than I did," I tell him, looking out on the ice at the guys all hugging and talking, most of them putting on their new hats. I grab mine and put it on my head, and the red carpet comes out, and we know the Cup will be here in just a bit. Evan comes up to us, and we do a group hug with all of us smiling so big.

We hear the commissioner start talking, and all of us turn to look at him as we stand in a line. I look down both sides, and all the guys have smiles on their faces. I look up and see my mother and Vivienne holding each other's hands while Vivienne smiles and wipes away a tear. I'm so entranced by her, I don't even hear what is going on until Evan smacks me on the shoulder. "Go get it."

"What?" I ask, shocked. Looking around, I see I was named the VIP for the playoffs. I skate to him and shake his hand and then look at the camera. The guys come over and smack me on the shoulder, and then the moment most of us dream of but seldom achieve is here—the Stanley Cup comes out.

Evan skates to the cup, posing for a picture, and then he finally lifts it in the air over his head, and everything is a blur. The families come on the ice, and my father and mother are the first ones I see. I hug my father and then my mother, and then I see Chris holding Vivienne's hand while he helps her walk to us. I lean down, and I suddenly feel all eyes on us, so instead of kissing her on the lips like I want to, I kiss her on the side. No one is really paying attention to us.

"I am so proud of you," she tells me and hugs me around my waist, pressing her cheek to my chest. She lets me go so I can shake my brother's hand, and she walks over to Evan and then to Matthew and Max. The whole time our eyes meet each other's, and I want to go over to her and pull her next to me, but I don't. This isn't the place to come out or make a scene.

Evan, Viktor, and I are the last ones on the ice, and when

we finally start walking back to the locker room, I am not expecting for everyone to go fucking nuts. Bottles of champagne are popped, and it's raining down all over us. We raise our hands in the air, and when I look back, Evan comes in with the Cup and hoists it in the air while champagne is just sprayed everywhere.

I don't know who, but someone just pours a bottle of champagne over my head, and when I finally get to my locker, the gray Stanley Cup shirt that they left hanging is all wet. I laugh and take off my pads while Evan places the cup in the middle of the table in the room. The center table is empty, but the buckets of champagne bottles are everywhere. I undress and take another dry T-shirt from the pile and put it on along with my shorts.

When I look up, I see that they are filling the top of the Cup with champagne, and everyone is taking a drink from it. I still can't see as everyone is up, and people are still spraying champagne everywhere. The music now goes on with "We are the Champions," and everyone sings at the top of their lungs. I don't know how long I stay in the locker room, but when we finally leave, it's no surprise that we are the last ones in the buildings. All the wives and children have gone home, and when I finally walk into my apartment, wearing my suit and baseball hat, I'm not expecting her to be waiting up.

"Hey," I say quietly, walking to her. "Why did you wait up?"

"Are you kidding me?" she says, wrapping her arms around me. "I didn't even get to kiss you."

"I know," I tell her and lean my head down and kiss her like I wanted to kiss her on the ice. I kiss her with all the love

I have for her. "I didn't know if it was okay for me to kiss you or not," I tell her. "I didn't know how to act, and I think we should have talked about it before."

"Mark, they call you Private Mark for a reason," she says, smiling. "I didn't expect you to break out of that role. Besides, what we have is private, and it's ours, so it was more than okay."

"Where are my parents?" I ask her, taking off the hat.

"They are staying at my place," she says, and then she turns and walks out of the room, and it's only then I realize she's wearing one of my jerseys. "I also took it upon myself to have some champagne chilled," she says, walking up the stairs, and we don't sleep that whole night. There is champagne everywhere. The bed is soaked in so many places, I laugh when I reach over for her and my hand sticks to her.

"What time is the party?" I ask her, and she just looks over at me, her chest rising and falling. "We have to go. It's a big deal."

"I know," she says. "We also need to order a new bed."

"Good thing we leave tomorrow," I tell her as she gets up, and I see her ass all pink from all the times I smacked her. I didn't think I was doing it that hard, and she kept telling me to do it harder.

"I haven't even packed," she says, and I look over at her. "I thought we had more time. I didn't think you would win in five games," she says. We said that we would take off for three weeks just the two of us to a secluded island where I wanted her to have no tan lines. I had it all set up, and after last night's win, all I had to do was the confirmation, which I did as soon as I was dressed and headed out. "I told your parents we would call them for dinner."

"I have to nap after this party," I say to her, getting into the shower with her, and when we finally walk out of the apartment, my hand grabs her, and I bring it to my lips. We get in the car and make our way over to Viktor's party. We arrive there, and no one really says anything about us arriving together. She walks over to Karrie and hugs her, and I look around and see the guy at the bar. All of us look rough. "Who actually slept last night?" I ask, grabbing a water bottle from the bar.

Evan puts his hand up. "I crashed as soon as I got home." And all of us look at him. "Hey, we have a newborn. Do you know how precious sleep is to us?" I shake my head and laugh while everyone comes in, and we wait for Viktor. It's a surprise party that Zoe set up for him to celebrate his one year.

When he walks in, he is more surprised than ever, but he also looks like he didn't sleep. Everyone sits down, and when I look over, I see the women are all sitting together, so I grab a seat next to Max and Matthew. All of us are still pretty much riding the wave from last night. When I see people start to slowly leave, I try to catch Vivienne's attention, but she is laughing away with Karrie, and now Matthew has joined them, sitting next to Karrie.

I push away from the table and walk up to Viktor and shake his hand. "Congrats," I tell him smiling. "I'm going to head out." Viktor shakes my hand and thanks me for coming.

I look around, and then my eyes land on Vivienne, and I don't know what to do, and as I look around, I finally take a deep breath, not giving a shit who sees anymore. Vivienne looks at me, and I see her saying something to Karrie. I shake my head and walk over to her, stopping right in front of their table. Matthew's eyes come to mine, and then I look at Vivienne, who just smiles. "Are you ready?" I ask her.

I don't even realize that everyone has gotten quiet or that all eyes are on us. The only thing I know is that it's time to leave, and I'm not leaving without my woman beside me. "Yes," she says, flipping her hair behind her shoulder.

"Good, now let's go." I motion with my head. She pushes her chair away from the table and gets up, walking around the table with her purse in her hand. She walks around the table, her hand slipping in mine just like she does every single time we leave.

"What in the fuck is that?" Matthew is the first one to ask, then looks at Karrie. I smile; the secret's finally out.

Karrie shrugs her shoulder. "I don't think she's thirsty anymore," she says, and just like that, everyone starts to laugh.

She drops her hand from mine and does one even bigger, wrapping her arms around my waist. "I am not thirsty in the least." She looks at me while she says that and then turns to look at Matthew and Karrie. Standing in the middle of the restaurant with her closest friends, she looks around and says, "I'm in love."

EPILOGUE ONE

VIVIENNE

One Year Later . . .

"*I*'M SO SORRY, are we late?" I say, hugging Karrie and kissing her on the cheek. "Traffic was a nightmare."

"And it's just starting," Karrie says. "Summer combined with getting out of the city is a mess."

"Well, thankfully we won't be here." I smile at her and look around to see where Mark is.

After I declared my love for him in front of everyone, we didn't leave the party. In fact, they popped more champagne. Everyone was so curious as to how long it was going on, but the only one really in shock was Matthew, who sat there looking at Karrie.

"You knew about this?" He pointed at me and Mark, and she shrugged. "We aren't supposed to keep secrets from each other, Karrie."

"It wasn't my secret," she said and then leaned over and kissed his lips. "Now be happy for her. Do you know how long we've waited for this?"

He looked at me. "I never thought it would happen," he said, taking a long pull of his beer. "Who would be crazy enough to deal with her?" he asked the question that everyone has been asking for over a year. We came out to our friends and family and then finally had our picture taken at a red carpet event for his company, and that was online everywhere.

"Are you really staying in Greece for a month?" Karrie asks me and hands me a glass of wine. I look down at it and then look back at her again.

"We haven't really decided," I tell her and put the glass of wine down. "We are going to wing it. It might give me hives since I need a plan, but for now, we are going to Greece for the month. His mother and father are also coming, and eventually, his brother will pop up."

"Look at you," Karrie says. "The family girl."

I shrug. "What can I say?" I don't add in that I wouldn't change it for anything. I don't add that my life is so much more complete with him in it. Instead, I look around and spot Zara and Zoe huddled together in their chairs while Zoe bounces baby Zoey on her lap.

"Can you remember how small they were when Matthew and I met?" Karrie says of the twins, and I shake my head.

"What are you two chatting about?" Allison comes over with her glass of wine.

"How the twins have grown," Karrie says, and I look back over at them.

"It really is crazy how they've settled down," Allison says.

"Except now they are teaching my kids all the shit they did."

"How is that going?" I ask Allison who glares at me.

"I put salt in my coffee this morning." She takes another sip of her wine. "Let me go and yell at them for that." She walks over to the twins, and we just laugh.

"I brought you some water," Mark says, coming to me and leaning down to kiss my neck.

"Thank you," I tell him, and Karrie looks at me.

"But I got you wine," she says, and then I look at Mark and then at Karrie, who is now looking at me with huge eyes. "Vivienne," she says my name.

Mark hugs my shoulder, his hand rubbing my arm, and brings me close to him. "Well, that lasted what, an hour."

"I didn't even say anything," I tell him and then turn to look at Karrie. "I didn't say anything."

"Oh my God," Karrie says with tears in her eyes. She just looks at me, and I look at my best friend who would hold my hand through everything … well, almost anything. "Vivienne," she says softly, coming over to me. "Are you …?"

"What is going on over here?" Matthew says, coming to us and seeing Karrie with tears in her eyes. "Oh my God, please don't tell me that you're pregnant again, Karrie. I swear, I don't think …" he says, taking the baseball hat off his head and scratching his head. "I mean, if you are, I'm super happy."

"Dude, shut up," Karrie says to him. "I'm not pregnant."

"Oh, thank fuck," he says, putting the hat back on, and going to hug her, and she pushes him away. "So why are you crying then?" he asks.

I turn to Mark and then back to them, and I finally say,

"I'm pregnant." Two words I never thought I would ever say. "We're pregnant. I keep forgetting I have half of you living inside my uterus."

"Oh, dear God," Matthew says at the same time Karrie takes me in her arms.

"I'm so, so happy for you," she tells me and then looks at me. "You are glowing."

"Oh, that's because we had sex before we came here," I tell her. "Not because of the baby." Matthew now groans out. "Matthew, how do you think we got the baby in there?"

"There are things I don't want to think of in my life, and this is one of those things," Matthew says and then smacks Mark on the shoulder. "Never thought I would see this happen."

"I helped," I say, putting up my hand. "I probably did all the work, too."

"Honey," Mark says softly, shaking his head. "I love you. Let's go get you something to eat."

I nod at him and look around and see eyes on us, and I have no idea what is going on. But then I spot Mark's family, and I look over at him and then everything finally clicks into place. The tent, the balloons, all the flowers—this isn't just a family barbecue. I turn and see Mark, but now he isn't beside me, he's on his knee.

"Vivienne Paradis, you came into my world, and you made it complete. I want to hold your hand for the rest of my life. Until we are old and gray and can't remember anything except that we love each other," he says, and the tears just pour down my face. "I want to wipe your tears. I want to hold you up when you can't do it yourself. I want to be the man you deserve now and forever." My hand goes to my mouth to stop the sob coming and my hands shake, my knees get weak. "Would you make me the happiest man in the world and spend the rest of your life with me?" he says and then laughs. "I mean, you make me happy every day, but if you say yes, it will be extra special."

"Yes," I say the one word that comes to mind. I always watched others get proposed to, and I never thought it would happen to me, and I was okay with it. But this past year just being with him, I knew that I wanted to do it official-ly. I wanted to walk down the aisle and promise to love him until my last breath. I don't even look down at the ring that he slips on my finger because my hands grip his face, and I bend to kiss him. A minute later, our families come and give us all the hugs and kisses, and when I finally look down, I see the most beautiful ring I've ever seen.

It's not a diamond; it's the color blue like my eyes, prin-cess cut with two heart-shaped white diamonds on each side. I grab my purse, taking out my phone and snapping a picture of me holding up the ring next to my face. "What are you doing?" Mark asks, and I look over at him, and I smile.

The serial dater has finally crossed her name off the list. Get ready for all things wedding.

I attach it with the picture I just took, and I put it back in my purse.

"Oh my God." I hear Evan shriek from somewhere, and then he walks to us. "You're the serial dater."

"Um," I tell him. "You follow me?"

"You are the guy who bought her the fish?" he says, laughing and pointing at Mark.

"Let's have a toast," Karrie says, lifting her glass of champagne. "To Mark and Vivienne."

"To love," I say, looking up at Mark. "To forever love."

EPILOGUE TWO

MARK

Five years later . . .

I WALK INTO the bathroom and click the door closed, and my wife looks up at me. My wife, I gave her the fiancée title for two weeks, and then I just said fuck it and threw another "barbecue," but this time at my parents' house and with all my family and her family there. With Karrie at her side and Chris at mine, I vowed to love her forever. "You look like you're on a mission." She smiles and turns around, looking at me. She's wearing her robe, and it's hanging open with nothing under it.

"I am on a mission," I tell her and pick her up, putting her on the counter. "The mission to get inside you for more than five seconds before someone comes looking for us." My hands rub her bare legs, and she opens for me. "Are you ready?" I ask her, praying she is, and she just nods her head.

"Always," she says, taking my cock into her hand and placing it at her entrance. I slide into her as slowly as I can. Both of us let out a moan when I get all the way in. "Markos." She whispers my name, and I move now, my head buried in her neck, and then I put my mouth on hers to stop her from moaning out loud.

"I'm there," she tells me, and I know she is as I look into her blue eyes that I can get lost in. I watch her the whole time I fall over, and then I kiss her lips. "I'm going to need another shower," she says when I slip out of her, and she walks over to the shower and turns it on. "Where are the kids?"

"I put on some cartoon I found on Netflix," I tell her and smile when I think about my children. That's right, more than one. I wash my hands and walk to the door, opening it in case one of the kids calls us. We had Karrie six months after we got engaged. She came out with black hair and the bluest eyes I have ever seen. I was in love the minute they placed her in my arms, and my mother was over the moon she finally had a girl to spoil, it would be bows and dresses.

It was also when The Serial Dater became The Serial Mommy, and well, her following just went crazy. It went even crazier when two months after having Karrie, she found out she was pregnant again. She thought it was a mistake because no one gets pregnant while breastfeeding. She didn't believe the five tests she did, and it was only when the doctor confirmed it did she admit defeat.

So three days before Karrie turned one, she gave birth to my son Stefano, who looks like the stamp of me. They are almost like twins, and just when I thought we were done and one got ahead of us, and two years after Stefano, we had our little princess Angelica. Who looks like a mixture of both of us except with crystal green eyes.

"Ma mere." Angelica comes walking into the bathroom with her blanket trailing her under her arm. "Je suis fatigué." *I'm tired,* she says. Another thing, our kids speak French and English. And if my father has anything to say about it, they are going to speak Greek.

"D'accord, princesse," she says, turning off the shower and drying herself. Angelica comes over to me and holds up her hands, and I pick her up and she lays her head on my shoulder. "All that sugar they ate at Karrie's and now comes the down part."

"No one to blame but yourself." I smile at my wife as she glares. "If you didn't spoil Karrie, she wouldn't want to do it back to you."

"You know, sometimes I have to wonder whose side you're on," she tells me, putting on one of my T-shirts and then holds out her hands to Angelica.

"You never have to wonder because I'm always on your side," I tell her, and she rolls her eyes. "There was a time your mother used to get hearts in her eyes," I tell Angelica who just smiles at me.

"I'm going to put her to bed. Can you get the other two?" she asks me, and I kiss her and then kiss my daughter, who wants me to kiss her lips also. "bonne nuit papa."

"Bonne nuit," she says in her soft voice, and then Vivienne goes off to take them to bed. Another thing that we did was move to the suburbs. I mean, with three kids, it was hard for them to run around in the city, so I bought us a decent-size house in Long Island. Actually, it's like a ranch, and my parents have their own house on the ten acres of land I bought.

I walk back down to the kids' playroom and see them trying to keep their eyes open. "Okay, let's go, you two. Time for bed." I clap my hands together, and they don't even fight me this time. They just get up and walk to their room. When I turn off the television and walk to Stefano's room, he is already under the covers. "Bonne nuit," I tell him, and he smiles at me. "Je t'aime." *I love you,* I tell him, kissing him.

"Boone nuit, Papa," he says, and I turn off his light and close his door just a bit, and then I walk into Karrie's room.

"What are you doing?" I ask her and see that she is putting cream on her leg.

"I'm hydrating," she says, and I look at her. "It's so I don't get scaly like a mermaid."

"You're four," I tell her. "I don't think you have to worry about that for many years to come."

"Yaya told me she has scaly skin, and Maman said it's because she doesn't hydrate enough. I don't want legs like Yaya." I close my eyes, and I can imagine my daughter's face of horror when my mother told her all about her scaly legs.

"You are going to be fine," I tell her. "Look at Maman's legs; they are perfect," I tell her, and she shrugs and gets into bed.

"That's because she hydrates, Papa," she tells me matter-of-factly, and I can't even argue with her because she's right. "Bonne nit." She smiles at me, and I kiss her, and she turns over. I close her door also and walk back to my bedroom and see my wife doing the same thing my daughter was just doing.

"You know that I just found Karrie putting cream on her legs," I tell her, and my wife laughs. "She doesn't want to have mermaid legs."

"That is your mother's fault," she tells me and slides into bed next to me. "I'm exhausted," she says, and I look over at her. Being outside, she has a gorgeous tan, and the little freckles on her nose are coming out. "Who would have thought that I would be going to bed at seven thirty, and I am not even sorry about it."

"Didn't you nap today, too?" I point out, and she looks at me. "For two hours."

"What day is it?" she asks, sitting up in bed. Looking over at me, she then grabs her phone, going on something, and then chants, "No, no, no, nonononononono." Getting out of bed, she squeezes her nipples. "They hurt," she says to me, and I look at her so confused when she runs to the bathroom and then comes back a minute later.

"Are you going to tell me what's going on?" I ask her as she paces the floor in front of me.

"I'm late," she says.

"For what?' I ask her. "Pretty sure you had nothing to do today since it's Sunday."

"I don't mean that, Markos. I mean, I'm late," she says, pointing at her vagina, and now I get it.

"How late are we talking?" I ask her, and she just continues pacing in front of me.

"About three weeks," she says. "I mean, with the kids not in daycare anymore, and with your parents here, I don't know it slipped my mind." She stops and looks at me. "How many times did we have sex?"

375

"Since when?" I ask her, getting up now. "This week? Ten, maybe eleven times. But you're on the pill," I tell her. "I mean, you take the pill every single night."

"I do," she tells me and then looks down. "I mean, I do except for the time I forgot." She looks at me. "Hey, I was drunk, and you were all handsy, and I was all up in there." She points at my cock, and I cover myself now. "I forgot one time. Maybe two."

"It only takes one time," I tell her, and then she puts her hands on her hips.

"Wow, who is teaching sex education now," she hisses, and the phone rings from the bathroom. "Well, I guess we get to see if you put a bun in the oven." She walks over, and I grab her hand to stop her and see the tears well up in her eyes. "I'm sorry. It's all my fault."

"Don't cry," I tell her and grab her in my arms.

"I know that you weren't expecting this, and neither was I, but it's our baby."

"Vivienne," I say, grabbing her face. "I want to have as many kids as you want to give me. Be it three, four, or seven, I don't care."

"Oh, I can tell you if that test is positive, then there is no fucking five. You are going to go and get snipped."

I cringe at her. "Don't talk like that. God gave me the gift. I can't just give it back."

"God also gave you two hands. Do you want to only use those to get pleasure?" she asks me, and I roll my eyes. "Now let me go see the answer."

I don't wait for her. Instead, I follow her, and right on top of where I just look at her, the smile on my face so big. "And just like that, we are a family of six," she says with tears of joy in her eyes.

"This is crazy and wild?" she asks me, and I look at her.

"No, it isn't," I tell her, grabbing her around her waist.

"You're right." She wraps her arms around my neck. "This is love."

Other title by Natasha Madison

This Is
This Is Crazy
This Is Wild
This Is Love

Hollywood Royalty
Hollywood Playboy
Hollywood Princess
Hollywood Prince

Something Series
Something So Right
Something So Perfect
Something So Irresistible
Something So Unscripted

Tempt Series
Tempt The Boss
Tempt The Playboy

Heaven & Hell Series
Hell and Back
Pieces of Heaven
Heaven & Hell Box Set

Love Series
Perfect Love Story
Unexpected Love Story
Broken Love Story
Mixed Up Love
Faux Pas

Made in the USA
Columbia, SC
13 January 2024

30456760R00226